DOWNRIVER

A Tale of Moving Pictures Before Hollywood

Evan Anderson

Miriam—
thanks *so* much for
your support, encourage-
ment & great
suggestions!
♡ Scott/Evan

Alice Guy Blache's talk was excerpted from her article "Women's Place in Photoplay Production" as published in *Moving Picture World,* July 11, 1914, vol. XX1, no. 3

Vachel Lindsay's poems (excerpted) are in the public domain. "The Blackhawk War of the Artists" appears in Vachel Lindsay's collection "The Congo and Other Poems" published by Dover Thrift Editions, 1992.

Acknowledgements

Sincere thanks to Ray Bradbury, whose stories, enthusiasm and in-person encounters did a great deal to steer me toward the writing life, and to Shirley Windward, who gave me the equivalent in school. I'm also grateful to the late Gunnard Nelson, who helped instill a love of golden age cinema, to Plumflower for her support and inspiration, and especially, to the Glaring Ommisions, without whose encouragement, guidance and oversight this book would never have come to be. A particular nod to Nancy Rullo for suggesting that this story could be more than just a scene on a river bank.

To Robert Lovelace Barrett, vaudevillian,
film actor, studio projectionist and grandfather.

And to the actress Dawn O'Day, later known as
Anne Shirley, for providing the spark.

Chapter One

Four women in black picked their way along the wooden footpath, skirts hoisted ankle high above the estuary mud. By the time Anne caught sight of them it was too late to step back and hide among the cattails. When they came around a bend in the path she faced them dead on.

"Anne Blackstone!" Miss Hutchins, pillar of the Ladies Aid Society, was in the lead. Anne smoothed her skirt, took a breath, and gave a slight curtsy. When Miss Hutchins drew close she blocked not only the three ladies standing behind her but the sun as well. Anne found it almost impossible to look her in the face.

"Good day, Miss." She bowed her head ever so slightly.

"Unfortunate, Anne, we did not find you at home," said Miss Hutchins. "We have just paid a social call to the Meadows. We hoped you could show us about, introduce us to your neighbors."

Strange request, Anne thought. The Ladies Aid didn't usually venture into the Meadows except at Christmas time.

"I'm sorry…" said Anne, looking up for a moment. "I've been in town on errands."

"Errands on your mother's behalf, I'm sure," Miss Hutchins replied, clutching her string purse tighter. "We were most pleased to find her in such good spirits."

"How old are you now, fifteen?" asked another of the Ladies, whom Anne could not see clearly.

"Sixteen, Miss."

"And do you take your mother's temperature regular?"

"Yes Miss, once in the morning, once when I get home from school and twice at night."

"It is a blessed thing," said the lady who stood second from last, "when an ailing mother is looked after so well by an only child."

"And as we know," said Miss Hutchins, "human aid takes us only so far." She made a slight move towards Anne. "Then we must lay our trust in the hand of Providence." Anne inched away as the hand reached to stroke her hair. Miss Hutchins straightened. "We look forward to our next meeting, Anne. And speaking of what lies ahead."

Anne was about to ask *and what is that, please?* when Miss Hutchins said to her companions, "Well, ladies? Day is getting short. We must return to the Home."

Anne curtsied and let them pass. Her entire life she'd stayed clear of these women who, from behind the high brick walls of the Children's Home, ruled the town of Marion with the support of the church, the charity ward and the mayor himself. The Home itself was little better than a workhouse. But as a result there were fewer homeless children in Missouri River towns.

The church ladies looked vulnerable as they stepped past her. The slightest push and they'd topple to the mud, to flail on their backs like turtles.

Once they had walked a ways on the planks, with her fingers Anne made the sign of the Devil and Snakes and swore if she ever became a river pilot she'd ferry the pack of them to the gates of Hell.

*** *** ***

The cabin was full of the smell of boiling potatoes when Anne stepped inside. Ma, in her big blue apron, stood by the stove. One hand on the counter steadied her as she reached into the pantry shelf.

"We had visitors while you were in town."

"I know," said Anne, tying on her own apron. "Miss Hutchins and the Ladies Aid Society. I ran into them at the marsh."

"Let's talk about it while we get your picnic together. You'll need an early start to make that excursion boat, so we may as well do everything tonight. We'll start with the potato salad; that will be easiest."

Anne was sent down to the root cellar for celery, capers and onions, up to the rafters for dried parsley, and off to the neighbors for eggs and one plump white chicken, to be delivered later that afternoon.

Back in the kitchen, she plucked boiled potatoes from the kettle, nearly dropping one when her fingers brushed it. She sliced them up with oil and vinegar, chopped onion and celery very fine, and added capers, parsley, salt and pepper. Mother stood across from her blending oil, egg yolks, lemon juice and vinegar into mayonnaise, which Anne ground into the potatoes with a big wooden spoon.

"Did they talk about me much?" asked Anne.

"Who?"

"The church ladies."

"That's not a fair or a truthful name, Anne. I don't believe they're as dreadful as you make them out to be. They seem to have your best interests at heart."

"Then they *did* talk about me…"

A neighbor girl came to the door with a freshly killed chicken dangling from her fist. Ma took it, thanked her, handed it to Anne. Conversation was at an end.

Anne sat on an upturned pail and started to pluck the feathers. Halfway through she was distracted by a smell that she realized couldn't be coming from their cabin. Then she saw smoke drifting from the direction of the riverbank. The old man who lived down there had a lot of nerve, she thought, smoking his fish outside while a population of hungry folks lived within smelling range, not to mention the stray dogs about, who could be a lot more vocal than the neighbors.

Ma cut up the bird, then rinsed and patted it dry, while Anne whisked milk and an egg in a cooking bowl. Ma showed Anne how to take the chicken pieces, dripping with milk and egg, and roll them in a shallow bowl of flour, salt and pepper. They fried the chicken in shortening until the skin was a golden brown, and the aroma too much to bear for the dogs, who began a howling and whining from the double assault of smoking fish and frying chicken in the air.

Then came the part Anne looked forward to most: the baking of the mince pie. The secret lay in the contents of the mysterious jar on the top pantry shelf, which Ma had added to over time. By now it was a potent mixture of beef suet, raisins, apples, orange-peel, lemon juice, orange juice, sugar, nutmeg, cinnamon, and a pinch of salt.

The mincemeat also called for two glasses of brandy. "I'd like to get one of sherry," said Ma, "but we'll just have to make do." Fortunately, a small brown bottle of brandy had been saved for medicinal purposes. The making of the pie took them into the night, later than either of them were used to staying up.

But in the morning, a fine basket of food was waiting, and as Ma helped her put on a long pleated dress and big sunbonnet with a long yellow ribbon, Anne felt that success was assured.

"I think it's going to be fine," said Ma. "Fine enough for the Heights."

Anne turned from the little silver plate mirror above her bed. "You knew I was going with Eddie, didn't you?"

"Eddie sounds like a fine boy. I'm sorry you haven't been able to bring him here for a visit," Ma looked away so Anne couldn't see her face in the mirror. "But I understand."

As Anne understood why she hadn't been invited to the house where Eddie lived, up on the Heights, overlooking the river, the Meadows, the town itself. She imagined it had dark wood paneling, oil paintings, carpets, ferns, and bookcases five shelves tall.

That was the kind of house where, years ago, her mother used to take in laundry. There were two possible ways her daughter could enter a house such as that. One was through the servant's quarters. The other was through the front door, on the arm of the young man of the house.

"Sit up now," said Ma.

Anne sat on a tall stool, as Ma took her one precious item, a comb with a pearl handle, and ran it through her daughter's long auburn hair, twisting a few locks into a braid and tying it with green ribbons.

*** *** ***

The big sternwheeler was waiting when Anne arrived at the crowded waterfront. Her classmates were already in line. Most of them, like her, clutched picnic baskets and looked expectant. They were dressed, if not in Sunday best, then a shade better than school clothes. She thought her bonnet and freshly polished shoes looked smarter than any of the other girls' outfits.

Eddie carried his contribution, a jug of cider, and a red and white blanket folded across one arm. She hadn't expected him to provide food, although, as a boy from the Heights, he had access to food served on silver plates alongside fine wines. That was one reason she liked Eddie – he'd rather eat lunch with her at school than with any of the stuck-up girls in their class. If she'd ask Eddie *why* he wanted to share a basket he wouldn't have a ready answer, at least one that could be believed. He only wanted to be sure she was going with him.

When he caught her eye he looked more intrigued by her picnic basket than by what she was wearing. She had tucked a blue cloth napkin over the basket, and refused to give a clue as to what she'd brought. Once they were aboard, she did not protest when he drifted off to join the other boys his age.

She climbed the stairs all the way to the hurricane deck. Even at that height she felt the giant pistons throbbing through her boots. Before her, the Missouri's horizon spread to the mouth of the Little Sioux River. Spray from the bow speckled her face.

As they pulled from the wharf, above the cottonwood trees she could see the slate roof and chimneys of the Children's Home. It looked peaceful enough from this distance. But below that roof were walls and a courtyard where children lived and, she assumed, played, though she could not recall ever hearing happy sounds behind those walls.

She glanced from the rail to see Eddie in a close huddle with the other boys. It was her first chance to see how he behaved with friends and classmates outside school. She'd only been with him to the library, a band concert and a street fair, all very public places. And, of course, the walks beside the river, but those were the times they spent alone.

He looked up at her every once in a while, perhaps to see if she was still there, or if she was looking down at him.

The girls were talking in a small knot a little distance from the boys. She might be among them this moment, acting modest and gracious but ever so intriguing, giving those girls, who did everything short of openly snub her, a look at what she and her mother had prepared. If they asked "Who else is this for?" she wouldn't quite know what to answer, though she might ask in turn which boys *they* planned to share their picnic baskets with.

When the sternwheeler let them out at the picnic grounds, she was impressed that Eddie slung the basket over his arm without once looking at what was inside. Walking a bit farther than the rest, they found a spot where she spread out the red and white checkered blanket. Anne opened the basket, and brought out the dishes of fried chicken, potato salad and mince pie. She watched for his reaction, trying not to be too obvious about it.

"It looks grand," he said simply. Anne wasn't certain if he meant the food itself, or the plain pottery cookware.

"Wait 'till you taste it," said Anne.

As they ate, they watched the river, placid as a band of gray green silk compared to its usual wild and turbulent state. The only thing to break the surface was a small-mouth bass lunging after flies.

They fell silent. She noticed Eddie watching her. Not staring *at* her, exactly, but at something just beyond her.

"What is it?" she asked.

"The mayflies."

She swatted the air with one hand.

"Don't," he said. "They're nice to look at, especially around your red hair."

"It's *not* red. It's reddish brown. And look there." She pointed out other flies, the bluebottle kind, closing in on their picnic. Eddie shooed them away, bending closer as he did. A group of swans flew past the landing place at the shore.

"Know much about swans?" she asked.

"Not much, except they can be nasty. Some on the riverbank tried to bite me."

"Not the ones I know."

"Bet they wouldn't let you pet them on the head."

"I bet they would, since I feed them cake. They follow me down the river bank when I bring cake."

"What makes you so particular about swans, anyway?"

She closed her eyes before answering. "I don't know... something about the way they pull their necks out of the water. How they float on the surface. Muskrats, frogs, water bugs, they seem to belong here. Not swans. They glide, like rich folks glide through life. I've had notions that heaven is full of swans." She looked away, laughing. "Then they wag their tails and break the spell."

He leaned back, one arm tucked behind his head. His other arm tickled next to hers in the long grass. He could smell baking powder and mincemeat on her hands, and something else, a soapy fragrance.

"Know much about rivers?" she asked.

"I know a few things about this old river."

"I was thinking of the Danube."

"The what?"

"The beautiful blue Danube?"

"Oh," he shifted. "Of course."

"I saw a picture in a book. It's the river that flows through Vienna." She sat up suddenly and folded her arms over her knees. "I'm going there one day. That's the place to get a well-rounded education."

"Like what?"

“A well-rounded education is a little of *everything.* Cooking, piano, singing lessons. And in the evening, there's concerts, and carriage rides through the Vienna Woods."

"Like that?" Eddie pointed with the chicken wing to a horse and hay wagon, weighed down with their classmates, setting out for a short drive.

"Nothing like that,” she replied. “A carriage in the Vienna Woods is... is like a gondola on the Venice Grand Canal."

“I’ve never been there, but my folks have.”

“Wouldn’t you like to go there one day?”

"What would *I* do in Vienna?"

"Oh, there's lots for a boy with brains and ambition… if you’ve got it," she said, more softly. She picked up the pie plate. "More mince pie?"

He shook his head. His eyes followed the green ribbons dangling from her hair.

She lay back on the blanket. Before Vienna, she realized, must come the means to get her to Vienna. It would have to do with money, of course, but it had even more to do with a boat, the largest sternwheeler on the Missouri, its wheel sliding like glass through her fingers as she steered for a wharf, crowded with people shouting and waving their hats in the air, while a brass band played and bright cloth streamers flapped in the wind.

Her thoughts were broken by the schoolteacher’s whistle, calling the students back from the pony ride, the song circle, from their blankets on the meadow. They gathered up the baskets, counted heads, and boarded the sternwheeler once more.

They were obliged to share the return trip with a group of Bible-toters headed for a camp meeting upriver. The deck was so cramped that, once they landed and class was dismissed for the day, both needed to take a walk beside the river. She did, at any rate; Eddie held a napkin full of bread and pie crumbs.

From the river came a whooshing sound, a spray of water, and suddenly a big male swan lept from the bulrushes right in front of Eddie, all beak, wings flapping like thunder.

"Get back!" Anne shouted, at the same moment Eddie cried "Do they bite?"

The angry swan flapped its wings again and swished back into the rushes. "I forgot it was nesting season," said Anne. "You can't go anywhere near them."

She tried not to feel sorry she'd suggested this spot. She'd received her share of hisses from the swans, and they'd come close to biting her. But they tolerated her presence, especially when she brought food. Usually she fed them as they glided off the riverbank, but sometimes the adults and their young ones ambled up the bank to where she sat waiting for them.

As they were about to leave, a single female, apparently not nesting, approached them with curiosity. Anne encouraged Eddie to offer some crumbs from the napkin he carried. Pie crumbs, they discovered, were just as good as cake.

"See that, now?" she smiled. "Peace has been declared between Eddie and the swans."

She returned to the Meadows with empty basket, but full of the day's events to tell Ma.

When she entered the cottage, Ma was sitting upright on her bed, one hand opened in her lap, eyes half closed. It was her breathing, deep, wracked, that Anne noticed first.

Anne called her, loudly. Ma did not move.

Chapter Two

COURT ORDER drawn up at Marion, Iowa this 25th day of May, 1898

Whereas Anne Blackstone, sixteen years of age, residing in the provisional common space referred to as "the Meadows," has, as of this day, no living relatives nor means of support, and

Whereas the Children's Home of the Town of Marion, a suitable and commodious house has been erected by the Ladies Aid Society of Marion for the shelter and maintenance of children of unfit parents, abandoned, or orphaned upon the death of parents

Therefore: the Court of Monona County, being satisfied about the *bona fide* intention of the Ladies Aid Society and also being satisfied that such guardianship will be for the welfare and benefit of Anne Blackstone,

The Court does hereby, pursuant to the Revised Statutes, chap. XI, title 1st, "for the relief and support of indigent persons," appoint the Ladies Aid Society of Marion as guardians of said orphan, Anne Blackstone, to be placed under their tutelage for training as junior teacher and custodian for younger children residing at the Children's Home.

IN WITNESS WHEREOF, the parties hereto have affixed their signature on the day, month and year hereinabove written.

*** *** ***

There were certain special things – Ma's comb, for one – that Anne would not let them have. She stuffed the keepsakes in Ma's big carpetbag and left it with the Westerbury's, their neighbors just down the path towards the river. Anne was walking back from there when the ladies, court order in hand, pulled up in their coach.

It had the air of the funeral parlor about it as Anne stepped inside and took the one seat remaining, next to Miss Hutchins. Anne dared not speak; her heart was too much in her mouth. The three ladies were likewise quiet, though they did make attempts to smile. The coach rattled past the neighbors' cottages, chicken coops and small garden patches, places Anne wanted to imprint in her mind.

Miss Hutchins cleared her throat. "I will speak, Anne of your overall duties. Like the other older girls, you will be responsible for the younger children during certain parts of the day, primarily at bedtimes, mealtimes and at physical recreation in the courtyard. During the day they receive religious and social instruction."

"What is recreation, Miss?" asked Anne.

"Jump rope, hopscotch and stick ball," said the lady in the opposite seat.

"Amusement without laxity," said Miss Hutchins.

Anne was about to ask the meaning of "laxity," but held her tongue, not wishing to appear more ignorant than they already supposed her to be.

The coach pulled from the street and into a tunnel beneath a brick archway, a tunnel of darkest shadow. They drove into a large courtyard, with, at one side, swings, benches, and a small wooden platform. The Home itself was a three-story gabled fortress.

She was brought into the reception room, which had plush chairs, red velvet curtains, and a fireplace that gave a ruddy glow to the room. A silver tea service sat on a counter. Perhaps, she thought, Ma *had* been right - the Ladies did have her best interests at heart.

Miss Hutchins introduced Anne to the head teacher, Miss Radcliffe, and Miss Atwater, in charge of all things "household," whose upward-arching eyebrows made Anne think the woman had just been struck from behind.

Miss Atwater entrusted her to a matronly woman dressed like a laundress. The woman, keys jangling at her hip, took Anne down a passageway so dimly lit that Anne only knew by the sound of her shoes that they walked first on a carpet, then a wooden floor. They continued up a steep flight of stairs, darker still.

At the top of the stairs, the woman fished through her key ring, inserted one of the largest keys, and opened the door. "Dormitory," said the woman. "It's usually empty in the afternoon, but today we're giving the classroom a wipe down."

The beds were scrunched close together in three long uneven rows. There were windows, but they were small, segmented by a lattice of wooden crosses.

The children sat on beds, some alone, some in small groups. Anne guessed there were about thirty of them, most wearing the school uniform of gray and white. She had seen the children in those uniforms before, marching in two straight lines down the side of the road on a Sunday afternoon. She had never been close enough to see their faces.

Now there was curiosity in these faces – also fatigue, boredom, mild interest – but no joy. Was this, she wondered, the reaction to all new arrivals? Or to one they thought of as a hireling, who would beat them down?

"Let's have those clothes," said the woman with the keys. From a drawer she pulled out a starched uniform of gray, with white collars and cuffs. Anne looked about for a place to change. At this hesitation, the woman spoke louder.

"Off with them, now!"

Anne withdrew to one end of the large room. She undid her coat, stepped out of her dress, and stood for a cold, eternal moment in her underclothes. The children's expressions had hardly changed, yet they still watched her. She was grateful they were noticeably younger than she.

The woman pulled the uniform roughly over Anne's body, then stuffed her clothes into a sack. "For the laundry," she said. "You'll be getting them back someday."

She picked up the sack with Anne's clothes, opened the door and said, "Miss Hutchins will be sending for you," then locked the door, leaving Anne alone with the children. They brightened, slowly but noticeably, once the woman's steps receded down the stairs.

One little girl, who looked about six, her hair in brown curls, approached her. "Are you the new Glad Girl?" she asked.

Anne knelt down to look the girl in the eye. "What's a Glad Girl?"

"There's three Glad Girls," said a boy sitting on a nearby bed. He looked about eleven. "Three dormitories, three Glad Girls. The Ladies call them Monitors. The last one tried to run away, but they caught her."

Anne sat on the bed next to him. "What happened to her?"

The girl with brown curls shook her head. "We didn't see her ever again. And nobody ever told us what a-happened to her."

Anne drew a deep breath. "Well, I can't say if I'm the Glad Girl or not, but my name's Anne." She offered a hand. The girl hesitated, then shook it slowly, as if she'd forgotten how. "I'm Eugenie. That's James," she said, pointing to the boy.

"When did you come here, James?" Out of the corner of her eye, she noticed the children slowly gathering round, sitting on the nearby beds or standing nearby.

"Two years ago, on the Orphan Train."

"Orphan Train?"

"Dad answered an advertisement in the newspaper, from a family in Nebraska."

"Why, then you were no orphan at all!"

"But Dad couldn't afford to keep me no more, and this family, the Hinchcliffes, wanted to adopt me. So I went on a train, what they called the Orphan Train, out of Baltimore."

He looked down. "They said they wanted a boy, but they didn't neither. They wanted a hired hand. They made me sleep in the barn, and Old Man Hinchcliffe beat me with a leather belt when I wouldn't work, and fed me half as much as his own kids ate. So I ran away, but they caught up with me, and sent me here."

“I'm Annabelle,” said a girl in pigtails, about his same age. “Our train came out of Philadelphia.”

“And you ran away too?”

Annabelle nodded.

“Why?”

“I can’t say.” She whispered in Anne’s ear. “I’ll never, ever say.”

Anne looked closely at the children gathered about her - orphans, foundlings, the dispossessed – children she’d heard whispers about but never imagined becoming.

A key rattled in the door. It was unlocked by a different laundress-woman, who scanned the room quickly before settling on Anne.

“Anne Blackstone.”

“Yes?”

“Miss Hutchins wants you.” She raised her voice suddenly. “And the rest of you, dressed and ready for class in fifteen minutes. Cleaning’s over.”

The large embroidered sampler above Miss Hutchins’ desk was the first thing Anne noticed, perhaps the first thing anyone was intended to notice.

GREATER OBEDIENCE

GREATER TRUST

GREATER PRIVILEGES

Miss Hutchins wore reading glasses, lowered to her nose. She looked up from her papers.

"So. You have met the children. I have mentioned your duties preparing them for class, for mealtimes and recreation. You will, of course, stay in their quarters, to be available for their needs in the morning and at night."

"Miss Hutchins," Anne spoke quickly. "I understand there are other groups of children, looked after by older girls, like myself."

"That is true. They are other monitors, with their charges, in other sections of the building. You do not sit together at meal times; you will be seated with the children in your own dormitory. Your interactions with the other Monitors will be limited. The occasions when the children come together as a whole are well regulated."

She stood, and walked toward a corner. "The Children's Home is precisely that, a home for children who have no other homes. We have other functions as well. We are not a church, yet we provide religious instruction. We are not a school, yet we provide lessons in geography, mathematics, American History, and, of course, the Bible. We are not a workhouse, despite things you may have heard. There are institutions for the manual trades that employ older children, such as yourself.

"This is a home for younger children, for the innocents, whose characters have not fully formed." She leaned slightly closer, seizing Anne's attention as fully as if she had grabbed her by the collar. "We have been given a sacred trust: the development of young souls and minds. We accept this with the utmost seriousness. I trust you will too."

Anne found the children in the dining hall when her interview was done. They were sitting at three long rows of tables and benches, each of which seated ten to twelve, elbow to elbow.

The woman who had come to fetch her for the interview explained the protocol of meals. She was not, as Anne thought, a laundress, but was known as Staff, as Anne was known as Monitor. The Staff dished out meals, assisted by either a Monitor or one of the children – if not an older child, then a husky one, who doled out portions with a ladle, or poured the large pitchers of milk, water or tea. As they waited, the children, except for the very youngest, sat in silence, hands folded.

Obedience, Trust, Privilege. Rewards, Anne thought, that were worth the effort.

"Dear Lord, from Whom all blessings flow..." the children recited in messy unison. "Make us truly grateful for this food we are about to receive. A-men."

Today Anne received the same food as her charges - thin stew of uncertain origin, potatoes, and to drink, watered-down milk served in stained crockery. There were, she guessed, almost three times as many children in the dining room as she had met in the sleeping room. The entire room continued to eat, in silence. She looked the room over thoroughly for other Glad Girls. It was not a term Miss Hutchins or the Staff woman had used; Anne supposed the children had made it up.

Far across the room she saw the other Monitors - two older girls, sitting, like her, at the end of a table. She kept looking in their direction, hoping they would look up as well. But there was little looking up on anyone's part. She sensed it would be forbidden to so much as cross the room and stand before them.

At the farthest end of the large room was a separate quarter, like an elevated stage, concealed behind a screen, but partly visible. She noticed a smaller table, with chairs instead of benches, a large bowl of fruit, and the silver tea service she'd first seen in the reception room. One by one, the ladies in black took their seats around that table.

When it was time for bed, she had noses to wipe, hands to wash, and faces to scrub. It was, she was told, permissible to tell bedtime stories. She made one up about a little swan who won a race against the larger, stronger swans when they decided to see who was the greatest swan on the river.

The story satisfied the children, but they wanted more.

"Suppose you tell me one?"

Eugenie sat down next to her. "We can tell you what happens to the *bad* children."

"There's the bad," said James, joining them on the bed, "and the really bad."

"You hold your hands like this," said Eugenie, hands face up. "Then they hit you with a belt."

Other children chimed in, providing detail upon detail. "And they make you bend over, grab your ankles, and hit you with a paddle!"

"Or they lock you in a closet with Mrs. Jones!"

"Mrs. Jones? Who's that?"

"Her husband gave the money to build this place," said Eugenie. Her voice fell to a whisper. "They say he died of poison, then she got sick, and shriveled away. Now they keep her here, locked away in the dark."

"*Now* I think you're making things up," said Anne. "I can believe the paddles and the belt; they do that at other schools. But a Mrs. Jones in a closet -"

"Just watch," said James. "They take her out sometimes. Sometimes in the carriage."

"Sometimes in a hearse," said Eugenie.

"No!" said Anne.

"And sometimes to walk."

"She's shriveled and old, but still walks!" said James. "You'll see."

Eugenie climbed on the bed next to Anne. "But the *really, really* bad children, they put on a shelf, in the dark."

"Only bread and water to drink, and not even that, sometimes."

"Now this has to stop!" said Anne. "I don't want you giving us nightmares. I can believe everything else, even in Mrs. Jones, but I can't believe anyone's seen or heard children put away on a shelf."

"We didn't make it up," said Eugenie. "One of the Misses told us about it."

"They're just trying to scare you into doing things their way, like ghost stories and fairy tales, telling what happens to wicked little girls and boys."

Eugenie only stared, with a weariness that belied anything Anne could say.

"Miss Anne," James' voice fell to a dead whisper. "You've only been here a day. You don't know what they do when everyone's asleep."

"Do you believe those stories, too?" Anne asked, trying to smile.

"I believe in God," said James, "who makes the sun to shine, the grass to grow, cows to give milk, and puts food on the table."

"And keep away sin, wickedness and idolators," said Annabelle. "I believe in the Saints, the Apostles and the Lamb of God."

"And Jesus?" said Anne. "Do they tell you about Jesus, who preached mercy and forgiveness?"

"On Sundays," said James. "They take us to church on Sundays."

That night, Anne dreamt she was suffocating in blackness. Light entered when a very small door was opened, to reveal the profile of a woman with hair pulled tightly back. She held a candle aloft. In its light, she had pinched-up eyes and a sneering lip. She peered into the blackness as if checking a tray of cookies in the oven.

When the woman turned away, the door was left open. Anne squeezed out of it, then walked through rooms and down passageways, cold floorboards creaking beneath her bare feet. There was no moon, no candles burning, but the outlines of things were seen in a dull silvery glow.

She heard a moaning from inside one room. Thinking it was a child, she opened the door. The room itself was pitch black, but in the center of it, suspended, as if in thin air, was a small ferret-faced, wizened head. The person – if this was a person – did not seem to notice her, or that the door had opened, but was immersed in conversation with someone not in the room. Then she saw hands, fluttering, gesturing in the air.

The head and hands, so pale white, belonged to a body encased in black as deep as the room.

*** *** ***

In the days, weeks and months to come, demarcated by the Currier and Ives calendar hanging in Miss Hutchin's office, Anne learned to drop everything and report for duty whenever she heard the word "Monitor!" in her presence. She met the other girl monitors (for they were only girls, like herself) at afternoon recess time or for brief moments during meals. One's name was Lizzie, the other Isabelle. Both had come to the Home as small children, and had no other family. They were, like Anne, true orphans.

She discovered there really was a Mrs. Jones – Mrs. Edward Jones, in fact. Not only did her husband's money provide a trust fund for the Home, but it had once actually been their home. Not long after Mr. Jones passed away, his widow had been persuaded to turn the house into, as it was then known, the School for Orphans. Though Mrs. Jones did not take active part in the Home's operation, she continued to live there. Then she herself took ill, and was not seen for many months.

When she emerged, it was as the shuffling little creature, seen only behind the protective black skirts of the Ladies. Anne rarely got a glimpse of her face, but from what she did see, there was a resemblance to the creature in her dream. Beneath her dark veils, she was, in Lizzie's words, "frightening as ectoplasm at a séance." Despite this, she did go outside the grounds, sometimes in the carriage, sometimes on foot, though always escorted, and sometimes in a custom-built vehicle that resembled an oversized baby buggy with black curtains.

The only occasions when Anne did leave the Home were, in fact, to go to church on Sundays. At least two of the Ladies walked in front of the two lines of children, two walked behind, and the Staff walked at either side. Anne watched the faces along the street, and in church, searching for Eddie's face, or any familiar face, but at other times hoping no one she knew would be on the street, and recognize her. For as long as the eyes were upon her from in front, from behind, and from the side, she dared not change her step.

Anne learned the cost of any infractions, of any sloppiness or misbehavior by the children in her care. "Modesty in dress, in speech, in manners," was the doctrine of appearance, according to Miss Atwater. "The clothes must be orderly and free of wrinkles. The hair parted just to the side for the boys, trimmed straight on both sides of the face for the girls, tied back with a neat bow if it is long. There can be no exceptions."

For general misbehavior, the children were made to stand on a chair in the place of their transgression - in a corner of the classroom, at one end of the dining hall, or, if they were at recess, on a box in the corner of the yard, while the other children played around them.

One autumn morning Anne was instructed to wash and scrub the children especially well. The Staff delivered their uniforms laundered and fluffed. One of the Home's benefactors, a Mr. Sturgood, would be paying a visit, accompanied by the Mayor himself. Anne was directed with having the children on their best behavior, by any means possible.

The classroom had been decorated with oval portraits of the Presidents, a map of the United States, letters of the alphabet, and multiplication tables. At Miss Radcliffe's instruction, Anne sat at the rear of the classroom, ready to remove any child from the room who demonstrated anything less than perfect manners and posture.

Soon after the geography lesson began there was a polite tapping at the door. Miss Hutchins announced the presence of the Mayor and Mr. Sturgood. Two bearded men stepped inside.

"Isn't this *wonderful*, children?" asked Miss Radcliffe, in an affected voice. "We have special visitors. Aren't we grateful, children?"

"Yes, Miss Radcliffe," they replied, in messy unison.

"Thank you, thank you, children," said Mr. Sturgood. The teacher ushered him to a place that faced the rows of desks, then eased herself into a seat where she could face the entire class.

The benefactor placed his thumbs under his lapels. "Children… I want you to think of me as your friend, just as," he glanced at the two ladies, "these two good Ladies are, I'm certain, your friends."

A nervous look was exchanged between the Misses Hutchins and Radcliffe. The latter cleared her throat abruptly, and looked down at Tabitha, who stood abruptly by her desk.

"If you please, Mr. Sturgood," quavered Tabitha, "I will recite a poem."

Miss Hutchins nodded again.

"How lovely, how charming the sight,
When children their teacher obey;
The angels look down with delight
This beautiful scene to survey."

"Charming, indeed," said the Mayor. "Do we know anything of the major poets?"

"The children," said Miss Radcliffe, "are not well-versed in the classics. Not yet," as she scanned the class. "But they have committed to memory certain homilies. Angelica?"

Angelica Wilkes, eight years old, stood at attention. She looked straight forward as she recited:

"Here's a lesson all should heed -- try, try, try again.
If at first you don't succeed -- try, try, try again.

Let your courage well appear,
If you only persevere,
You will conquer -- never fear - try, try again."

"Excellent!" said Mr. Sturgood, as he and the Mayor responded with spontaneous applause, which prompted a slight curtsy from Angelica. The children, unused to applause for any occasion, were uncertain if they were supposed to respond in kind, yet a private, withering look from Miss Hutchins urged silence.

The afternoon meal was, as Anne expected, a horn of plenty compared to the regular fare. There were pan-fried snap peas, a warm and flavorsome bread, roast turkey, and *pie* for dessert. Once the Mayor and the Benefactor had observed and heartily approved the menu, they took their chairs at the Ladies' table, where the bounty of food could only be imagined. Anne, Lizzie and Isabelle had been told by the Staff that, after the blessing, reasonable conversation among the children would be permitted, though the Monitors would be strictly accountable for their behavior.

So she remained at the table of the children under her charge, looking up every once in a while toward the tables of Lizzie and Isabelle. This time they returned her glances. The looks on their faces were joyful, sometimes comical, but most of all, expressed a desire to sit at the same table, heads close together, lost in gossip and the confidences girls yearn to share with one another.

Chapter Three

The day had begun – as had a number of days in Anne's ten months at the Home – with the sound of Hannah's crying. It had not been loud enough to alert the Staff, but enough to send a ripple through the children within hearing distance. When Anne got out of bed to put her arms around Hannah the children in the neighboring beds were crying as well, as one who hears a cough in a crowded room is compelled to cough.

But Anne could not bring back Hannah's mother, or make Miss Hutchins or Miss Atwater behave any more kindly, and Anne was a poor liar. Besides, she could think of little else but the plan for today. While drying Hannah's tears, she went over the details in her mind: items sown into the lining of a coat, a cheery smile, an appearance at the right place and time.

Weak tea was already being poured as the children, in two straight lines, filed in. An older girl stood at the rear of the dining room ladling porridge. Except for an occasional sniffle from a tall, thin girl at the end of the table, the children ate in silence.

Close to the end of the meal, there was a commotion from the Ladies' dining room, and Miss Atwater entered the hall carrying a silver platter. On it was a large apple tart, still steaming from the oven. She walked slowly behind the row of seated children, then stopped behind the chair of freckled, round-cheeked Caleb Prescott and placed the tart before him.

"For *merit*," said Miss Atwater. Her voice echoed in the dining hall, breaking the silence. "For scholarship, and…" as she tapped the back of his head, he blinked in surprise, "…for committing to memory *three* Old Testament stories."

In the returning silence, eyes grew wide and fingers clutched the tablecloth hanging below the table.

"Go on, Caleb," said Miss Atwater. "Eat. You deserve it."

Slowly, unsteadily, Caleb brought the spoon, with a small portion of the tart, to his lips. His hand shook. As it reached his quivering lips, an infinitesimal tremor could be felt along the length of the table, a gurgling, a contraction of throats and rumbling stomachs.

Caleb was unable to get more than two spoonfuls into his mouth before he burst into tears. Miss Atwater wasted no time in pulling him from the chair and escorting him from the room. One of the Staff brought the apple tart after them.

As they did after each breakfast, the children pushed back from the long table, stood, made an about face toward the aisle, and marched out to the courtyard for morning exercise. From the Ladies dining room Anne could hear Miss Atwater demanding that Caleb eat every last spoonful.

Anne wondered how, once the children were caught up in games of hopscotch, rolling hoops and jump rope, an episode such as that in the dining hall could be so quickly forgotten. But time and again she had seen it happen.

She walked the perimeter of the yard, grasping her elbows tight, her steps those of a caged animal let free into a larger, but no less enclosed pen. She imagined herself in twenty, even fifteen years, a tighter-lipped, dowdier version of herself, barking at the children, wanting nothing so much as a crocheted shawl about her shoulders, a rocker and a cup of warm tea.

It was from an open window that she heard Miss Hutchin's voice.

"Just as I have told you. After being with us almost a year she is quite capable of maintaining discipline on her own."

"Anne?" replied Miss Atwater. "She's still one of them, only older."

“But on the threshold of becoming a young woman," said Miss Hutchins, undeterred.

"It is true, she reads her Bible, can quote passages if necessary. She plays 'the Glad Girl' well, very well."

Anne stopped completely, so they would not hear the crunch of her shoes on the courtyard's gravel.

“Still," continued Miss Radcliffe, "I do not find her stories entirely suitable for the children."

“She has a vivid imagination," said Miss Hutchins. "And she keeps the children entertained, far better than any Glad Girl I have seen. I could even say I find her most capable."

There was a pause, as Anne heard the director step even closer to the open window. Anne stepped back, her feet turning softly on the gravel.

The younger children were stretched out for their afternoon naps, sleeping, or lying with eyes closed, pretending to sleep. Some of the older children drew pictures, counted on their fingers or sang softly to themselves. It did not matter, so long as they were quiet.

Anne gazed through the big picture window, the only one in her ward that did not have bars across it. It was at such moments she thought about Ma, Eddie, and her few childhood friends, like Missy Carlton. She looked past the cottonwood trees, towards the rooftops of town, and beyond them, to the gray plume rising from a steamboat at the landing.

When Pa was still alive and working on the river, there was a favorite place of his, a place at the heart of Marion's landing, where he returned to without fail when he returned from his work trips. Everyone in town knew Fantine's.

Anne had first stepped through its swinging doors one Saturday night over ten years ago, when Ma went to fetch Pa from the poker tables and, in case persuasion was needed, had brought Anne with her. She taught the child to clasp her hands together and, with tears in her eyes, beg father to come home.

On that first visit Anne caught only a glimpse of Fantine, from far across the room. She had a black lace collar around her throat. Her hair was piled atop her head. She wore a dress probably made in Kansas City, though it may well have come from Paris. She stood behind the long oak bar at the back of the room, where river men stood elbow to elbow with the pariahs of Marion. It was Harry, the barman, who returned Pa to them, hair still damp from the dousing beneath the water pump.

After Pa died, when the boiler on their boat cracked only two miles from port and eight men died in the explosion, Fantine's became her amusement, her theater, her life. It was also located at the heart of the Marion landing - a synonym, to the church ladies, for the gutter.

And that, Anne thought, might be the safest place imagineable.

Below stairs, the bell sounded for the afternoon meal. With a shrug, she turned from the window and gathered up her charges.

After the morning's incident, the afternoon meal was more subdued. The Ladies presented no awards. There were mashed peas in a watery broth, hard bread, and on each child's plate was a wedge of cheese.

Did it have something to do, Anne wondered, with Religious Instruction, the next class period? Perhaps there was some parable or citation having to do with cheese. Was cheese served at the Last Supper? The appearance of it on their humble plates was a small miracle.

While leading the children to class, she passed the door to the Ladies' dining room. It was open just enough to hear a snatch of conversation. It was brief, but precisely what Anne had hoped to hear.

"Will she ride today?

"No, the pram has a wobble to it. And it is so pleasant out. I think she will walk today."

At precisely three o'clock, Anne appeared at the door to the reception room. Inside the room were Miss Hutchins, Miss Atwater, two of the staff and a small figure covered by a shawl, crowned with a black bonnet.

"I cannot understand it," said Miss Hutchins, "and I'm not quite sure we can excuse such absenteeism. But regardless, Mrs. Jones must have her walk."

She stepped slowly into the doorway. Miss Hutchins noticed her first.

"Anne?"

The Staff looked up as well, and drew to the side. Mrs. Jones stood in their midst, blankly facing the reception room wall.

"Anne, you know the route we take for Mrs. Jones' walk?"

"Yes, Miss Hutchins."

"Describe it, please."

"Down High Street, around the park, east on Maple Street, and return."

"That is correct." She placed her hands on Mrs. Jones' shoulders, and turned her slowly until she faced Anne. "Go fetch your coat, Anne. You may take her for a short walk. The Staff will look after the children while you are out."

Those two words summoned Mrs. Jones from her impenetrable state. Her face broke into fresh wrinkles as she smiled, and held out her hand.

Anne dashed, when she dared to dash, down the hall and up the stairs to the sleeping room, grabbed her coat, her mind all the while racing through the fragments of her plan: images of streets, of the carpetbag tucked in her neighbor's closet at the Meadows, of whether she dared say goodbye to James, Eugenie, Hannah, even a quick embrace or a smile and a squeeze of the hand…

But they were only fleeting thoughts.

In a moment, she stood outside the courtyard door, Mrs. Jones' cold, bony hand in hers, the two of them blinking by the side of the road. There were the distant neighbor's houses, and the clip-clop of horses and sounds of children playing, which, if Mrs. Jones did hear, she made no sign of recognizing. But realizing that she was in the presence of someone new, she moved her small, trembling hands about Anne's shoulders.

"And are you one of the Glad Girls?" she quavered, in a voice to match her smallness.

"Yes," said Anne, practically into her ear.

"And what is your name?" she asked.

So she could hear!

"My name is *Anne.*"

"I knew a woman named Anne. She went on the stage. That was the last we heard of her."

Before they had taken a few steps, Mrs. Jones asked if she could feel Anne's face. Anne bent over slightly, as the woman's tendril-like fingers, still atremble, passed over her mouth, her nose, through the curls of her hair. As the tiny old woman nodded in approval, Anne had the distinct feeling that she was not entirely blind, just as she was not completely deaf and dumb.

The "quick walk" was neither quick nor careless, but a slow, shuffling pace of tiny steps and veering feet, which Anne had to guide every so often back to the sidewalk, all the while keeping an eye for any familiar people on the street. Would they recognize her, and without intention make a ruin of her plan?

A horse and carriage drove past; she felt compelled to see if there was a familiar face, but at the same instant, dared not, as she had not dared on the Sunday walks to church.

Though she tended to veer and needed steering, much as a small boat would, Mrs. Jones knew the route well. She made the turn at High Street before Anne did, and brightened at the sounds of dogs and children in the park.

As Anne bent to sip from a drinking fountain she let go of Mrs. Jones' hand for only a moment. Though she weaved ever so slightly, the woman did not fall or stumble. So she could stand – perhaps even walk – unaided.

Anne took her hand with a lighter touch this time, prompting Mrs. Jones to place less weight on Anne's arm. At the same time, rather than turning east on Maple, she continued straight across the street from the park, onto Arnold Street.

Does she feel anything like I do? Anne wondered. The elation, the wind blown from the river that buoys you up like a swan, gliding above the town? How long had it been since she had felt this happy?

In a playful, rather than malicious way, Anne felt the urge to grasp Mrs. Jones by her cardboard thin shoulders and give her a spin, round and round, until, without good sight or sound to aid her, she was as good as lost, and it would take the Ladies the better part of a day to locate her, by which time Anne would be far away.

"Mrs. Jones!"

"We haven't returned yet, have we, child?"

"Mrs. Jones, I'm going to leave you here!" She raised her voice, and was not sure why, since she'd found that she didn't need to speak this loudly for Mrs. Jones to hear. "Please don't stray into the road. I don't want the carriages to hit you. But if you like, Mrs. Jones, keep walking!"

Mrs. Jones smiled, appearing to be in the grip of a game that she hadn't played in almost eighty years

"*Run,* Mrs. Jones, if you can!" The old woman probably did not hear, but stood there, blinking like a mole that had stumbled into sunlight.

Anne gathered her cloak about her throat, covering the white collar of the uniform she wore beneath. Turning towards the river, she kept her eyes level. She could not stand out, not be stopped by anyone as long as she wore the uniform. They would wonder what she was doing so far from the Children's Home, perhaps tell someone about the girl orphan who had lost her way.

The nearer she came to the landing, the less important her appearance became. The path wound past young sports lounging on the corner, peddlers with dime remedies and the peepshow at the Mutoscope Parlor, where the turn of a crank made a series of photographs flip around a wheel. The proprietor told her that back in

Chicago and New York there were pictures that moved “just like real life,” but he never did anything about bringing them to Marion. It was years since he’d bothered to change the photos in the Mutoscopes. By now everyone in town had seen the young lady who lifted her skirts above the knee and the cook who fell into a barrel of flour and came out looking like a ghost.

She walked past an abandoned sawmill, until she came in sight of the boat houses, the wharf, and down the street to the right, next to a rundown building with ROOMS painted in dark red letters all along the front porch, was Fantine’s.

She wanted only to see Fantine or her barman, Harry. He was Fantine’s partner as well, and had a talent for putting together impromptu vaudeville shows. Anne had helped with the shows a number of times, pushing back the chairs, turning the kerosene lamps down low, and on one occasion assisting the magician.

That was what she could offer now. Or, as on nights when Fantine shushed the boys and gave Anne the stage, she could recite poems she’d learned at school, like "Barbara Alan," "Excelsior," and "Annie Laurie." When the boys coughed up the dollar coins and bills, Fantine let her keep whatever they threw. It might be no more than a pocket full of change, but was a great deal more than she’d ever seen at the Children’s Home.

The sun had just gone down when she knocked at Fantine’s door.

Chapter Four

The door opened a mere second. A hand shot out, grabbed Anne by the forearm and pulled her inside.

Fantine was decked out for the evening: pinned-up hair, lace collar, and her dress, while not exactly dripping with pearls, sparkled like green jade when she turned in the lamplight. There was a scent of toilet water in the air. Anne plopped into a stuffed chair and told Fantine the day's adventures.

"Brimstone and cinders!" Fantine tapped a cigarette on an abalone case "What are we going to do with you?"

"I can't go back to the Meadows. They'd look for me there sure."

"You… tell anybody at that Home about my place?"

Anne shook her head.

"They wouldn't look for you here?"

"Oh, I *hope* not! For your sake!"

"Well then…" Fantine scraped a match on her heel, and lit the cigarette. "First thing is to get some new clothes on you."

Anne pulled at the cuff of her gray uniform. "You can burn this, for all I care."

Fantine puffed awhile, then looked towards her dressing room down the hall. "I got a couple things would fit you, but not enough for a full get up."

"All my clothes are in a carpetbag in Mrs. Westerbury's closet."

"Who's she?"

"Our neighbor at the Meadows, old friend of Ma's."

"Then we get that carpetbag."

For the first time that day, Anne smiled.

"Tomorrow morning." Fantine flicked ash into a copper bowl at her elbow. "Let's make that *late* morning."

"Is it a good house tonight, Fantine?"

"If you call a coal barge crew *good*, sure." She scratched her scalp. "There must be something in my closet that'll fit you, just for tonight."

She looked the uniform up and down. "Rest up a bit, then come give a hand in the kitchen. Lord knows what they eat on a coal barge; they'll probably be famished. When food's about done you can slip into my dress and have a seat at the back. The boys will keep an eye on you."

Over steam rising from a pot of boiling potatoes Anne caught a glimpse of the barge crew. A hole in the wall between the kitchen and the bar gave her a good peek at the gaming room. The crew pounded fists on the bar and hoisted each other aloft to see the liquor on the top shelf and, higher still, the legs of the girls who watched from the balcony.

When her pile of potatoes was done, Anne slipped into the kitchen bathroom and changed into the dress Fantine set aside. It had none of the bright colors and spangled brocade the upstairs girls wore, but was the most elegant thing Anne had put on since the day Pa came home with a pocketful of cash and bought everyone new clothes.

She entered the room near the back, where her Pa's old drinking pals - Jack, Horace, Big Steve and Willie - played a game of five-card stud. When Anne visited Fantine's, these were the boys that kept an eye on her.

"Hey-ya Annie!" Big Steve called.

Anne lifted her chin higher. Miss Hutchins and her minions couldn't touch her in this place. She had protectors.

One stranger in the room was definitely not from the barge. He wore a loud checker-striped jacket, and spoke in a voice to match. He tacked up a poster at the back of the room, then pulled a wad of papers out of his pocket and passed them amongst the crowd. Anne stepped closer to the poster. It was a drawing of a woman in tights, her hair up, right arm gesturing in an arc, and beneath her a horse or an elephant, Anne couldn't tell which in the dim gaslight. But the words were prominent:

PRESENTING

THE SPECTACULAR RIVER QUEEN

PERFORMING COMPANY

in the stirring drama

"HEART'S WOUNDS"

with comedic interludes

Dancers, Juggling, and Buffoonery

Adults 25¢ Children 10¢

FRIDAY NIGHT, ON THE RIVER

PROMPTLY AT 7:30

Anne caught Harry's eye at the bar. She was just about to take an empty chair when a bargeman stumbled against her. On instinct, she jumped back to see if he'd rifled her pockets. As she looked at his hands, dirty but empty, he put one of them across her knee.

"Now see here!" she hissed. He laughed and stuck his face close to hers. His breath was a furnace of onions and rank whiskey.

"Now see here!" she cried, three times as loud.

Quiet descended in a wave from the gaming tables to the bar, until the only sound came from the player piano. Big Steve hoisted the bargeman by his armpits and whisked him away so quickly Anne wasn't sure if he went out by the front doors or the back alley.

*** *** ***

"There's no doubt in my mind. This means you're of age."

"Of age for what, Fantine?" Anne sat in the carriage between Fantine and Toinette, an old friend of hers from Kansas City.

"Why, to take care of yourself." Fantine's glance at 'Toinette appealed for help. "You can't… stay in the kitchen forever."

"You mean – "

The horse bucked at the sound of an automobile's horn. Harry eased the coach over just in time for the vehicle, billowing dust, to zoom past.

"What is it, a Duryea?" asked Fantine, peering through the dust.

"Damn nuisance," muttered Harry.

“I don’t know,” said ‘Toinette. “If some nice gentleman offered me a ride in a Duryea, I doubt I’d refuse.”

“That a fact?” Fantine looked at her friend with a hint of surprise. “Maybe we’ll just have to go up to Kansas City and try one out.”

“Fantine, an automobile!” Anne exclaimed.

“I don’t see as why not. Lady ought to travel in style, if she has the means. Which reminds me…” Fantine lowered her voice. "This young man…”

“Eddie?”

“His folks must be pretty well off."

"Them up in the Heights?" Anne sat straight up in the seat. "I don't aim to ask any favors of them." In truth she hoped to see Eddie, planned to write him. But as long as she remained at Fantine's Place she couldn't see him, not yet.

“Never hurts to ask,” said Fantine. “You know,” she glanced sideways at ‘Toinette, “it took a string of favors to put me where I am today.”

Anne’s feet touched her old carpetbag, Ma's pearl-handled comb tucked safely inside, sitting on the carriage floor. She smiled at the thought of Mrs. Westerbury when she’d opened the door to the two women in smart dresses and feathered hats. She'd looked so surprised she hadn’t even noticed Anne standing between them.

*** *** ***

Kept busy with kitchen knife, broom and wash buckets, Anne found herself spending more time with the girls upstairs. They had names like Flossie, Lil, Dubuque Mary, and Waterloo Sal. One named Cassie was the nearest her own age.

On Friday morning, she asked Cassie to fix her hair. She hadn't slept well; Flossie and Sal had been laughing their heads off for hours upstairs. Cassie combed out Anne's auburn tresses, and stuck a scalloped comb at the side of her head.

"That's not how I usually comb it," said Anne.

"We'd like to see your face."

"Why?"

"You know." Cassie gave Anne's cheek a light pinch. "You won't be slicing potatoes in the kitchen forever. You wouldn't want to, neither." She wet her thumb and forefinger. "Face facts." She curled three locks on Anne's forehead into the shape of slender rings. "You can travel with captains and first mates, get treated like a lady and wake up in the morning with a nice wad of dollars - twenty times more than a girl makes at the mills or the cannery.

"Or, you can wake up on your back in a coal barge with your dress tored off." She took Anne's chin between her thumb and forefinger. "Either way, Annie, you're in the flesh trade. You might as well go first class."

The Whore of Babylon, only three years her senior, spoke to Anne while combing her hair. The Ladies had alluded to her, though not by such names, in Bible studies class. To them, the struggle was clear cut: the spirit and the flesh, the fields of the Lamb, or the cesspool of the unrighteous.

Anne must have spoken to women like that dozens of times before she went to the Home. She only knew them as the jolly, reckless girls who leaned from the balcony and laughed too much.

Cassie's fingers slipped away from Anne's chin. "Don't worry, Annie. Things ain't nearly as rough as they were in Fantine's day…" she looked away, with an amused smile, "… or in my Mom's day."

Anne took her hand. "Will you do me a favor, Cassie?"

Cassie nodded.

"Can I go to the milliner's with you?"

Cassie let go of her hand, and turned away. "I don't know…"

"Fantine said it was all right, just at the landing. And I'll wear a hat."

So with a borrowed hat, she walked with Cassie through the front doors of Fantine's Place, past the decrepit building with **ROOMS** painted in red along its side, and into the street. She could only see well directly in front of her; the hat was conveniently draped at the side.

Halfway to the milliner's they heard music, floating from downriver.

"Pipe organ," said Cassie. Anne had no idea what she was talking about; the only organ she knew belonged in a church.

Young boys raced past them, running towards the water. The man who owned the livery stable across the street came out in his doorway, a customer peering over his shoulder.

Two columns of smoke rose just beyond the bend. What pulled into the clearing was like nothing that had been seen in Marion before: a two-storied barge with a gingerbread house, frosted windows, cloth banners and streamers glistening in the wind. A chugging towboat only half its size pushed the decorated cake box ahead. On the top deck a man wearing rubber gloves played a steam calliope, whose sound was somewhere between a whistle and water gurgling down a throat.

As the craft pulled to the landing, three musicians in pale yellow uniforms took up the calliope's tune on cornet, trumpet and bugle. A rope was tossed, a plank was laid to the wharf, and a small troupe of fancy dressed people stepped down.

"Show folks," she heard someone in the crowd say.

A tall man carrying a banner with tassels and fringe was the first down the gangplank. "The River Queen," said the banner. "Tonight on the Landing." A small wind band followed him, some with little music stands attached to their instruments.

Dancers came down the plank. A man in long tails took a bow, while his partner did a small pirouette. One dressed in an acrobat's tights did a back flip and flexed his muscles. A little man in a band uniform scurried ashore, a sheaf of large handbills under his arm. He tacked one to the first wood piling he came to.

He saw Anne watching, and handed her a piece of paper. It was the same handbill that the man in the loud suit had passed out at Fantine's, only the emphasis was "Moral and Refined Entertainment, **Tonight** on the River."

A man in a captain's uniform followed the band and leafleteers. He tipped his hat to Anne as he passed, appearing to mouth *A pleasure!* though the drums were so loud she couldn't hear.

She discovered change in her pocket, and was quite ready to spend 25 cents for a ticket. A rather out of breath man in the band told her not to worry, there would be plenty of tickets available at show time.

When the small entourage from Fantine's arrived for the evening's performance, the showboat's upper deck and entryway were braided with torches. Just inside the boat, the little man who had been passing out handbills sat in a cubicle – it would surely have constrained a normal sized person – and sold tickets for the evening show.

The Captain stood just behind the booth, in the center of the red-carpeted aisle, tipping his hat to the ladies, shaking a hand when he appeared to know someone. The people flowed around him like a stream around a rock. Anne caught his eye, but he did not appear to recognize her from the morning.

Their seats were about ten rows back. Once seated, Anne looked over her shoulder. The theater itself looked larger than the outside of the boat. Townsfolk filled its boxes and rows of benches, stretching to the rear wall. Some benches had cushions, some were long, hard planks anchored to each side of the theater. The band came down the aisle to take their seats in the orchestra pit. There was an overture, acrobats, a "Singer of Sentimental Song" with magic lantern slides, a soft shoe dance and a magician. After intermission came the drama itself, "Heart's Wounds." It was rather like a dime novel Anne had once read: a poor young couple wish to marry, a miserly landowner, and a sudden inheritance that brings about the happy ending. The one aspect that really surprised her was that the leading lady, a beautiful dark-haired woman, was the only one to break character and acknowledge the applause when she walked onstage.

Most of the entourage wanted to leave the moment the curtain came down. Anne wished to stay and meet the cast and crew. But she knew she'd return the following day, when the *River Queen* was open for public viewing.

Anne didn't sleep well that night. Lights were going off in her head; electric lights on the street, torches on the bank, lamps at the foot of the stage. She remembered the faces, costumes, and sets in the glow of that light, the steam hissing from the calliope. How could she sleep?

Wrapped in a cloak, she raced to the dock by 10:30, for the one scheduled tour of the day. A handful of people were already gathered on the wharf – fortunately, no one she knew among them. The little man from the day before, in his hat and coat, carrying a suitcase, walked down the plank. He waved farewell to someone on the boat, blew a loud raspberry to a man who'd hurled some oath after him, and vanished into the landing.

The guide asked the people to gather round. He introduced himself as Arthur, a member of the *River Queen* touring show.

"This," he raised his voice, "is the first visit by a showboat of the first rank to towns big and small on the Missouri River. *The River Queen* plays all the major stops along the upper and lower

Mississippi, and the Ohio." He led them up the plank, and past the cubicle. "The dangers and swift current of the Missouri have made such a voyage practically impossible – until now."

There was a narrow stairway set off to one side that she hadn't noticed last night. She asked Arthur about it.

"That? It goes up to the Crow's Nest."

"Crow's…?" Anne look puzzled.

"Where the colored folks sit."

Anne began to ask a question, but the tour guide had already led the small group down a hallway, carpeted in red, with gold leaf patterns of breaking waves on the walls. Without the motion and press of the audience, she could see the plush chairs in the first five rows.

"Total capacity," said Arthur, "four hundred and fifty, not counting standing room." He walked them down toward the orchestra pit. "Gas lamps," he said, tapping the sides of the stage.

As he led them backstage, he pointed out the huge canvas sets propped against a wall. "The four basic scenes: saloon, parlor, village street and a clearing in the woods." He showed them the backs, also painted.

At the back of the stage were dressing rooms, with an assortment of wigs, glasses and props for each character. "Also double as bedrooms," said Arthur, opening one door and allowing a peek before he closed it quickly.

They exited at the stern, looking directly toward the towboat, *Sally Ann.* It had, Anne noticed, a pilothouse of glass and tarpaper sticking above hurricane deck, and a squared-off bow, to make for a snug push. She was heading for a closer look when Arthur ushered everyone toward the upper deck, which was ringed by a picket fence and dotted with life preservers.

He directed their attention to the calliope, a spiral formation of shiny silver bottles, just behind the pilothouse. They were attached to a keyboard, in front of which was a small stool. Each of them hissed with gusts of steam. He reached down, turned a small valve and shut off the steam.

"On a day with a favorable wind you can hear the calliope a good ten minutes before we land. And let me tell you, there isn't a more pleasing sight than a crowd jumpin' and waving as you pull to shore."

Walking back to Fantine's, Anne still heard the sound of the calliope, the wind instruments, the song about the faded rose, and lines from "Heart's Wounds" that stayed with her: "Let go of that poor child!… Do you think your coins will buy you passage into Heaven?… Such injustice cannot remain buried forever!…" and the gasps, sighs, laughs and muffled sobs from the people in the dark around her. Most of all she imagined the applause, and how it would be to *receive* that applause.

"We're going to have a special dinner," said Cassie, breaking Anne's reverie. A friend of Cassie's was visiting town, and Cassie wanted to show her "as good a time as we can get in Marion." Her friend Alexandra being in the same line of work as Cassie, they weren't about to take supper at one of the three nice restaurants in town, two of them located at "respectable" hotels. So it would be upstairs, in one of the private rooms.

Cassie's description of it brought Anne firmly back to earth: "Scallops and shrimp in a wine sauce, baby new potatoes, an endive salad, and hot apple tarts!" Alexandra found the tarts amusing in the extreme; the two of them laughed about it for quite a while.

Though the faces were familiar by now, at least the female faces, for Anne didn't know any of the gentlemen – to be seated at a large table in a smallish room, in this company, was a moment she wanted to press firmly in an album of memories.

To think this came within a day of the showboat's arrival! Her life must have turned a newer, grander page. The feeling was, admittedly carried aloft by the seafood in wine sauce, the champagne and brandy making their rounds of the table, the laughter and stories about cities far away.

This was an event that, at most any time in her life, she would have cooked for, or served at. This was the sort of dinner her mother imagined taking place in one of the modest mansions on the Heights, and Anne would have been a servant at best, as much a part of it as a fly on the wall. Now she tasted it, drank it, giggled at its stories.

It was near the end of the brandy and hot apple tarts – which still inspired merriment – that most of the dinner party decided to go for a spin in the carriage. With the clatter and swaying as they got to their feet, Anne was grateful that they were not getting behind the wheel of an automobile. They could do less damage by racing down the landing in a horse and carriage.

Anne pushed back her chair, thinking that she would join them, when Cassie, at her elbow, whispered "Let the old ones go off. We young folk will have a good time." The "young folk" also included friend Alexandra, and Mr. Sterling, a young professional man from St. Joseph.

"First, you need to get those sin-chasers out of your system," said Cassie, when the four of them were alone. "It's a whole lot easier if you start by having a little fun. No money exchanged, no promises made, just a fare-thee-well in the morning."

Cassie sat in Mr. Sterling's lap, tousling his hair. Alexandra made gurgling sounds, then reached from behind to unbutton his shirt. Cassie lowered her head, and glowered at Anne from over the young man's shoulder.

It wasn't that the women were evil to begin with, even the Ladies had to admit that. They were forced into the life, fleeing a drunken father or kidnapped by white slavers.

Not Cassie and Alexandra. This moment, they weren't forced into anything. They smiled. They *enjoyed* themselves.

"You'll see what it's like," said Cassie, "in no time at all."

They purred like oversized cats. In that slow, unblinking cat-like way, they looked at Anne, expecting something from her.

"Oh?" said Alexandra, both a question and an utterance of delight, as she reached farther down the man's chest.

All were looking at Anne now. Cassie beckoned her with a black-gloved index finger.

"Excuse me," Anne muttered as she backed into the furniture, one hand out to clutch the edge of the couch.

"Have to go?" Mr. Sterling reached out and grabbed her arm. "We were just getting acquainted…" There was a tiny growl beneath his words.

Anne shook herself free. She stumbled from the room, and back to her own bed. She took off Fantine's dress and left it on the bedpost.

She put everything she could into the big carpetbag - socks, a blouse and a nightdress Fantine had lent her, and wouldn't be needing back. That, and a pair of soft deerskin gloves, were all she took with her from Fantine's Place.

Chapter Five

In the blue light of dawn, the *River Queen* was still tied at the wharf. On its upper deck a middle aged woman emptied a bucket into the river, then vanished behind the railing.

Anne walked toward the boat, carpetbag swinging in her hands like a pendulum. She cleared her throat, and called "Hello!"

The woman was scrubbing the deck, and had to sit up on her knees to see Anne above the railing. "Sorry, we don't take passengers."

"I'm not… looking for passage. Anne Blackstone's my name."

"Pleased to meet you. Hettie Altweiser." She put down the pail. "If you don't want passage, what's the bag for?"

Anne licked her lips before speaking. "You see, the fact is this - there was a man, he left this boat suddenly –

"Jimmy? The little guy? He had family business to attend to. Very sudden."

"Wasn't he a performer?"

"'Course. Everyone performs." She wrung out a towel. "So you're lookin' to fill Jimmy's shoes?"

"At the local place of entertainment, I personally assisted a variety of theatrical artists."

"Theatrical artists, is it?" Hettie returned to her scrubbing. "The boat's full of 'em."

"The real situation is…" Anne stepped closer to the boat. "Is there… a gentleman named Arthur aboard?"

"*Gentleman?*" Hettie looked like she was going to spit. "Did *he* make you any promises?"

"Not exactly."

Hettie picked up the pail and the mop. "Well… better hide the bag, anyway. You don't want to give Arthur a fright this early in the morning."

When they knocked at his door Arthur was tucking in his shirttail.

"This young lady – " Hettie began.

"You… remember me," said Anne, with as much sunshine in her voice as she could manage.

"From the tour, aren't you?" he asked.

"She's here on account of Jimmy."

"Jimmy told you to see me?"

"Not exactly," said Anne, "but I remember he worked on the boat, and I thought, since he left, you being a hand short…"

Arthur rubbed his neck. "I see."

Anne shifted the carpetbag behind her back. She shut her eyes briefly, summoning psychic resources. "I have also performed. Locally, of course."

Arthur glanced at Hettie. "Yes, I told her we're full up with theater folk," she said.

Anne's eyes shut tighter yet.

Arthur let out a long, deep breath. "Can you cook?" he asked.

"Was Jimmy the cook?"

"*No*. Can you cook?"

She placed the bag on the deck, and nodded.

"Can you sew?"

She nodded, crossing her fingers.

"Well…you look sturdy. Might be useful somewhere. References?"

"Not with me. Sir."

"Person of good character to vouch for you?"

"My aunt." She looked at the carpetbag. "She's apt not to be awake yet. Needs her sleep awful bad; she was up all night nursing a sick friend."

"Never mind; we shove off within the hour. We'll telegraph from Council Bluffs. Say, you're of age, aren't you?"

"Certainly."

"Hettie, after breakfast you show Anne where to bunk."

"Not where Jimmy slept?"

"'Course not. Just… clear a space in the ladies' room." Shirt tucked in, he gestured for Anne to follow. "Pay's eight dollars a week. Come on, I'll introduce you to Cook. You may as well start by helping with breakfast."

The galley was tucked behind a crate of onions and wilted cabbages. Cook was a pale, weathered man with the stub of a cigarette wedged in the corner of his mouth. When he looked Anne up and down his narrow eyes became mere slits.

That appraisal made her feel more a nuisance than anything, but in fact he had no time for pleasantries, and put her directly to work slicing French bread. It was needed on the foredeck in fifteen minutes, with butter and jam, coffee, tea and a bowl of fruit, for the actors' breakfast.

As she sliced the loaves, Anne felt the snout of the *Sally Ann* thump against the boat, and they were gently nudged downriver. Through the small galley window she watched the world she might never return to slip past: wharf pilings, boat shelters, a row of cottonwood trees, the bank where her water birds waited for food and at the very last a shack and cooking fire at the Meadows.

Cook handed her a tray of food and aimed her toward the foredeck, where a table and a few folding chairs had been set up. A stout, middle-aged man was waiting at the table.

"You must be the new girl," he said.

She looked at him, puzzled.

"Word travels fast on a boat," he quickly added. "Jimmy skipped off, and you're here." Coffee cup in hand, he made an awkward bow. "Roy Bolting, company villain. But actually I'm a tender soul at heart."

"Don't believe him," said a voice just behind Anne. It belonged to a tall man she glimpsed standing in a doorway on her way to the galley. "A villain, on stage or off, is still a villain."

"Drat your hide, Zachariah Wilkes," said Mr. Bolting.

"Mr. Wilkes?" asked Anne. "Is that your real last name?"

"I'm afraid so. Sometimes it helps, sometimes it doesn't. At least it's not 'Booth.'"

"Your family," said Bolting, "must be truly grateful."

"Either way," said Mr. Wilkes, "I'm the Prodigal Son. I play the hero, or the brother."

"He also sings," Bolting added.

As she placed the breakfast tray on the outdoor table Anne glimpsed Hettie with a similar tray, cautiously stepping across a narrow plank that joined the showboat with the towboat *Sally Ann.* The towboat's crew, she'd been told, were gnarled river men, a breed apart from the showboat folks. Even from this distance she saw the coal smudges on the faces and overalls of the short, stocky men who helped Hettie unload her tray.

Two actresses arrived at the breakfast table; Anne remembered their faces from the melodrama. They were followed by the one person Anne recognized without question: Constance Margaret, the leading lady, whose name and face had been featured prominently in the advertising. Her face was ringed with perfectly formed curls; a tasseled umbrella protected her porcelain skin.

"So you're the new girl," said Constance Margaret, more observation than greeting. She kept her face shaded beneath her sun parasol. "Arthur told me about you. I like my coffee not too hot."

Mr. Wilkes inhaled impatiently.

"And cocoa in the evenings," she said, reaching a gloved hand for the bowl of fruit.

On the way to Anne's new quarters after cleanup, Hettie led her past the ticket booth, a tiny cubicle with a window. "You'll likely be spending some time here. Almost all of us do."

"Hettie, I don't know how I'm going to make eight dollars a week last."

"Here's how. You've got no real expenses. You'd be surprised how much take-home pay there is at the end of the season. Free room and board, and you won't need to pack many clothes – not that you've got much in the first place, I notice."

They walked past the business office, packed with shelves, open file drawers and slots for holding coins.

"Where *did* Jimmy sleep?"

"On the *Sally Ann*. Single actors, coal stokers, deckhands – it's no place for a young lady." She stopped. "Here we are. Wardrobe department. Accommodations for single girls and women."

It looked incredibly small for a place to share with four others, who were probably not going to be happy about it. She was given a bunk with a straw mattress, a stool, a small mirror and half of one shelf. A tiny oil stove and a sink stood not far from her bed. A bucket at the end of a rope dangled from an open window.

"Running water wherever we go," said Hettie. "Dip in the river when you need a washing up." She stepped down from the window. "You've got to excuse me now, still plenty to do."

Anne unpacked her carpetbag, curled up in the bunk and took out her small bound writing book. She thought to write Eddie a letter. She owed much more than the little note she had penned to him just before she left, apologizing for not letting him know her whereabouts, and a request to feed the swans while she was away. Instead, she wrote a note to herself.

What am I reaching for?

A life far from small town minds, sleepless nights and the walls of an orphanage.

Eddie's probably courting some rich girl from the Heights with a floppy pink bow trailing from her curls.

And I am on the river, waiting to be called on deck for morning laundry.

*** *** ***

A clothesline, loaded with corsets, costumes, stockings and work clothes from the *Sally Ann*'s crew flapped across the rear deck. The perspiration stain on the silky green dress Anne worked over wasn't coming out easily.

"Constance Margaret," said Hettie, peering into Anne's washtub. "That's her stage dress."

"Really," said Anne. "She seems cool to me."

"That's all high hat. It's the public gives her the sweat."

Anne blinked. "The public?"

"The *applaus*e." Hettie glanced around the rear deck, lowering her voice. "Watch when she takes her curtain calls. She gets pelted with flowers. Fact is she gives nickels to the local boys to throw them. Then she scoops up the flowers, sticks 'em in a pail and they're ready for the next town. 'Course, every other town she has to buy fresh flowers, or they'd all be dead."

Anne remembered that first night in Marion, when Constance Margaret made her entrance. At the sound of polite applause, she gave a nod and a smile to the audience, something none of the other players did.

"How 'bout you, Hettie?"

"How 'bout what?"

"You like applause?"

"Only time I'm onstage is in a crowd."

"What's a crowd onstage?"

"Eight, maybe nine people, all from the crew. And I *don't* march in the parade."

"What's the parade?"

"When we get to Thebes," Hettie picked up a basket full of clothes. "You'll see."

She moved the basket aside just as the cook came out of the galley with a bucket of kitchen slops. They pushed the remaining baskets aside and made sure he tossed far enough so the scraps wouldn't splatter the clothes drying on the line.

They were done in time for Anne to help with lunch, where she consoled herself that she still had the early afternoon off. From the kitchen, where she prepared a large salad, she could feel anticipation building in the cast for the next scheduled stop, even as they hungered for her food. Hands deep in a bowl of salad greens, Anne came to a realization about the *River Queen.*

It was its own sovereign world. It provided the essentials of life: food, clothing, shelter… a place to work, sleep, perfect one's craft… or merely fish. The people here lived by a series of elaborate agreements, disagreements and compromises. This world had almost everything except what came out of the ground… like salad greens. Like trees.

As close as one hundred yards away, willow and cottonwood trees glided past, appearing to float between river and sky. Their motion came close to hypnotizing her.

After lunch, Anne sat in a canvas deck chair, writing book in her lap. On the other side of the boat someone began to pluck on a banjo. At the far end of her deck two actors walked together slowly, rehearsing lines from the play. She began to write.

I've been told the boat is one hundred ten feet long, almost forty feet wide, two levels, is surrounded by a white fence, and draws three feet of water.

I had always known my Missouri as a broad and tranquil river that flowed past the town. It was the barge men who first introduced me to the Missouri of steamboat wrecks, river pirates, ghosts, treasure buried in sand bars, and the wild stretches of the upper river, where white cliffs tower over logs that lay scattered like bones on the riverbank.

Nothing like the Missouri we drift upon today.

She looked up at the brown rippling of the river. It was its happy, placid self, enjoying its own day off.

About six feet away someone leaned against the rail. She quickly stuffed her journal beneath the chair's cushion, creating more of a noise than if she'd simply kept writing.

"Hope you don't mind," said Mr. Wilkes, tipping the edge of his broad-brimmed hat. He took in a deep breath. "We call this our little holiday. These few hours… I treasure them most. Simply doing *nothing.*"

Yet Mr. Wilkes appeared to be a fine example of doing something. The clay pipe that hung easily from his mouth, the slight fishing pole balanced in the palm of his hand, how his body balanced itself on the rail on the strength of one buttock.

Anne blushed at the mere fact of her noticing. Mr. Wilkes was, after all, a professional, the one actor on the boat to have big city stage experience *and* a degree of talent. He looked at her, and she felt caught off guard a second time.

"You know, this morning at breakfast, I said to myself, girl as pretty as she… must have some nice young fellow waiting for her at home."

"I don't know as I have any home."

"But there is a fellow."

She could see there was no denying anything with this person. "We never had that discussion: if he *is* my fellow, or if he's a friend."

"Ah." He puffed at his pipe. "That's a discussion you shouldn't wait too long to have."

"And you, Mister Wilkes?"

"A girl in Paducah. We don't plan on marrying anytime soon." Anne gave him a quizzical look.

"When you work on the river," he explained, "you can't expect to have a married life as real people do. If you have children, unless you put them in the act you may never see them. Which," he squinted at his fishing line, "may not be such a bad idea."

"What do you mean, 'real people'?" she asked. "Aren't we real people?"

She watched as he pretended not to watch her.

"That's something you'll simply have to discover for yourself. And you… aren't you here nursing an ambition to be an actress?"

"Is that the ambition of every woman who comes aboard?"

"Well, are you?"

"I don't know." She closed her eyes. "I thought I'd become a riverboat pilot. I wanted to go to Vienna."

He gestured to the cushion beneath her. "Is that what the… book is about?"

She shook her head. "It's not a book." Deftly, she pulled it out and laid it closed beside her. "I wish I could read more books, especially of travel and distant places."

"Ah, geography." He tapped the pipe on the rail, flicking the cold ashes in the river. "Please, feel free to borrow some books of mine. I have plenty to spare. I'm going to school myself."

"Going to *school?* On the boat?"

He cast his line toward a patch of still water.

"Not actually. I'm going to get a degree without going to school. Through the mail. It's called Chautauqua."

Anne rolled the word over in her mind. “Doesn’t sound like any school I’ve ever heard of.”

“It isn’t. It’s a lake in western New York state.” He propped the fishing rod against the rail, and with his fingers traced an arch above his head. “A great canvas tent, like the big top of the circus. But inside…” he closed his eyes a moment. “Greater than any circus… the world of the mind.”

His fishing line grew suddenly taut “Dang!” Wilkes struggled with his line. “Excuse me, Miss,” he lifted his hat. “Not supposed to swear aboard the boat. I’ve just caught a snag.”

“I don’t know as I’d call that swearing.” She played a bit with the pen, then resumed writing.

Nothing like the Missouri we drift upon today. Which is. dishes in the sink, baskets of laundry, serving the table, rather than sitting at it with the actors, scrubbing vegetables, peeling potatoes, sweeping peanut husks and bread crumbs from the theatre.

*** *** ***

“Here you go,” said Arthur, as he handed Anne rolls of lithograph paper, a paste bucket, brush, and satchel full of printed handbills. “Just be grateful I’m not putting you in the band. I’m giving you window work instead.”

Anne clutched the heavy rolls and the glue bucket awkwardly.

"You'll do just fine," said Arthur." The calliope whistled into action above their heads. "Time to go. Make us proud of you."

When the gangplank thunked on the dock at Thebes Anne was the first ashore. The posters had to go up first, on fences, walls, intersections, storefronts.

While all eyes in town were fixed on the gigantic cake box that glided toward the Thebes waterfront, Anne put the lithographed posters up alongside advertisements for auctions, river excursions and dry goods sales. While pasting them up she had to admit the posters for that evening's melodrama, *Miranda, the Woodman's Daughter,* did look splendid in their vivid colors. Constance Margaret was featured prominently in the advertising, more so than in *Heart's Wounds*.

From the river, she heard the band on the *River Queen's* top deck strike up a tune. "When you hear the band start to play," Arthur had said, "head back to the boat and leave your postering tools, or, if you're nowhere near, ditch them and take off into the crowd." She found a park bench where she expected they'd be safe, and headed back to the thoroughfare to await the band as they stepped into town.

She took a fistful of handbills from the satchel. She'd been told to put one into every open hand she saw, to anyone who looked at her, to anyone standing still, to the mildly curious, to anyone listening to the band.

Since the crew of the *Sally Anne* had been pressed into service the band had swelled to fifteen, though there were only eight people in the maroon and gold-braided uniforms who actually played their instruments. Even Hettie had put on a uniform, something she swore she'd never do, and was given a triangle, which she swore she wouldn't play.

Anne kept at least twenty steps ahead of the band. When they reached an intersection there was a pause for a brief concert. After a march and a Stephen Foster song, Captain Newcomb held up one arm, and arced a finger through the air. The band stopped.

"My friends!" His stentorian voice rang through the square, bringing the crowd to a near silence. "Tonight at 7:30, on the landing, we, the traveling company of the *River Queen,* the floating theater that travels the length of the Mississippi, the Ohio, the Green, the Wabash, and now for the first time on the Missouri…" He paused, as if waiting for applause, though there was none. "…We bring you a **feast** of sweet music, tuneful singers and thrilling melodrama, as enacted by as illustrious a troupe of artists as you will find on this or any river!"

The principal players, dressed in their stage costumes, emerged from behind the band. "Among our sterling cast, you will meet… "Zachariah Wilkes! Stalwart hero, ringing baritone, and consummate actor!" Mr. Wilkes stepped forward to doff his hat, clutching a cane that Anne noticed had not been with him on the boat.

"That thrilling songbird, dimpled heroine, the toast of New Orleans and Baton Rouge… Miss Constance Margaret!" As the actress took her steps forward, twirling her parasol, Anne noticed some lusty cries from the crowd that did not sound entirely spontaneous.

"And what is a story to thrill the heart, without that most dastardly of scoundrels, that schemer and rogue, our villain supreme… Mister Guy Bolting."

Both cheers and hisses went up for the elegantly tailored Mr. Bolting, who snapped his fingers, and immediately produced a deck of cards in each hand. Over a layer of astonished cries, the Captain said loudly, "Did I forget to mention that he's an accomplished magician?!" More applause greeted Mr. Bolting, and the brief show continued.

But Anne was already on her way back to the boat. She reclaimed her posters, bucket and brush from the park bench, and lugged them up the gangplank. The *Sally Ann's* crew had already returned, those hunched, powerful men, who, like the rest of the doublers in brass, had given up pretending a while ago. Now they tore off their uniforms, doused themselves with a rinse bucket and changed back into their work clothes.

Anne took her place in the ticket booth, ready to sell tickets to those who couldn't wait until the evening. She was still there, selling tickets at a slow but steady pace, when the oil lamps that illuminated a path to the stageplank were lit. First there was the strong smell of lamp oil, then a gradually lengthening string of lights reflecting on the wide doorways leading to the boat's interior.

The lighting of the lamps was the signal for the musicians to take their places. The calliope gave them the downbeat, and they began to play "Good Night, My Lady Love."

Anne had not been warned about the barter system in these small river towns. In place of money, some of the older folk carried pies, fresh baked bread, baskets of fruit and homemade cider in exchange for a seat.

She banged on the window of the booth to get Arthur's attention. "It's OK," Arthur mouthed above the playing of the band and the din in the foyer. He pointed to a nearby corner. "Tell them to put it *over there.*"

A small pile of food and beverage grew next to the ticket booth, a very good thing, Anne realized, as it made less work for the Cook and herself tomorrow.

Yet it was not, she realized, an especially poor town. There were also fine ladies and gentlemen buying tickets, and churchgoing types who could conceivably belong to a Ladies' Aid Society, if Thebes harbored such a viperous company as that.

At show time, Anne found a place to stand beside a curtain at the rear of the theater, where she could see both stage and audience. She stayed alert for a tap on the shoulder just before intermission, when she was needed in the lobby to sell refreshments.

Once the last customer was seated, the band filed into the crawlspace below the lip of the stage, and the gaslights were turned low. Mr. Wilkes strode onstage wearing a fancy traveling coat, and launched into "Shenandoah." A sea chantey seemed a strange choice at first – until the refrain.

Oh Shenandoah

I long to see you

a-way I'm bound to go

across the wide Missouri

After spirited applause, he began "The Picture of My Mother on the Wall." Anne smiled as she watched the audience. A boy put his arm around a girl, an older couple gazed at each other, and an arm was wrapped around practically every mother in the audience by the song's end.

It was a fine mood-setter for *Miranda the Woodman's Daughter*, which Anne had only seen in disconnected scenes. Ashton Farnaby, played by Guy Bolting, was a city speculator buying up parcels of a peaceful valley for some secret purpose. He wore a cape that swirled to good effect, made frequent asides to the audience, and advances to Miranda / Constance Margaret.

"Why should you suffer?" he pleaded. "Why work those pretty fingers to the bone… you were born for good food, fine clothes, satin sheets…"

Anne closed her eyes. The rise and fall of Miranda's and Farnaby's voices felt like music.

"We'll let it be our little *secret,"* said Mr. Bolting. "Won't we…?" at which point Miranda sighed, almost in a near-faint.

Anne opened her eyes, when Mr. Wilkes made his appearance as Jonathan Rideout (to applause, as he'd done so well with the songs.) His voice added a new current, buoyant as a cloud, full of chaste love and rapture.

"I hear, Miss Miranda, that the rich schemer Ashton Farnaby has been seen about these parts." The piano rumbled. "I advise you to keep your windows closed and your door barred, especially at night."

Miranda gasped, putting a hand to her mouth. "Oh you don't think he'd stoop so low as…"

"There is no telling what that fiend is capable of. But if he so much as harms a hair on that sweet head…" He gripped his rifle. "He'll have to answer…"

"Stop!" Miranda cried, one arm extended, clutching. "It means certain death!"

"Either to Heaven…" he continued. "…Or to me…" …and left the cottage suddenly.

Piano crescendo. Miranda rushed to the door and put up a hand, as if to wave goodbye. Curtain, Act 1.

Anne took her place behind a small table that served as the concession stand. The townsfolk seemed thoroughly caught up in the play, exuberant as they handed over small bills and coins in exchange for nuts, cherry tarts, apples and horehound candy sticks. She did not sell many apples; most customers had brought their own fruit.

The play galloped along through forest glade, village square, courtroom, and finally to humble cottage. Towards the end of Act Two, when Farnaby forced his attentions on Miranda, Jonathan, riding not far away, heard her cry for help.

"Can it be her voice?" he exclaimed. Four or five women in the audience simultaneously replied "Yes!!" He burst into the room just as Farnaby had her on the floor.

Mr. Wilkes didn't dare use a stage gun with this crowd; the sound of a shot might wake a sleeping child, who'd cry all the way to the finale. So there was a wild tussle, blows were exchanged, not realistically, but punctuated by convincing cries when fist and jaw were supposed to meet. A portion of the audience, the backwater folks, threw themselves heart and soul into the fight.

After goodness triumphed, curtain calls and the waking of the last sleeping patron, Anne swept nutshells from beneath the seats. The actors went ashore, to find a bit of adventure, perhaps even love in the town of Thebes.

Hettie told Anne that they would stay up half the night consuming the excess energy that remained after the show. When the actors returned to the *River Queen*, some at a slight tilt, it would soon be time to pull from shore.

In the dark of morning, the actors, tossing in their bunks, cursed the ringing of bells and tramping of feet on deck. The towboat *Sally Ann* pushed the boatload of actors from the shore. Not long after, Anne got up to take Constance Margaret her cocoa, and another day on the river began.

*** *** ***

"So what'll it be?" Hettie's voice broke the long spell of quiet that had settled over the laundry room. "Seamstress or actress?"

Anne had no ready answer. Actress? A respectable girl who still had family in a small town would bring shame upon them if she took to the stage back home. But she could get on a boat, float a thousand miles from home and be held respectable in any other small town on the river.

"Guess if I have to pick one," Anne said finally, "I'd say actress."

"Twenty dollars a week," said Hettie. "Beats eight. You could start by understudying the female parts – *all* of 'em. Would be a help if you'd blown in from somewhere special – no offense, you understand – like from a big city. Theater folks get all excited about news from the big city." Hettie let the silence sink in a bit. "You'd be a lot more popular."

Anne looked at her uneasily. "I don't know as I'd want to be popular. I wouldn't have time for it."

Hettie began to brush out a costume of thick velour, a riding outfit. "Oh, being popular can sometimes add up to less work, more time to be sociable. That Mr. Wilkes, he seems to kind of takin' a shine to you."

"You don't *understand*." Anne shut her eyes before she could form the words. "When I left town that morning, I just came from a fancy house…"

Hettie looked up quickly from her brushing. "You ain't one yourself?"

"'Course not!!" Anne wiped her nose on her sleeve, and squinted out the one small window.

"I wouldn't have asked, you understand, if I thought you were. I can spot those women three miles away. Made a study of them. Not only on this boat, but all the ships I ever worked on. Some of these ladies with a past think they leave that past behind when they take a job on the boat. And you know what? They're right. They can play themselves, character parts, and get paid for it, clean and honest."

Hettie leaned her elbows on the costume mannequin to whisper in Anne's ear. "But I can tell you… there's one aboard now… who walked up that plank a fallen woman, and hasn't picked herself up any degree since."

She was suddenly quiet, like she'd said too much. But as they were preparing a bag of clean work shirts for Anne to carry over the *Sally Ann*, Hettie did need to clarify that this woman was no common harlot, but had been known to take a producer in Des Moines upstairs, and when she came down, it was as a different sort of lady, with the promise of an acting job. When that opportunity soured, she secured a job on this boat.

"So she *had* to leave town?" asked Anne.

"As fast as possible." Hettie leaned over to whisper. "See? *She* had to get out of town, too."

"Maybe that's why she takes such a dislike to me. I remind her of that."

"All the same, I wouldn't rub it in her face. Remember, we run a clean ship in all senses of the word. A clean show, clean jokes, no racy things. That's what brings the dollars and coins a-flowing." She passed Anne a basket. "Here's your shirts, now off with you to the *Sally Ann.*"

Anne tossed the laundry aboard the towboat first, then made her way over the narrow plank between the two vessels. Anne had never been on the towboat, had only seen a crew member up close once, as he spoke with the Captain on cabin deck while she watched from the stairs above.

"No Visitors Allowed" read the sign on the pilothouse door. It was, she assumed, for anyone on the boat tour who had wandered aboard. She opened it, then climbed the narrow stairs that spiraled to the pilothouse.

Anne was surprised at how much of the feminine touch these coarse-looking men possessed. There were drapes over the portholes and white pull-down curtains over the windows, which gave a princely view in every direction. She did a quick turn around the tiny room. It was filled with the gleaming instruments she remembered from her Pa's boat – brass gauges, signal bells and speaking tube.

The pilot, Hamish, received the laundry with thanks, and introduced her to the engineer and the first mate. Like Hamish, they were stubby little men, like pug dogs in need of bathing.

"We've got a visitor, boys," said Hamish. "So remember, we'll have no cussin' here." He winked at Anne. "Fact is, we cuss all we please on *this* tub, but we got to watch our mouths the moment we set foot on Your Majesty."

"That's what you call her?" Anne reached out to touch the pilot wheel, then stopped and pulled away.

"Can't bring ourselves to call her by the name painted on her side."

"Truth is," said Hamish, "there's bigger things to worry about."

"You mean… the river?" Anne's voice dropped.

Hamish nodded. "I don't mind tellin' you, this Missouri makes me nervous. A boat's a fragile thing against its damned unpredictableness – you'll pardon my language, Miss. River's wrecked nearly 500 steamboats, what with snags, eddys…"

"Explodin' boilers…" said the engineer.

"Smashed steampipes under a bridge," added the first mate.

"And sawyers," said Anne

Hamish raised his white eyebrows handsomely. "So you know about sawyers, do you?"

"Pa called them the Devil's hands. Trees wedged in the riverbed by the roots, their branches floating on the surface."

"Stumps and floating logs," Hamish nodded. "Act like a rifle shot and steer true when you see those cussed things. They can skewer the hull like a battering ram. Only a fool takes her out in a storm, or *after* a storm."

"Tell me, Miss," said the first mate. "Do you know what the 'dead men' are?" He gave a wink to the engineer.

"Dead men?" Anne looked out the porthole. "Aren't they the trees part-buried in the mud, so'se you can tie up to them when you can't reach the wharf?"

"She's practically a pilot now," chuckled the engineer.

High praise, thought Anne. But she had doubts she had what it took for even a cub pilot. A working pilot needed a memory of landmarks up and down the river, and a dead-keen sense of judgment. She had to know a wind reef from a sand reef, see how the water curls off it, read the pattern of the curl, read the current. Moving at four times the speed of the current, you needed to think three or four times as fast. And that's how you advanced, from deckhand to watch to mate. Who knew after that? Maybe pilot or Captain?

"So your Pa was a river man?" Hamish asked.

"He's still a river man." She looked at her hands.

"How d'you mean?"

"After the explosion… they never found his body. All together, I mean."

Hamish shrugged, like his collar itched. "Here," he said. "It's only 'cause you're a river man's daughter I'm doing this." He slid his hands to one side, and placed hers on the great wheel. It was smooth, though not glass-smooth as the pilot wheel in her daydream.

Hamish stepped away.

Except for the crew's breathing and tobacco-chewing, for close to two minutes the pilothouse was completely quiet. She saw the bow, the ripples downstream, the safe passage below, and, to either side, the tree lined shore. On the starboard side a deck hand took the river's measurement with a long painted stick. Then, something was dropped on her head. A pilot's cap slipped over one eye.

“A bit like Cap’n Callie, don’t you think?” asked the first mate.

“I don’t know,” said the engineer. “If you was looking through the window behind me – “

“…a *dirty* window…”

“Then she might be Callie French.”

Don’t be makin’ fun of me, Anne thought. "Who’s Callie French?" she asked.

"Oh,” said Hamish, almost casually, “a pilot.”

“*And* a captain,” said the engineer.

Anne turned her head an inch. As she looked over her shoulder, the cap fell from her head.

“Don’t pay us no mind, Miss,” Hamish said, softly.

“There’s only the three of us,” said the engineer. “We run out of lies after a while.”

Anne glared at the cap laying on the floor. Hamish picked it up, tossed it in the air, then resumed his place at the wheel.

The first mate caught the hat. “Where’s she been sailing, Hamish?” he asked.

“Sailing? Who?”

“Callie. On the Mississippi?”

“Naw, the Ohio.”

“And what’s her boat’s name?” said the engineer.

“Showboat’s name,” Hamish corrected. “*French’s New Sensation*,’ after her husband, Augustus French.”

Out tumbled the stories, like work-clothes falling from a cabin closet. How Callie, dressed like an old woman, would walk tightrope above the deck. How she took that boat through twenty-five years of flood, hurricane and ice jams so they could bring two hours of entertainment to people far, far up river.

They were well-versed in stories because they had the memories of the ever-changing features of the river. It wasn't a soaring, high-falutin' kind of memory, but it had precision for names, places, details, and practiced with many years of telling.

When life on the *River Queen* became crushingly small, now Anne knew where to go. On the *Sally Ann* she could split the kindling, stoke the wood stove, clean the windows, bring coffee – and find refuge in a house with a view of the whole river, a smaller but no less intoxicating version of Fantine's.

"But how about that?" the engineer gestured to the spittoon.

"If you expect me to clean that," Anne squinted at it, "you'll just be waiting forever."

Chapter Six

In its mildly ornate way the stairwell at the rear of the lobby reminded Anne of a fire escape. Until now she hadn't set a foot on it.

As she climbed its steps, she ran her dust cloth along its handrail, the black paint worn smooth to the metal by a multitude of hands. During her climb, the structure lurched a few inches. Anne held her breath, and waited before taking the next step.

On crowded nights, she'd been told, the balcony was for overflow seating. But Anne also knew once they reached Osceola, from there south it would be, as Arthur called it, "the Crow's Nest" - reserved for colored folks only.

"I don't like it any better than you," she remembered Arthur saying. "But that's how it's gotta be south of the Mason-Dixon!" followed by a slammed door.

Once she reached the top she could see no seat backs sticking up. She thought at first they had been removed. In fact there were benches, but placed so low in the dark she hadn't seen them at first.

"Can't dust what I can't see," she muttered. As she was polishing the balcony's front rail, a squeal from the rafters high above the stage startled her. Up there, a rope spooled through a giant pulley. Anne watched as it lowered a painted backdrop to the stage.

Against the painted Main Street backdrop, actors in costume took their places at various parts of the stage. The deckhands rolled in cargo barrels, set up in stacks of three and four. Arthur was pacing at the front of the stage, a script in hand.

"Now... quiet, *please...* can we get together on this... *pah-leese!"* he cried. "We are here for '*Violet the Garment Girl.*'" He held up his copy of the script. "I know, we've had two rehearsals of this opening scene alone, and we're *itching*, just itching to get to something more substantial, but I don't want to move ahead without one more try. Remember, it's a *prologue.* It's *pantomime.* That doesn't mean it's twenty-three lead actors on stage.

"I know you're good. We *all* know you're good. But please – ladies and gentlemen. Let's have no mugging, no upstaging and no hokum. 'Violet' has to look *real,* from this very first scene." He looked once around the room, hoping for a smile, a nod of agreement.

"That's clear, then?" He found Constance Margaret in the crowd, and pointed an index finger at her. "Violet, we'll take it from your entrance."

As she dusted the long rail, Anne noticed these stage people didn't look like they were on any Main Street she'd ever known. They bumped into things, they crowded too much in one place and too little in another, they looked distracted, immersed in themselves.

Constance Margaret's entrance looked worst of all. She wove around the props like a tavern drunkard, looking over her shoulder as if a bag would be dropped from the wings and lay her out cold.

"Stop!" cried Arthur. "Now, can we get toge-?" He paused, swallowed, closed his eyes. "If I have to, I'll get a piece of chalk, and we'll draw lines on the floor!"

They went through the motions again. Constance Margaret bumped into a painted flat and tripped over her own dress.

Anne let out half a giggle before she could suppress it. Constance looked up. Her gaze found Anne, in the front row of the balcony. “What is *she* doing up there*?”*

Arthur squinted up to the first row balcony where Anne sat. “Well?” He waited. “What *are* you doing up there?”

“Dusting… sir.” She flicked at the rail with the dust cloth, and went to pick up her broom.

“Wait!”

Anne paused at the top of the stairway.

“Where are you going?”

“Why, I’ve got to finish my cleaning – “

“Cleaning, hell, there’s always time for – were you watching what was going on here?”

“I…” Anne swallowed. “Maybe some… I was dusting.”

“Then were you *listening?*”

“Maybe some.”

“Then what’d you think?”

Behind him, Constance Margaret gasped. “What does she *think?*” A wave of Arthur's hand cut her off.

“I don’t know,” said Anne. “It just seems that, maybe some of them move too much, and some don’t move enough. Maybe like they’re not sure where they’re supposed to go. Or not paying attention.”

"*Not paying attention,*" Arthur said over his shoulder, loudly. "You," he indicated Anne. "Do me a favor. Sit up there."

She stepped back a few rows.

"No, farther up." Anne took a seat two rows from the back. "Ladies and gentlemen, action!"

Most of the actors stood still, looking at their shoes, while a couple of women did extravagant moves with the furs about their shoulders. Anne also noticed a great deal of waving and shaking their hands, like they were compensating with too *much* motion now.

Arthur directed one man to stick his hands in his pockets, another to wave to someone offstage. He had two men who were talking together suddenly stop, one of them walk across the stage to two others and interact with them. When Arthur wondered what to do about one man standing resolutely at the corner, doing nothing, Anne volunteered her broom. It was tossed to the stage, the man picked it up and began to sweep.

Then she was told to take a seat at the extreme right. By this time Arthur felt ready for Constance Margaret's re-entrance. When she appeared this time the cast was directed to tone their actions down, notice her, become yet more still, and watch her.

But whatever the crowd on Main Street had learned was lost on Constance Margaret. She was all disjointedness and nervous energy, a grasshopper against the tranquility of the crowd. Arthur turned to Anne, to ask her perspective of the scene, when Constance Margaret interrupted him at twice his volume.

"Do you think I'm just going to stand back and be directed by one of my own sex?" The words made a dry snap in the air, still swimming with dust motes, above Anne's head.

*** *** ***

"Here you are." Arthur plopped a large notebook in her hands. '*Violet, the Garment Girl'*. Prompter's book."

Anne felt the density, the importance of the bound pages – full of cross-outs, underlines and red pencil marks – in her hand.

"That's where we change things we don't like, where the cast gets their cues, entrances, exits. Until the routine's in their heads, they get it from me. But when they forget… or when *I* forget, it comes from you."

Anne looked up, the smile in her eyes reflecting thanks.

He returned to the pages. "If someone misses a cue, if they can't remember a line, you speak up. And you watch for accidents about to happen, like Constance Margaret's entrance today."

Anne noticed the dust rag draped on the stairway where she'd left it. "I can't imagine what Cook will say." She picked up the rag. "And there's the laundry."

"I'll square it with the laundress... and Cook," said Arthur. "When we're in rehearsal, you're my assistant stage manager. Oh, don't look so surprised; I've had my eye on you since you talked yourself aboard." He lowered his voice. "There was no aunt to vouch for you, was there?"

Anne looked down, and shook her head. “I was awful 'fraid you'd find out, and put me ashore. After a few days, I just thought you'd forgot about her.”

“Well, if all the secrets aboard this boat came out we'd be in a fine stew, wouldn't we?” Arthur cleared his throat. “So tell me... what do you know about 'the business?'”

“That’s… well, if you’re in business for yourself, you own a store – “

Arthur shook his head. *“The* business. Something to explain the situation. The character.”

He demonstrated from the stage: leaning on a lamppost, looking at his watch, lighting an invisible cigarette. He looked across at Anne. “What does that tell you?”

“He’s impatient?”

“Impatient, yes, but something else?”

She blinked; against her will, her curls fluttered.

“He’s expecting someone!” he said.

“Of course,” she said, trying to look as if she’d known it all along.

*** *** ***

At her first true rehearsal Anne was so busy trying to find the “business,” the little things everyone would do, that she missed cues and mixed up stages left and right.

Dialogue was the thing that tripped her up most. The business that worked best, at least for her, wasn't spoken.

Violet's story was of a girl who toiled in a mercantile store. Its owner had vanished under suspicious circumstances. The new owner of the store, Mr. Treacher, had designs on poor Violet.

Mr. Bolting's ripe performance was tolerated, up to a point. Constance Margaret was not so much directed as prompted. Mr. Wilkes, as Violet's village beloved, Phillip, was himself thrown off balance by all the attention paid to his co-star.

At his first confrontation with Bolting, Wilkes entered suddenly, took off his hat and threw it to the floor. The hat ricocheted and struck a painted flat, causing it to quake.

"Nice gesture, Mr. Wilkes," said Arthur. "But we don't want to repeat that on opening night. We'll take it from your next line."

Mr. Wilkes stood there a moment, chewing his lip. "Line."

Anne looked wide-eyed at Arthur, who snapped his fingers. Without a beat, she read aloud "Thank Heaven… "

"Thank Heaven I arrived in time!" Wilkes continued, and began to roll up his sleeves.

Anne noticed the extravagant gestures with his arm, a fluttering motion that occurred at moments of triumph, an arm pointed to the skies, index finger extended, or clasped to the heart. If the gestures were not in absolute sync with the words, such as his line "I have nothing to offer you - but an honest and a willing heart," then the effect seemed patently absurd.

In the second act Wilkes struck Bolton, who fell to the floor, injuring his left elbow. The action was stopped while Anne went to fetch him liniment and a sarsaparilla. He was encouraged to resume the tussle, climaxed at last by his jumping through a window.

Violet rushed to Phillip's arms. "Can you ever forgive me?"

"Hold it!" Arthur yelled. "Constance, if I can barely hear you from here how can paying customers in the balcony hear you at *all?"*

Her jaw clenched. "It's a *tender moment.* I am not required to shout."

"We don't need to hear you across the river," Arthur smiled. "Only as far as the *Sally Ann."*

"Rrrrgghhh!" Constance Margaret stamped her feet. She stepped back, and cleared her throat. "Phillip!" Mr. Wilkes jumped a few inches in the air. "Can you ever forgive me!!" She turned quickly toward Arthur. "You are going to see such a *storm,"* she hissed.

*** *** ***

From Anne's galley window the evening clouds were dark at the horizon, not at all like the cotton-candy clouds she'd seen on the stage cyclorama. Spring rains upriver had swollen the Missouri by a hundred creeks, eight inches of rain on banks already saturated with snow melt.

By now, fifteen miles from the town of White Cloud, the water was already the color of filthy milk. Tree trunks, boulders, and the cargoes of half a dozen barges floated by.

The *River Queen* hadn't a chance of reaching port in time. Captain Newcombe had them steer close to shore, while he looked for a protected mooring place along the banks.

A small cove was spotted and a scouting boat sent ashore. The crew chopped down small cottonwoods, broke their branches and wove them into a fence that was strung across the cove's mouth. From end to end it looked to Anne like a flimsy protection against wind and wave. She and the rest of the crew spent the rest of the day stuffing newspapers and old playbills into cracks in the hull, or bailing the water that puddled on the floor as long as the rain kept up and the waves lashed against the hull.

While waiting for the storm to clear the cast and crew passed the time with cards, a bushel of bruised apples from their last play date, and well-worn copies of the *Police Gazette* passed around the cabins. A popular spot was beside the camp stove set up on deck.

It was here that Mr. Bolting claimed the storm was "just a squall" compared to the flood of '92, when he watched half the town of Gold Dust, Tennessee, float by.

Anne was still getting to know Mr. Bolton's place in the *River Queen's* universe. He seemed to provoke the strongest audience reaction. He'd been threatened more than once for simply doing his job. At first he thought it was because he was a poor actor. Then he wondered if it might be because they believed every word he said.

One night, he'd told Anne, a fellow watched him from a box close to the stage. It looked as if he held a walking cane, but at one of the moments when Bolting threatened Constance Margaret, the fellow stood up, puffed out his chest, to reveal a shillelagh in his right first. He leapt upon the lip of the stage, and yelled, "Touch one hair o' her head and I'll brain ye, sure!"

Half the people in the theater thought it was part of the act. Then down the aisle stormed Cap'n Newcombe, but by that time the fellow's more cautious friends had pulled him back to his seat. From then on, every man with a gun or a club had to check it at the stage plank before they stepped aboard the boat – unless they carried a badge.

Mr. Bolting's stories, Anne realized, strove to impress, to win one's confidence, to bluff, like the magician he played on stage.

"I remember," said Mr. Wilkes after a long pause, "in the days when I played the Maritime Provinces, way up Hudson's Bay. It might have been the closest theater to the Arctic Circle, real theater, that is, plush seats and curtains… and when we looked outside, there were icebergs floating by."

Anne giggled. He was just like Hamish and Hettie and all the rest. They told stories because that's what they were supposed to do on the river. Not that she minded a good story.

When it was decided to try the river again, the deckhands jumped in and took apart the branch barricade. In front of them was a floating carpet of tree trunks, branches and debris.

All hands were called on deck. Twelve pikes were pulled from the hold and distributed to the hardiest. The rest, like Anne, took mops and broom handles. They crouched and sprawled on the main deck, and with pikes and mops pushed at the wreckage – pieces of houses, piers and fences, driftwood and dead livestock, snakes and rats swimming for their lives; fish floating belly-up. Anne thanked God they did not come across a human arm or foot tangled in the debris.

Mr. Wilkes, shirtsleeves rolled, pike in hand, took position on the port bow to be the first to strike the floating hazards that met them head-on. Inspired by his example, Arthur lowered himself from the starboard bow, and swung his pike into battle. Those on deck cheered lustily above the frequent shouts directed to Hamish in the *Sally Ann's* pilothouse: "Slow she goes! Back up!" and finally "Full Speed!"

Once the boats were past the worst debris and into clear water again, Mr. Wilkes and Arthur were given a hero's thanks. Both had their trousers completely soaked, so a drying station was set up around the cook stove. Steam rose from the towels draped over their heads and across their shoulders as they sat by the fire.

Now they could see the marks of the storm on the riverbanks. Water oozed from one slope. Green scum clung halfway up a steep hillside, and another seemed as if long sharp fingers had scarred it all the way to the water line. The river uprooted trees, tore houses off foundations, and pulled animals from the corral and into the foaming water.

That night Anne fell asleep to the sound of mosquitoes as she lay on deck in a hammock. The first thing in the morning, they woke her with a melodic hum.

*** *** ***

January 1, 1900

Dear Eddie,

Let's only say I'm on the river. I want you to have this card for the date alone. I don't feel like anchoring the turn of a new century with a place.

What does it mean, now that we've rounded the bend and the nine has changed to zero? Now that I'm seventeen, you're eighteen... does the world seem any different?

Will trains in 1900 run any faster, telegraphs and telephones tie us all together, automobiles finally take the place of horses? Will we be any happier?

What do you think the new century will bring? What do you wish for? Wish for it, Eddie. It might come true.

I'm sorry you can't break away from your studies, but I understand.

River life's about to change, and soon. Just after Saint Louis, we'll be on the Mississippi, *Mecha Seba*, Father of Waters. At the Ohio River half our company changes to a sister boat, the *Louisville Belle,* to play the Kentucky riverfront towns. If I continue with them, the *River Queen* continues south to Memphis, Natchez, the bayou country west of Baton Rouge, and finally to New Orleans.

Too tired to think of anything else for long enough to write it down. I will try to do better next time.

Sincerely,

Anne

Chapter Seven

Anne stood in the shadows of the penny arcade, one hand on a smooth metal crank. When she turned it, Sadie Leonard, female boxer, jabbed a punching bag again and again.

In the two weeks since they'd landed in Paducah nothing had caught Anne's fancy like the Mutoscope machines. Drop a penny in the slot, turn the handle and look through the peephole: *The Jealous Model…How Bridget Served the Salad Undressed… The Way French Bathing Girls Bathe... Bag Punching by Sadie Leonard…*

Miss Radcliffe had once held up a newspaper during class at the Children's Home. "Picture Galleries of Hell!" was its headline. Inside was a cartoon of boys and girls handing their coins to an overweight man before they vanished behind a curtain.

Miss Radcliffe had said that Mister Anthony Comstock and other right-minded civic leaders of New York City, with the help of newspaper editorials, had closed down those peep shows. She and the other Church Ladies wanted the Mutoscopes on Marion's waterfront to be next.

Here in Paducah there were at least three times more of the machines. In fact, there was more of everything within trolley distance of the boarding house on Carlyle Street where Anne lodged with the *River Queen's* single women.

Paducah was her first opportunity to savor what a city had to offer. They had stopped in Kansas City and Saint Louis, but her time off the boat was brief, while postering or on closely supervised errands.

When they pulled into port two weeks earlier Paducah looked anything but promising. A gray-white smoke swirled above everything. Signs on the brick buildings, some twenty feet high, announced distilleries, ironworks and coal yards. The *River Queen* was greeted by a carpet of floating debris so thick that Anne wondered if the ships that preceded them had crashed into the bank and left scraps of wood to float up and down the rivers.

"May I have your attention *please!"* A barker's voice from the boardwalk broke the drone of a distant barrel organ. "Step right this way!" He lured the crowd into the arcade, a big dark building smelling of fish and tobacco juice. There was a poster of a veiled Arab woman reclining on a mound of pillows, a wisp of smoke circling her body.

The Mutoscope machines were directly below the poster. Signs taped over them, hand-lettered but made to look like print, proclaimed "This is a Hot One!" and "Don't Miss This!"

Anne stopped turning the crank. Sadie Leonard halted in mid-punch.

Fun, Thrills, Sensation… the price of only a penny…

Anne stepped away from the Mutoscope. Squinting, she walked through the doors and into the boardwalk's sunlight, to the human river that swirled about the Paducah waterfront, past Mike's Saloon, where the showboat's actors had recently joined the *Sally Ann's* crew in a concentrated binge. For seven months they'd held fast to Cap'n Newcomb's law of no liquor aboard the *River Queen*. Though there was an entire winter in which to achieve obliteration they successfully achieved it within two weeks.

Anne crossed the tracks of the Illinois Central to the wharf where the big boats docked, at the juncture of the Ohio and Tennessee rivers. Since the *River Queen* had gone into dry dock for repairs no other floating theaters were in sight.

There was a new towboat at the docks, a bit larger than the *Sally Ann*. She went closer to read the name stenciled on her side - the *Mary Stewart.* Why did it sound familiar? One of Hamish's stories, probably.

She asked a stoker, a big man with a child-like face, if the *Mary Stewart* happened to push a showboat.

“Sure does.”

“What’s her name?” Anne asked, more quietly.

“*New Sensation. Number 2.*”

“Her Captain?”

The stoker cracked an amused smile as he wiped his greasy hands with a rag. “Why, Callie French, a’course.”

“She on board?”

“Nope, gone ashore.”

Stokers and roustabouts, Anne had learned by now, didn’t concern themselves with the comings and goings of captains. Still, it wouldn’t hurt to ask.

“Know where?”

“Nope. But they might be up at the ticketing office.”

The ticket agent said the *New Sensation* was in town for just a few days. He suggested she try the Gilroy, a hotel on North Second Street that catered to captains and first mates. Anne set out for it on foot.

The Gilroy! By all accounts it was the nearest thing to "Monkey Wrench Corners" in New Orleans, where captains, ship owners and theater people drank and swapped tall tales, sometimes for the benefit of a group of boys, cub pilots and their friends, who stood in an outer circle, or sat against the rail, listening with eager ears.

The Gilroy had a big white porch with frilly ironwork that would have been at home on the deck or in the hallway of any showboat. Men sat in tall rattan chairs or leaned against the rail. One who stood by the Gilroy's front door looked like he might have been an engineer, or a stoker after a good bath.

"It was so small you couldn't find it on the map." It was a woman's voice. Anne edged closer to hear more. "Most fun we had was when a twister came to town and blew the houses a quarter-mile away. So when Mr. French's circus came to town, well, you can imagine."

A man spoke up. "So *that's* how you ran away with the circus, eh, Callie?"

"Thirty years older than me, but he was the best, kindest man I'd met in all my young life. *And* he had a traveling circus." Some of the men on the porch laughed. "So… he asked me to marry him. I said yes, we stopped by the justice of the peace, hopped in a circus wagon and took the road out of town."

She paused, as if taking a long swallow. "And that, friends, *is* how I joined the circus."

Anne sidestepped to an alcove where she could see the woman from the side. Yes, it was Callie, tightrope walker Callie, Captain Callie!

"Now we're off to Europe!" said the man on the porch.

"Yeah…" Callie chuckled. "Going to see all those *grand* places."

Anne tried to picture the slight woman in her late 30's in the high-backed rattan chair in a pilothouse at night, where by an oil lamp's light she gripped the big wheel.

"Maybe a pot of coffee before I put aboard," said Callie. "You know I can't hold the brandy like I used to."

"Coffee it is, Callie!" A brief wave of ragtime music and a cloud of smoke came from the Gilroy's lobby as the man pushed the double doors aside, and some of the other men followed him in.

From behind a post Anne watched Callie and one gentleman sitting at the table. For the moment neither of them said a word. Anne stayed well hidden, mostly because of things Ma taught her about showing up and disappearing at the right times, and what the Ladies had drilled into her about speaking when spoken to, especially by elders and persons of importance.

And Callie French, who had steamed up and down the rivers and had her share of grand moments in the light of the stage oil lamps, was just about the most important person at this moment. If Anne turned and walked quietly back to her rooms on Carlyle Street, Callie would cast off with the *New Sensation* and be far down river and then overseas, maybe to Vienna.

Anne shut her eyes, took a deep breath, stepped from behind the post, and up the porch steps. When she opened them she faced the hotel's front door. She could have kept walking forward. But what would she do in a room filled with men, smoke and clinking glasses?

"Hello!" It came out like an actor's voice, not her own voice at all. In fact, she was incapable of saying anything else.

Callie lifted her brows above two dark eyes, round as an owl's, as she took her measure of the girl. "Do I *know* you, Miss?" she asked.

"Hamish says hello… and mind the snags," Anne blurted.

"Hamish!" Callie French leaned forward from the rattan chair. "Don't tell me the *Sally Ann's* in Paducah?"

"Captain French… Anne Blackstone is my name. May I…?" Callie pushed a newspaper aside and motioned Anne to sit. "I joined the *River Queen* up on the Missouri. Above Kansas City."

"So you're with the *River Queen…?"* Callie French stretched out the name like pearls on a string. "Why didn't you say so? Thought you were a bill collector the way you upped and surprised me like that." She turned to her companion. "Horace! Get this young lady a drink, she looks thirsty."

Horace looked Anne up and down quickly. "A *drink*, Captain?"

"Oh, you know, something like mineral water, phosphate, birch beer…"

While Callie's eyes were averted, Anne noticed the silver pin at her collar. At first it looked like an ordinary circle, but now she noticed it was the shape of a pilot's wheel.

Callie's eyes crinkled in a friendly sort of way, or one that tried to be. "So tell me, then… where's Hamish staying? With that *Sally Ann*, I'll bet."

"Yes," said Anne. "Doing paint and repairs in dry dock at Walker Boatyard."

"And you're in town for the winter?"

"Yes, Ma'am."

"Ma'am, nonsense. Aunt Callie to my friends, though there's absolutely no family relation." She picked at wispy strands of brown hair. "You starting rehearsals?"

"Yes, Aunt Callie. A few weeks from now."

"How you fixed till then? Money, I mean."

"Cap'n gives us a weekly allowance."

Callie leaned forward in her chair. "I won't ask. We Captains keep those secrets to ourselves." She leaned even closer. "Now tell me – mind you, just between us – how's the business?"

"Good. I should say… fair."

"Fair?" Callie's eyes projected feigned shock. "Business on the *New Sensation* is lousy. It's that Illinois Central."

"You mean the railroad?"

"Of course! It's *always* the railroad! We can't make a decent showing between here and Omaha!" She gestured toward the river. "You have to cross the blasted tracks just to get to your boat. It's embarrassing!"

Anne played with her hands in her lap. "I hope… I *really* hope it isn't as bad as all that."

The Captain smiled. "You really like this business, don't you?"

Anne nodded. "Most of the time."

“You’re going to have to, and more’n most of the time. It’s no excursion down the river, that’s sure. You may’ve heard the line: ‘once you wear out a pair of work boats, you know you’re on the river to stay.'”

“Ma’am, I only got one pair of boots, and they’re pretty wore out already.”

Callie smiled. “You’re not really in it for the money, are you?”

“Money?” Anne had to smile this time.

“If not… what’cha in it for?”

Anne saw the swinging hotel doors that could at any moment be pushed aside by any sort of man. So what came out was the first thing on her mind.

“To do what you do.”

“*Why?*”

A man returned with Callie’s coffee. He stepped quietly when he saw the women in close conversation.

Anne thought she knew why, but the words, stuck in her head, wouldn't come out of her mouth. Horace came through the door with a fizzing drink, and put it in front of Anne. Now she put her hands in her lap and remained silent. The men were watching her, she knew it.

“Child, there’s nothing to be afraid of…” Callie leaned forward, and lowered her voice. “I have my own stories I don't care to brag out, even here at the Gilroy.” She closed her eyes and took a quick jolt of the remaining swirl of liquid in her glass. “Do you know what my maiden name was?”

“I’m afraid I don’t.”

“Leach.” She exhaled at the end of the word. “Isn’t *that* a name to leave ashore! I remind Mr. French about that when he gets on my nerves. After all, I could have picked him for his last name alone.”

“From Leach to French!” said another of the cronies, above a wave of laughter.

“And what’s your name, young lady?” a man who looked like a banker asked.

Callie spoke immediately. “This is Anne Blackstone, of *The River Queen.*”

Anne heard little else as the gentlemen and the boat men – who might have been wearing gentlemen’s clothes – stepped forward to take her hand, sometimes with a bow, and a good word as well. It wasn’t until she heard a direct question from Callie that she was able to focus again.

“And what’s your next season’s show, Anne?”

“Virtue’s Reward.”

“Good. I’ve never heard of it. Any of you boys heard of it?” Callie asked the men. They shook their heads. “That’s double good. No competition.”

Anne drank her phosphate. Though it was in a tall glass, she stretched it out as long as possible – for one thing to avoid the hiccups, and also to hear as much of the porch talk as she could before, as Ma had taught her, it was the right time to disappear. She did learn that the *New Sensation No. 2* wasn’t in Paducah after all, but she was promised a full tour when their paths crossed again.

Anne didn't take the trolley to her boarding house. This time, she walked. There were interesting sights aplenty: an organ grinder with a monkey, two sailors in striped shirts engaged in a mock brawl, a street vendor with the latest hats and feathered boas. But all stayed at the periphery of her vision, swept aside by the memory of Callie French.

*** *** ***

The backdrop was a range of snowy mountains, and in the foreground, spread across the stage, large wooden flats representing snow-covered boulders. After four months of work at the Paducah dry-dock the crew was not pleased about working overtime to paint them, but had done a credible job all the same.

At this point in the drama, the heroine, Josephine, has been banished from her small town. She staggers through a mountain pass; snow drifts down from above, then from all sides. Above the eerie, banshee-like moan of the mountain wind she hears wolves howling … while at the other end of the stage, Gerald, the hero, fights through the blinding snow to find her.

This, in any event, was what Arthur called "the million dollar scene." It was the heart-stopping image on the poster, and Ohio River audiences would expect to see it faithfully rendered.

Every member of the crew either stood in the wings or clung to a platform above the stage. Each hand clutched a fistful of finely cut paper. A wolf's call, instigated by Anne, was their cue to toss, and for a yank to the rope that dangled from a burlap sack, sending drifts of snow to cover Constance Margaret and the neighboring boulders in floating white paper.

The difficulty at this first rehearsal was not the howls, but the snow. Constance Margaret didn't so much speak her lines ("Lost!... Forsaken!...") as spit them through pieces of tiny paper.

"All right, Constance, what *is* the matter?" Arthur called. She shook her head vigorously, trying to get the stuff out of her hair. "Is it the snow? We can tell everyone not to lay it on so thick."

Constance Margaret stomped on the boards. "It isn't just that! Look at this ridiculous outfit she's given me! Is this the sort of thing you'd expect a person to wear in a snowy mountain pass?"

Half the people within earshot knew very well that Constance meant Anne, up late making alterations to the costume. But it wasn't about the costume, really. Constance resented being given direction, however modest, by a girl half her age, of "no breeding, no proper theatrical education."

The stage extras swept the fallen snow into large canning jars. Mr. Bolting stepped from his dressing room to stand beside Constance Margaret. "She's right," he said. "Constance is absolutely right. This girl's not even been through one full season, and already she's telling us how to stand, how loud or soft to speak, how to dress..."

"*God's sake*, you sound as if you can't dress yourself!" Hettie's voice came from somewhere behind a painted boulder.

"*People,"* cried Arthur. "Now can we get together, please!"

From her place in the wings Anne was somehow able to observe this tirade as badly written dialogue with no motivation spoken by actors with no sense of their lines. For in truth, she'd heard the lines before: "Anne, fetch me the scripts buried in the sea chest, will you?... Anne, can you tend to this button? Miss Abigail needs it by 3 p.m. rehearsal.... Anne, be a good girl and get this letter to the post office? And while you're downtown, would you mind putting up these posters?"

At first she was in awe of the company. Now she felt sorry for them. Especially for Constance, who had been heard to loudly exclaim that she didn't understand why a person with as many responsibilities as Anne should spend as much time as she did loafing on the *Sally Ann.* How could Anne be found if they needed her all of a sudden?

It was the final word in today's harangue, said almost as a throwaway, that roused Anne to something more than passive listening.

"Well," said Constance Margaret, "you know what to expect from those shanty boat girls."

"What?" Anne stepped from behind the wings. Her fists were clenched, and not with paper snow.

"What do you mean *what?"*

"*What* comes of shanty boat girls?"

Constance Margaret half-turned away from her. “I wouldn’t know.” Her eyes narrowed. “I don’t associate with them.”

“Might do you a world of good,” Anne replied.

In the ensuing silence Anne turned on her heel, walked off stage, went to her tiny bed and sobbed, grateful that the women she shared the room with were still at rehearsal.

No kindly older person arrived to put a hand on her shoulder, offer her a handkerchief, cluck "There, there, dear..." Anne simply cried until no more tears came, got up, made herself a cup of tea and returned to sewing a costume that she knew full well wouldn’t be needed in today’s rehearsal, but she needed to keep her hands busy.

Anne, not Constance, knew what it was to be that orphan child up on that stage. Black clothes, evictions and howling wolves were only a part of it.

*** *** ***

Anne awoke in darkness. The costume she’d been sewing was draped over her shoulders, probably by one of her roommates when they found her sitting upright, asleep with needle and thread.

She opened the door looking toward the river. There was enough moonlight to see haystacks and grain silos. Except for the throb of the pistons from below decks there wasn't a sound on the ship. Deckhands, prop men, mechanics, the entire cast of "*Virtue’s Reward*" glided, as she had moments before, in sleep along the Kanawha River.

At the end of the Kanawha was a town named Deep Water. Yet the farther up this inbred waterway they steamed, the narrower and shallower it became, and the more numerous the shanty boats tied against the mulberry trees.

The river itself was deep green, placid, a welcome contrast to the turbid Missouri or crowded Mississippi. Afternoons the company sat on the deck, read newspapers, talked about the wars in China and the Philippines and watched dragonflies swoop across the water's surface.

Anne wrapped the costume around her shoulders and stepped outside her room. She'd rarely been awake on the boat at this hour, when all was still.

What had she learned in two years on the river? To miss life on land, even if it meant the small-minded people of Marion. That the notion of showfolks as cheap and conniving still lingered among folks who lived on the river.

She wanted to dissolve inside something, become absorbed in it completely. At rare moments on the *River Queen* she'd tasted it, but it never lasted.

She hung onto the rail, softly kicked at the life preserver emblazoned *River Queen,* and watched the boat's wake.

The boat moved forward. It had no reason to go back. Neither had she. Why hadn't she realized this before? So busy doing, never had the time to think.

This was the time given to her, in the dark of an early morning, two and a half hours before kitchen duty. After breakfast there would be the costume she'd fallen asleep over, waiting to be finished.

When Anne returned to her shared room, eyes now accustomed to the dark, something caught her eye at the foot of the bed: the glint of moonlight on the handle of her old carpetbag.

*** *** ***

May 18, 1902

Dear Eddie,

Only time for a postcard today. I'm near exhaustion. Heading west again on the Ohio River, towards Cincinnati. Next stop is Maysville, Kentucky, where I'll poster the town.

I don't know if I can keep going at this rate. I'm putting in long, hard hours that mostly go unrecognized. I'm quite sure the theatrical life is not for me.

Then what is? It could be around the next bend. That's what keeps me going.

Love, Anne

*** *** ***

The small two-color posters were rolled under her arm as she left the Maysville waterfront and passed through the morning bustle on South Mulberry Street. She was tacking them to the first fence she could find when a bunch of smarty-pants boys asked if she was with the circus.

"I got nothing to do with the circus! Shoo!" She put up one of the posters right in front of them to show she meant business.

West First Street seemed to have the most traffic, so she took a turn there and continued postering. It reminded her of the warehouse district in Marion, Fantine's neighborhood. Absent-mindedly, she tacked up posters along every block. Her arms began to hurt.

There, on the side of a small warehouse - though it could just as well have been a saloon or grange hall – was a very different poster.

SEE the Charging STEAM TRAIN

The CHARIOT RACE

The FORBIDDEN DANCE

A FIGHT WITH SABRES

And OUR FEATURE

DREAMS OF OLD VIENNA

with a Cast of Sterling Players

All this without leaving the Theatre

Through the Magic of THE MARVEL OF THE AGE

KINEMASCOPE

Guaranteed Family Entertainment at a Price All Can Afford

Posters covered the walls and doors around the warehouse entrance. No one was taking tickets at the moment. Anne quickly stepped inside.

A blaze of light against the wall blinded her for a moment. She left the posters just inside the door and stumbled to a wooden chair at the back that was, fortunately, empty.

So this was that new motion attraction of Edison's she'd heard about, the one sweeping carnival midways and poor sections of the big cities. For the next hour, trains whizzed past, stallions charged in a chariot race of Ancient Rome, hot air balloons and aero planes, and a fierce sword fight. It was followed by a scene that must have been shot locally, for some of the people in the audience laughed and pointed at the people on the screen, who seemed familiar to them. It was larger than life, in all senses of the word.

After a moment of suspense in the darkened room, the feature began. Unlike the first part of the program, all in silence except for the sighs and gasps from the audience, this was to the accompaniment of Strauss waltzes played on a piano somewhere behind the curtain.

It was, indeed, like an opiate dream of old Vienna, as a smartly dressed man and woman, both smoking thin cigars, moved through a fantasy that involved Johann Strauss conducting his own orchestra, a Ferris wheel, and a concert hall. Near the end, they were in a carriage, trotting briskly through the Vienna Woods. They threw their cigars over their shoulders, and slowly moved in for a kiss that had a number of the ladies gasping for air as the picture dissolved on a swoon.

The lights came up, to reveal what appeared more like the back room of a grocery store than an actual theater. Most of the audience filed out of the room, though a a few stood at the back, next to an older gentleman who appeared to be in charge. His younger assistant wound a shining ribbon of material onto a large reel.

As she walked by the contraption, Anne felt tingling at the ends of her fingers and the small hairs at the back of her neck, very much as they had when she stood on the front steps of the Gilroy Hotel, gathering the courage to speak to Callie French.

She began to introduce herself, but found herself tongue-tied, realizing suddenly that she'd walked in without paying.

The older man noticed her hesitation, and extended a hand. "How d'you do... Henry Harrison, of Harrison's Kinemascope. Will and I…" he indicated his assistant, still packing the apparatus, "we exhibit this attraction." He extended his hand. "I don't often have the privilege of meeting young ladies at these presentations, much less young ladies apparently curious about my work."

"Anne Blackstone." She looked toward the wall, now in semi-darkness and projecting only shadows. "This is the first time I ever..." Her feet felt unsteady.

"Would you like a chair?" asked Mr. Harrison.

Her shoulders did feel somewhat heavy, and her legs still tingled from walking. But she shook her head.

"I'm also in the theatre business." She picked up one of the showboat's flyer for *Virtue's Reward* to show him. "But the moment I stepped through that door and saw that…" she pointed to the white sheet against the wall... "I don't know why these posters are still in my hand."

“Well, you can see for yourself what sort of theater we have.” Mr. Harrison pointed out their surroundings, which now, with the lights up, was unmistakably a vacant store. "This is palatial for me. Usually I follow the county fairs, the carnivals, penny arcades, basements and saloons."

"Mister Harrison," Anne looked at him intently, "I'd like to know about this business."

"Miss Blackstone, Will and I are both too hungry to have that conversation here, so the only way to do that is to accompany an old man to dinner. Can you spare the time?"

"I do have a boat to catch." She looked at her watch. "But… well, maybe."

As they were walking down Walnut Street, she dumped the few remaining posters into a waste-bucket.

*** *** ***

“I don’t usually eat in such places,” Anne whispered to Mr. Harrison as he escorted her into the Exchange Hotel’s dining room.

“You’re my guest,” he replied. “There’s no obligation, of *any* kind.”

As she hadn't eaten since breakfast on the showboat, it seemed almost unnatural to protest.

She looked across the dining room to the hotel bar, realizing this bar was just the sort of place where Cap’n Newcombe would bend the elbow and talk up the showboat to the drinking class.

Something in the atmosphere reminded her of Fantine's; she felt a strange reassurance in the clean but worn surroundings.

As the waiter seated them at a table she noticed Will, the projectionist, engrossed in a game of cards at the bar. If Mr. Harrison also noticed, he didn't let on.

He folded his hands, and looked across the table at Anne. "So, Miss Blackstone, you said you were in the theater business...?"

Before answering she closed her eyes and took a deep breath. "Well, as I mentioned… the showboat that docked this afternoon… for a *time* I was the director's personal assistant. I stage managed, coached, had charge of stage properties, costumes, and special effects."

"Impressive." He snapped open his napkin, and unfolded it across his lap. "But you see, we're not in the theater business. All we have is a magic lantern, a shadow-maker that throws pictures against a white sheet on a wall. Tonight you saw a pretty accurate picture of where we're at after five years in the business.

"When I started in the business they called them 'peep shows.' Thirty seconds of anything that moved: boxers, strong men, jugglers and dancing girls."

"We called them "Olio Players" and "Bits" on the showboat," said Anne. She smiled uneasily at the imagined dancing girls.

"My first big showing," Henry continued, "was in New Jersey, at a little dry goods store I rented for the night. When I turned off the lights a few people went into a panic. They thought there were pickpockets in the audience and they'd been lured into a trap. A couple of them ran up and demanded their nickels back. But thank the Lord, most of them stayed, and I knew a business could be made of this thing somehow.

"We used to travel by buckboard wagon; now we go by train. It didn't take me long to realize I couldn't do it all on my own, so I took on Will." He nodded toward the bar. "He thought we should drum up business by throwing in tricks like speeding the film up, slowing it down, running it backward.

"It did work – for a while. I found a music publisher to supply me with songs, and a local vaudeville house offered their actors free exposure." He gestured towards the bar. "I don't sing; neither does Will. When we found a local singer for hire, we'd hire them on the spot. I carried lantern slides, and we'd have a sing-a-long.

"Tonight…" He leaned back as the soup arrived at the table. "…was not one of those lavish occasions." He stopped, seeming more conscious of her presence at the table. "What time does your boat sail?"

Anne sat up, attempting a shrug. "My agreement with them has terminated." The lie lodged in her throat like a peach pit.

"Oh?" Henry looked over his soup spoon. "Trouble of any kind?"

"Nothing really, from my end of things." She purposefully looked back at Will. "There was an actor on the boat."

"Unwelcome attentions?" he asked, leaning closer.

“Something like that. And aside from that, some professional jealousy.”

“And it goes without saying that’s a situation you don’t care to repeat.”

“That’s right, Mr. Harrison.”

He sipped his soup. “You said something about special effects.”

“Wind machines, voice effects. And I made explosions once or twice.”

“I’m exploring something new,” he said, leaning closer. “Synchronized sound. It’s Will’s idea. We’ll have props, wood blocks and things. Perhaps vocal effects.” He considered the soup that filled his spoon. “Can you take tickets? Usher?”

Picturing the tiny confines of any ticket booth she'd ever known, Anne’s shoulders melted, sighing with the rest of her body. “Yes,” she answered.

“Good. It’s not that I haven’t needed a ticket taker before. But, well… you’re easier on the eyes than most.”

She began to glower at him. “I’ll need accommodations for the night. Private.”

He was silent a moment. “Of course. There was another room available, I remember, when Will and I checked in. Modest, but it *is* private. Our train leaves in three days for Terre Haute; I can stake you for two nights, an advance on your salary. But we can talk particulars later. Please, eat.”

She tore her bread into smaller pieces. “How do you think Will takes the news?”

"Once he's had a few, it will be easier to tell him." He saw her look of concern. "He's told me often enough about a certain girl. I assume you have a fellow?"

"I got a… I have a young man. His name is Edward. But I call him Eddie." Whether that was as much a bald-faced lie as her termination on the *River Queen* she was not so sure, but it still felt like a pit was stuck in her throat.

After checking into the Exchange Hotel and looking at the room Anne returned to the *River Queen* to claim her bags. The band was in the midst of the concert following the melodrama, and few show-goers were still on the boat. Arthur was by the stairs as she went up to her cabin.

"Where the devil have you been?" he asked.

"At dinner," Anne said, and kept walking.

"What, a dinner lasting three hours?"

"Almost."

"What about your duties here?"

She paused for just a moment, turned and faced him. "The show still went ahead without me?"

"Yes - "

"And was I missed so much that a search party was sent out?"

"Of course not - "

"Of course not. Exactly." She continued to her cabin door.

"So you're *leaving?* Just like that?"

"Just like Jimmy."

"Jimmy? The little guy who jumped ship back in your hometown?"

"Sounds almost like you've forgotten him."

Arthur folded his arms. "Jimmy was a fair-weather kind of guy. I didn't think you were."

"This isn't about weather. It's about where I *belong.* I don't belong here, that's clear. And just watch; somebody else will climb aboard to take my place." Arthur drooped against the wall, out of patience, out of breath. "Thank you, Arthur, for your past courtesy. Now if you'll excuse me, I've come to get my things."

"You're right, Anne. There's always somebody else in the wings. Always has been."

Anne closed the door to her cabin, then quickly gathered up her belongings. As the band still played on the stage of the *River Queen* she stepped down the stage plank, her old carpetbag again in gloved hand.

You'd be surprised how much you save by the end of the tour.

She patted the purse, fat with coins, nestled inside her carpetbag. *And you're right, Hettie. I do have just enough. Good-bye, and thank you.*

Early the next morning, from her upstairs room at the Exchange Hotel, Anne heard the *Sally Ann's* steam whistle, announcing to anyone awake in town that the showboat was heading downriver.

*** *** ***

November 18, 1902

Dear Anne,

I'm hoping this letter finds you at the address in Danville that was in your telegram. Though I don't know much about the picture show business it does sound tailor-made for you, certainly better than what the showboat presented. I'm glad for your new opportunity.

I've been thinking of how to break this news to you but there seems to be no other way than to just come out and say it. Hermione and I were married this past April, and we've set up house here in Omaha, where I've gone to work for an up and coming insurance firm. She's a grand girl, and I wouldn't care to hurt her feelings one bit so I think for the time being it best that you and I not communicate. The times we've shared together will always remain close to my heart, but I'm afraid that's where they must stay for the near future.

Now that I know you've found a good path for yourself this letter has been a bit easier to write. It sounds like we've both found what we wanted, or at least have come close. Be happy Anne, always.

Sincerely

Edward

Chapter Eight

She was running through one of those carnival midways, down one hallway of mirrors after another. If there were pursuers she never caught sight of them, so it was possible she was not being followed after all. It was just her reflection, caught in the thousands upon thousands of mirrors in a gigantic magic lantern.

Then all the mirrors shattered at once, and she was sitting where she had dozed, on the 11 a.m. train for Terre Haute. Her single reflection played against a blur of houses, barns, fences, and water towers as they whizzed past the train window.

Will walked in the aisle outside her compartment, on his way to check the precious cargo of films and projector in the baggage car, to be sure the glass slides and special projector lenses survived the jolts of the train.

Anne had almost no appetite, and felt a bit of motion sickness. She thought it was the new routine of eating in restaurants and train stations after the months of fresh root vegetables, greens and potato stews from the showboat cookhouse. Or perhaps Eddie's letter, which on third reading still hit her in a place deep in her gut.

That must be it, she decided, that and her anxiety about tonight's show, a big open air performance sponsored by the Terre Haute Civic League. Until she fell asleep she'd been reviewing her sound cues, written across the backs of old envelopes.

Will hadn't made things easier with his talk about the hazards of the business. He seemed to think girls just naturally got scared, and he was out to prove it. She at first dismissed it as a young man's showing off, though he'd made it very clear that as far as Anne was concerned it was strictly business, and there would be no "funny stuff," as he called it.

Still, his tales were starting to get to her. She had no idea so many things could go wrong: film could snarl, the projector could freeze and there was constant danger of fire.

Henry, by contrast, radiated optimism. There had been worry that the moon would wash out their open air projection, but he'd checked the almanac and learned that it would be no more than a quarter full. And she continued to marvel how he'd elbowed his way into the Keith-Albee Vaudeville Circuit – the "Sunday School Circuit" he called it – by his talk of how Harrison's Kinemascope offered more clean, reliable, family entertainment than any stage vaudeville could offer.

When the train pulled into Terre Haute station there was no mistaking the Civic League. They stood in a tight group at the front of the platform – dark clothes, the men with monocles and umbrellas, the women with gloved hands folded discreetly across their stomachs. Pure church ladies, Anne thought.

Henry ignored them until he had the sea trunks safely stowed in a rented wagon. One man with a monocle, who introduced himself as Deacon Moore, took Henry aside.

While Anne was helping with the baggage she overheard as best she could. There was a touchy situation in town. The business community and the mayor's office and the better government people were all pointing fingers at each other.

"You can appreciate, I'm sure, that our name can only be linked with clean, wholesome entertainment," said the Deacon. "In this current atmosphere we must have nothing that even hints of vice. As we are lending our name to this evening's event, along with the tent, the ushers, the vocalist and the refreshments, we expect that in all ways you will represent the values of the Civic League."

"Brother, I share your concern," said Henry, hands outstretched like a preacher's. "I know all about those back alley projectionists with their peep shows, their boxing matches, their snake and belly dancers. That is a misuse of a great new instrument, one that can light a path uphill, through education, through pure and noble values."

"Exactly," said the Deacon, and out of the corner of her eye Anne could see Will smirking. As they followed the luggage cart Henry put an arm about the Deacon's shoulder.

"Deacon, I will only show pictures I would not be ashamed to project on the wall of a Sunday School."

"Is that a fact, Mr. Harrison?" The Deacon stopped. "Have you performed in churces?"

"Episcopalian, Methodist and Baptist, and school assemblies and temperance unions."

With that assurance, the Deacon introduced Henry and company to the rest of the Civic League, and they proceeded to the park, where the tent was being set up. Two men unrolled a wall-sized poster for the featured attraction, "The Coronation of Edward VII." It was a better choice, Anne thought, than "Dreams of Old Vienna," the one she'd seen, with its opium smoke and swooning.

But it did strike her as odd, like the audience would expect to see the honest-to-goodness King and Queen of England live on stage in Terre Haute.

She hopped from the wagon and went to work unloading the trunks, laying out the objects for the sound effects, setting up the folding chairs, rehearsing in her mind the evening's sound cues, making sure she didn't get the signals for the train whistle mixed up with the wood blocks for the clopping horses.

Before her turn in the ticket booth, she took a seat next to Will while he unpacked the film and wound them on the spools. Once she saw it up close, the film projector didn't look all that mysterious. The film wound through an oval-shaped box, round at the top, straight at the bottom. Will could get at the film through a small hinged door. He claimed that he just turned the crank and the machine did the rest, though he did have to make those turns at a steady, deliberate rate, constantly watching the speed of the film and the focus as the film unwound into a waiting basket.

"Got to always keep an eye out for the film." He held a crisp strand of it in his hand, like a curling caterpillar. "It's nitrate. Goes up in flames in an instant. Poof. I've heard of some operators got roasted alive when that happened. It's just like having the boiler go out from under you on a ship, maybe worse."

Anne pursed her lips and looked away. "I'm not sure whether to believe you or not."

"Yeah, well you'll believe this, 'cause it was in all the papers." He busied himself with the lenses as he spoke. "I didn't want to tell you before, but… six years ago there was a tent just like this one, in a park in Paris, France. Someone struck a match, a lamp filled with ether caught the spark, the vapors exploded and spread to the curtains, and within seconds nearly 180 people burned up, most of them French nobility. That's one big reason the swells in France don't like the pictures. It's only been six years, and some of those Frenchmen are still walking around, scarred for life."

"Will, we're going to start with 'Mosquito,'" said Henry, as he poked his head through the small curtain that separated them from the main tent. "And Anne…"

"I know," she said, standing up. "In fact, I don't think I'll mind the inside of that box as much as I thought I would."

As she took the dimes and five cent pieces from the good citizens of Terre Haute, she noticed what fine clothes they wore. She imagined it was their best set of clothes, or what they wore on Sundays. Their expressions came to match: earnest, polite, but not eager to be sitting in full view of everyone while the lights were still up and bright. They only wanted to sit down, for the lights to dim, and for the marvels to begin, for this night would, for many of them, be different from all other nights.

When the line began to dwindle to a few, she passed the ticketing duty to a member of the Civic League and ran behind the tent, now aglow and humming with anticipation. The opening feature would be simple for her; she had only one sound to make.

"Smashing a Jersey Mosquito," the title came across the screen. At the first appearance of the insect, two feet across in actual size, she let out a "*Bzzzzzz…*" and concentrated on following the insect's body as it flopped about the screen. Once it truly was smashed, she was glad. Buzzing was not easy to project out loud for very long.

The travel piece was "The Georgetown Loop," a cliffhanging ride through the Rockies, captured by a camera mounted on a train. When the train went under a bridge, just as another train crossed a trestle 200 feet above, some in the audience screamed. Henry had talked with her about making train sounds the entire way, but they decided it was not good policy to wear out either the audience or the latest employee. She ended up blowing a train whistle, secured to a string around her neck.

Between whistles, she could hear the audience out in the dark, building to a sustained, almost collective gasp. Anne felt an immense pride, almost a power, for it was partly her doing that made them gasp.

Once the train went around its final bend, it was time for the sing-along. Lamps were lit at the back of the tent, and a single one, dramatically, at the feet of Miss Huddleston, from the Terre Haute Oratorio Society. Her robust soprano voice trumpeted the first stanza of "Beautiful Isle of Somewhere." At the refrain, she raised two fingers and prompted the audience, "Now *everybody* sing..." and as the elegantly stenciled slides flashed on the screen, they did: "Somewhere… Somewhere… Beautiful Isle of Somewhere…Land of the true, where we live anew…."

After the applause, generous since this was one of their own on stage, the lights went down for "Rescued by Rover," an English picture. Anne was required to both bark like a dog and scrape two wood blocks together when horses clopped down the London streets. During one moment when both the barking dog and the clopping horse were on at the same time, Anne was grateful when Henry and a volunteer from the League stepped behind the curtain to help with the wood blocks.

King Edward's coronation required a local violinist, whose variations on "God Save the King" was not too painful for the ears of a small but robust town. As crowds of coronation watchers filled the screen, Anne, Henry and six more members of the League walked behind it, muttering. At the effect, there were yet more gasps from the audience.

There was a finale, "A Trip to the Moon," the most elaborate picture of the evening. Fresh volunteers from the League joined Anne in a big chorus of "Boom!" as the rocket took off. With no time for rehearsal, Henry had to time the signal precisely.

Anne settled in to watch the picture, since her few sound effects were far between. She watched the city skyline, representing Paris, chimneys belching smoke. There even seemed to be soot on the horizon. She appreciated it for the beauty of its detail, superb in the way that the best canvas backdrops on the *River Queen* were.

Her favorite scene by far was the dream of the astronomers. Set against the sky were a woman representing the Big Dipper, a crescent moon, Saturn with its ring, and two women holding aloft a star. Henry was right. It *was* absolute magic, beyond anything the stage was capable of.

As they packed up after the performance, she asked Will if he'd felt any of that since working with Henry.

"I don't know. I think it's like any other kind of work. If I wasn't with Henry I'd still be a telegraph boy in Kokomo. Or I'd be out on the road selling things just the same."

"I don't think," said Anne, "there's anything the same as this. It's like the theater, but it's not like you're sitting there watching it. You're right there, on a London street, right there, flying to the moon."

He stopped packing the projector for a moment. "Books. You read a lot of books, that's why you see everything in life like a book."

"I have *not* read all that many books."

"Anyway, since you asked, magic to me is a full house and a film with its sprocket holes intact."

"What's so important about sprocket holes?"

"If you're out on the road, and anything breaks, you can't send it to New York or Chicago for repair. You've got to have it working in two days, or you don't have a performance. You've got to fix it. You come prepared." He patted a leather sheath at his hip, where she knew he packed some pliers and a screwdriver.

The grateful Deacon and Civic League had secured rooms for them at a local boarding house. Utterly exhausted, she fell back on the firm bed, still fully dressed, stretching her toes as far as she could to the end of the bed, listening to the muffled conversations, the tread of feet on the stairs, the laughter somewhere upstairs.

Tired as she was, Anne felt a glowing tingle spread from the hollow of her back, down her calves, to the soles of her feet, to the ends of her fingers, like feeling drunk without champagne.

*** *** ***

The small triumph at Terre Haute only bolstered the success that Henry Harrison envisioned for his Kinemascope Company. Anne couldn't help but wonder if her arrival had something significant to do with it. It wasn't something she would ask either of them about directly, but the more she pondered it the more she wanted to be sure her decision to leave the showboat had been the right one.

As their exhibition tour took them south, the one topic on everyone's mind was the upcoming Louisiana Purchase Exposition, the biggest thing yet to hit Saint Louis, Missouri. Once he had a grasp of it, Henry couldn't stop talking about the possibilities, the audience, and the exposure, second to none in the Midwest. He had a plan for Will to document every bit of culture and scientific marvel, across exhibits from 43 nations, halls, lakes, and gardens, and twelve palaces of technological advances. From this they would create a grand moving picture document to bring in audiences for years and years.

As Anne expected, Will was dubious about hauling the camera apparatus around the many acres of the fair, and wasn't the least disappointed when word came to them that the official documentation of the Exposition had been granted to another company. So, Henry decided, they would attend as regular fairgoers, but take careful notes and always have the camera close at hand if needed.

The big highlight of their first day at the Fair, as far as Anne and Will were concerned, were the new food sensations, the ice cream cone and the hot dog. He was partial to the dog, she to the ice cream, but after some comparison tasting they decided it was close to a draw.

Edison himself was present for a demonstration in the Palace of Electricity. Surrounded by dignitaries and blue-uniformed policemen, the Wizard of Menlo Park was practically unapproachable, but gave some high-minded pronouncement about Prometheus and the Hand of God, then switched a lever that gave birth to a shower of tiny sparks and the illumination of of an entire wall of the Palace by a multitude of tiny, brightly-glowing bulbs.

It was at the "reservation," where over two thousand wild native people, some from as far as Bolivia and Japan, lived out their tribal ways in broad daylight, that Henry and Will both wished they had the camera on hand, if only for a few minutes. Anne stood in awe before the Eskimo village, with its huge painted backdrop, greater by far than anything she'd seen in any theater. In front of the canvas were the Eskimos' tents and sleds with husky dogs. She felt sorry for both the Eskimos and their dogs, probably stifling in their long furry coats.

The natives from southern latitudes were, however, close to naked. The women walked about with their blouses off, while their kids ran about without a stich on their backs.

“I can't imagine how their parents allow such a thing,” a woman said.

"Nonsense, dear," a man's voice replied. "That's how they are in their native state. Why pretend? East is east and west is west."

It didn't sound right, and certainly didn't feel right, but Anne noticed that her own reactions were not so far from the fairgoers beside her. It was as if, except for the cages, they were watching animals in a zoo. She realized that, apart from the few Midwest Tribes she knew of – the Pawnee, Osage, Omaha, and Ponca – she knew precious little about the Indians of North America. When the time came that she did know more, their real, true story would be a great moving picture subject.

As some consolation for their lost opportunity, Henry had managed to rent a modest but respectable St. Louis theater mid-point in the Exposition. The local citizens still swelled with pride at their World's Fair. They were eager for good entertainment. Eager enough, Henry hoped, to part with 75¢.

He plotted out all the sounds they'd need to make a cyclone of special sound effects, and had gone as far as writing out lines of dialogue separate from the few spoken lines in the title cards. He'd scoured Saint Louis for some willing actors who were a quick-study.

So it was that he'd found Mr. Tatum and Miss Parshall. Both had been very clear that no one, absolutely no one, from the Saint Louis theater world was to know of their participation.

Not to worry, said Henry. They would be standing behind the screen for the entire performance. Only their excellent, theatrically-trained voices would be heard. (Rather a pity, he told Anne, for they were not unpresentable on stage, though Mr. Tatum had a high forehead completely unlike the film actor whose voice he was dubbing.)

Anne's sound effects table was both incredibly sturdy and long enough to hold a trough of water, wood blocks of different sizes and shapes, bells, horns, a wind machine, a door that slammed and a metal sheet that sounded like thunder.

Mr. Tatum and Miss Parshall, sat in the backstage shadows like props themselves, upright, scripts spread neatly across their laps, waiting for their musical cue.

Once Will received his signal to ready the projector at the rear of the hall, the two actors performed their own little rehearsal, practicing quiet steps forward to the canvas sheet, readying themselves to speak their lines of passion, hopefully heard above Anne's sound effects and the piano trio's musical accompaniment. They took almost no notice of Anne or her armada of contraptions spread across the table, except to practice not bumping into any of it.

They took their seats when the soprano soloist began to sing, one more of those songs about a wilted rose, pretty in its own way though much too sad, Anne thought, for a sing-a-long. But it was Henry's choice, and this particular singer had no qualms about bringing her friends to the theater, to judge by the spirited applause she received.

Then projected light filled the screen. Anne was caught off guard, much as she'd been caught off guard by the light on the back wall of the Maysville warehouse, the day that confirmed this was where she was meant to be.

Quickly she put on waterproof gloves that reached as far as her elbow, then sloshed the water in the trough – not enough to drench herself or spill onto the wind machine, but enough to be heard. And so the opening scene, a small boat tossed in a tempest at sea, arrived to the actual sound of splashing waves.

Anne heard applause. Restrained, yet definitely there. She could feel Henry beaming from the other end of the theater.

She reached over to turn the crank on the wind machine – with one hand, while still splashing a bit with the other. The machine itself looked like a cross between a bellows and one of those zeppelin airships she'd seen in the magazines. It didn't sound exactly like a gale when she turned the crank, more like a basso wheeze.

It didn't matter. The scene was almost over, and she'd have another chance for the wind effects, combined with thunder, in the final scene.

Storm over, the piano trio took the burden of sound for a while. The time for the actors' first appearance had come. Anne watched as they left their straight-backed chairs and deftly tiptoed up to the screen, one standing at each end. Enough of the image could be seen through the canvas so that Mr. Tatum knew to stand on the right, and Miss Parshall to the left. God help them if they'd done otherwise.

"Evelyn! I love you."

Silence. Anne wondered if she could hear tittering. It may have been a tremolo in the strings.

"Oswald! You dare to speak?"

"*Yes!* I dare."

Mr. Tatum – now Oswald – stretched out the "d-a-r-e" into a cry of both defiance and despair. Anne hoped the man sounded as effective in the eighth row as he did ten feet away.

On screen, Oswald took leave of the sun-drenched estate and mounted his horse. Anne picked up two of the wooden blocks, medium size, and clopped them together as the horse galloped down the country road. The clopping dwindled as the horse gradually disappeared. Anne was grateful when the trio played a bit louder; she felt something lacking in her "galloping into the distance" effect.

It was wood blocks she'd played with on Missy Carlton's back porch. They'd gotten to be quite good friends in the third grade class, and it had been a major achievement in Anne's young life to be asked over to Missy's house along the main road that led up to the Heights.

It didn't occur to her that Missy's mother had not extended the invitation to play. *"How **could** you let that dirty little girl from the Meadows into our home? You didn't touch her did you?... You might catch a sickness, that's why. Typhoid... Send her out of the house this minute."*

Missy didn't have to; Anne had already fled the house.

Bells were her next effect. It was amazing how many times bells were needed - for door chimes, in a church steeple, for fire engines. This was for the steeple. It was a rather small bell, with a string tied to a clapper. When she pulled the string it sounded a bit like the bell on the *Sally Ann,* not really like the bell in a church tower.

Would anyone else notice? Or would they care? It was well past the point when a moment of impressive sound brought applause.

The actors took their places again, more choreographed this time. As the bodies moved about the screen, so did the embodiments of their voices behind the canvas.

"Evelyn! How could you believe such a thing about me?"

"Dearest… can you forgive…. oh! How could I ever doubt such a true heart as yours?"

Shades of the *River Queen,* Anne thought. In truth, she couldn't blame Mr. Tatum and Miss Parshall for being a little ashamed of their participation.

On the screen, the speeding car careened down the country lane, the villain at the wheel, Evelyn struggling frantically to jump out of the passenger seat.

Anne squeezed the bulb of the automobile horn, Miss Parshall gave a distressed yelp, and Anne cranked the wind machine once more. She wished she had something to simulate the sound of the tree that crashed in front of the car. But she couldn't do it all.

*** *** ***

A matinee and two nightly shows was good dependable work in a city still humming in the wake of its big moment on the world stage. But after two and a half weeks the behind-screen romantic ardor of Mr. Tatum and Miss Parshall began to fade, and Anne's effects sounded less special. When the two actors gave notice Henry did not renew his lease on the theater.

His attention was noticeably elsewhere. This morning it was with the headline of the latest *New York Clipper*.

"Nickel Madness Sweeps the Country," Will read the headline over Henry's shoulder in the hotel parlor.

"They've cleaned up in Pittsburgh," Henry read aloud. "There's a new one opening on Broadway every week; Manhattan's Lower East Side is full of them."

"Full of what?" called Anne, her back to them.

"The nickelodeons, of course."

He grabbed a sheet of paper and a stubby pencil. "Look at the numbers. We pay $25 per reel, per week. Projector, $350, with projectionist $18 additional. Pianist, $10 a week. Rent, $250 a month on average." He underlined the figures. "Fifteen shows a day; we'll clean up on weekends."

"Not Sundays," said Anne. 'Not in some of the towns we've played. The church folk'll shut us down soon as look at us."

"Then the Saturday shows more than make up for it. I've played church halls and Bible assemblies; they'll flock to it like anyone else. It will be different, clean, nothing like the shabby little holes we've seen so far." Henry looked at both of them. "I tell you, *the gold is in the nickel show*."

It took no more than a swift glance through the *Post Dispatch* to find the nearest representative of the nickel show. It was "The Rainbow's End," owned by the Skouras Brothers, open for business in south St. Louis.

Henry and Anne took the trolley down Cherokee Street, past horse drawn cabs, pushcarts loaded with buttons, laces, cantaloupe, apples and fish. Then they heard the din from the talking machines on Grand Boulevard, where the bell shaped speakers pointed toward the crowd.

Before the *Rainbow's End* was in sight they heard the particular music of the nickelodeon's hawker. He stood beneath an oversized rainbow of cheap metal, trimmed with colored lights, blinking "CONTINUOUS PERFORMANCE."

"This way," said Henry, "to the pot of gold."

Gaudy posters hung on either side of the doorway. Sticking out front like the prow of a ship was a small ticket booth. After they'd plunked down their nickels and gone inside there was barely enough light to find their way. Some unimaginable thing stuck under Anne's shoes, followed by a crunching sound. Anne put one cautious hand to her shoe. Peanut shells stuck to a layer of something like tar.

When she lurched back, Anne knocked Henry into the nearest seat. Fortunately it was an empty one, and Anne found another next to him.

"I didn't see any food for sale in the lobby, did you?" she whispered.

"You won't," he replied. "People bring their own."

"I don't think food was what I stepped in."

Henry glanced toward the floor. "Probably tobacco juice."

They could not have entered at a more dismaying time. A tired pianist played at the opposite end of the room. On screen was a fat woman trying on corsets, some nonsense about backstage at a burlesque theatre. This was followed by footage of the recent, tragic earthquake in San Francisco. The buildings, layers of broken brick, looked like magazine pictures Anne had seen of buttes in the Southwest. She could barely imagine what had happened to the people who once lived there.

The "feature," if one could call it that, was an obvious attempt to lift their spirits. It was a Lubin production called "Fun on the Farm." Anne found nothing in the least fun about it; if anything, it was dispiriting. It portrayed rural folk as one great cliché. After one reel of humorless farm frolicking, the lights came up.

“No *wonder* they look down on us," Henry said, as they got up from our seats. Anne noticed perhaps seven other people in the theater, one of them asleep.

Outside, a phonograph record blared tinny music to the neighborhood. They found the hawker inside an office, only three times the size of the ticket booth, counting the day's nickels. The man seemed genuinely pleased to meet someone in the same line of business.

“Fine newsreel,” said Henry. “Had no idea things were that bad in San Francisco.”

The hawker shook his head. “Wasn’t San Francisco. Done on a tabletop somewhere. Mighty good job, if you ask me. But…” his voice lowered, “please don’t tell the customers.”

“So... business is going well?” asked Anne, almost inconsequentially.

He winked “Yes, sir-ee...”

What else would he say? Anne thought. The man was a victim of his own ballyhoo.

"And when do you do your... best business?" Henry prompted.

"Depends on the season. In August it's like the Black Hole of Calcutta in here so we shut down. We got electric fans in the wall, but they only cool the place a little."

Anne gestured outside. "Why all the metal and flashing lights?" she asked.

"Reflects the sunlight by day and the colored lights by night."

"If I may ask… why not pay some of that attention to the theater? The floor looks like it's never been cleaned."

"Would *you* care to?" The hawker laughed. "People don't come for a clean floor, they come for quick, cheap amusement." He leaned a bit closer. "Besides, you know a lot of these people are kind of used to floors like that."

The poor man's amusement. Anne took one more look at the cheap metal, brightly painted rainbow. This way, it sang; forget your sorrows, leave your cares outside, come here, under the rainbow, into the magic world of beautiful dreams.

The next day, Anne and Will, at Henry's request, went in search of storefronts for sale at a reasonable price, well across town from the *Rainbow's End*. There was the foot traffic, the smell of pushcart food in the air, but a noticeable lack of anything for sale on the main streets.

It was just a block off of Broadway that Will glimpsed a hand-lettered sign: “For Sale or Best Offer.“ The location was humble in the extreme: a converted barn and feedlot, going to auction for back taxes, and available dirt cheap. The smell of livestock still lingered, and one half of the roof had collapsed.

“It's too big for a nickel place,” said Anne, squinting at the facade of blistered wood.

“Got something else in mind,” Will said. “C'mon, let's get Henry; I'll tell you on the way.”

With Henry in tow, they returned to the barn property in a horse cab.

“Henry,” Will asked, “Do you know the biggest draw in Midwest theaters?”

“What’s that?”

“‘Scenes from the Life of Jesus Christ.’ ”

"St. Louis isn't exactly the Bible belt, Will."

"Maybe not. But it's got a big German population. Ever hear of the Passion Play?"

"Sure. It did great business in Boston."

“The company that produces the moving picture Passion Play creates their own economic miracle.”

Henry shook his head. “I don't know...”

"What's that you were just telling us about the churchgoing folk?" Will asked. "We can beat the Skouras Brothers at their own game. Supply *them,* and the rest of the nickel theaters with product."

"Say goodbye to the roving life," Anne chimed in. "Go for that greater audience." Her voice dropped to a whisper. "The ones who pay good money to see great plays."

The cab pulled up to the barn, hunched behind tall weeds and a "FOR SALE" sign. The partly collapsed roof was evident the moment they climbed out of the cab.

"I know it doesn't look like much now," said Will. "But the barn's just big enough for moving picture production."

"*Production.*" Henry squinted at the protruding rafters. "What about when it rains?"

"We'll put up glass, when we can afford it."

"What about the smell?"

"The caretaker swore it had been swept clean through," said Will, nudging an exposed plank with his boot. "But I think we'll have a job of deodorizing ahead of us."

Henry glanced at the streaks of sun poking through the walls. "And a job pasting over the cracks and window sills."

Anne rummaged through a coat pocket. "I've got my own list." She produced several much-folded pages of yellow notepaper. "One reel, fourteen minutes, 905 feet. People won't sit still for longer than that."

"Ten cents a foot," Will chimed in. "That's the going rate for finished product."

"And finished product adds up," said Anne, glancing at Henry.

So here they were, opportunity staring them in the face, and if they only had half the money to put up, what of it? Minus the actors and special effects, they'd continue to exhibit films by night, even those that had lost their luster, and prepare for their move into the barn by day.

*** *** ***

From a few skilled carpenters, hired hands and temporarily out-of-work actors a crew was assembled. The gaping roof was the first problem to address. The glass roof would have to wait; in the meantime plain wooden scaffolding was put up. Will found a dark corner that would serve as the film developing room. A desk for film cutting was brought in, along with two large metal wheels to dry the film on. The largest room was subdivided into six different shooting stages.

"And what will we call our studio?" Henry asked. "Harrison and Blackstone?"

"Too stuffy," said Anne.

Will countered with P & B, because he liked the sound of it. They threw around names until Anne came up with a word combining pantomime and "graph" which gave some recognition with the big players like Biograph and their nearest competitor, Vitagraph, in Chicago.

"Pantograph." Henry rolled the name over on his tongue.

"*Pantograph Film Company*." Anne said the name aloud.

Once the splintered boards were patched and the roof stretched from one end of the barn to the other, they were open for business – a large, unprepossessing building with the canvas banner "Pantograph Moving Picture Company" tacked above the former barn doors. Now all they needed were actors.

*** *** ***

On a chilly morning in early November, a horse drawn wagon turned onto Market Street. Seated in back were a society matron, a bearded gentleman in dress coat and top hat, a governess in her bonnet, and a laborer in overalls – who had, in fact, been pulled from the stage crew that morning. Atop a box that held the camera, pressed against this cross section of Pantograph's stock company, sat Anne and Will.

Will had heard about a film shot on Manhattan's Seventh Avenue. A young child's abduction had been filmed by a concealed camera in front of astonished passers-by, who believed the scene was real. Will had an idea to repeat something like that here in the morning rush of downtown Saint Louis.

"Keep a lookout for a good chase location." Will said, though Anne was unsure if he spoke to her or the driver. "Train tracks, that sort of thing, And if there's action – parades, police wagons, fires – we drop everything and follow. We can cook up a story later."

Anne didn't care what the day's plans were, or what sort of footage they'd end up with. This was true location shooting, their first time away from artificial lights and painted backdrops.

Will gestured to the sidewalk. “Let's pull over here,” he called to the driver.

The society people were given instructions, Will stuck his head into the box, and the two began to stroll down the sidewalk, the wagon keeping an even pace so Will could capture their moves, along with the passers-by, for a full block. Anne tried not to giggle; from her view at the other side of the wagon Will's legs stuck out at a ridiculous angle.

She watched the passers-by, each unaware their likenesses would be projected onto screens far from Saint Louis – if, that is, anything of value came from this day's adventure.

The society couple reached the end of the block. They made their way back to the wagon, where Will pulled the laborer into a huddled discussion Anne was unable to hear.

In the next block Will told the driver to park in front of a store. The gentlemen and the laborer hopped out and walked to opposite ends of the block.

“What are you up to?” Anne asked.

“Not telling.”

“Why?”

“If I did you'd probably say no.”

“Would Henry say no?”

"Henry isn't here," said Will, and stuck his head and torso back into the box. The gentleman began to walk from the left, all swagger. The laborer came from the right, hunched and aimless. As Anne, too late, feared, they collided in front of the store. The startled expressions of people on the sidewalk were what mattered now; Will was undoubtedly smiling in the darkness of his box.

The laborer knocked the gentleman's hat off; the gentleman struck the laborer on the chest. The crowd stepped back in true alarm.

"Fantastic," said Will, muffled from inside the box. "First rate."

"Have you a license for this activity?" A St. Louis cop stood by the back of the wagon, hands on his hips.

Anne and Will gave each other a quick glance. Will cleared his throat. "Officer, we..."

"We weren't aware of that," Anne spoke up. "What sort of license do we need?"

"Let me see... It would be a... a... " The cop counted on two of his gloved fingers. "Oh, ask the Mayor's office! I'm going to let you go this time, but you'd best take your operation away from Market Street." A thumb went up to his chest. "That's *my* beat."

They drove to the city docks, where the players could walk, move and interact against a backdrop of the great steamboats. Within minutes of setting up, they attracted curiosity seekers, who had probably never seen a motion picture camera before, certainly along the St. Louis waterfront. They stood and watched as Will turned the crank on his camera. Concentration was lost; early as it was, the crew decided to call it a day.

Back at the Pantograph barn, projected against a sheet tacked onto the wall, the day's footage looked fine and realistic, but it seemed to Anne to have nothing to do with plays, acting, or telling a story.

Henry was generally enthusiastic, the exception being the ride through the streets on a carriage. "I don't know, Anne," he said. "It makes me feel dizzy watching it. How would an audience feel? This could leave them feeling a bit queasy."

Anne nodded, though not really sure she agreed. She was already making plans to shoot a racing horse from the back of the touring car. Cameras, she'd discovered, were wonderful for capturing motion going by – the streetcars, the ships, the trains whizzing past.

They were also well adapted to the grand scale, like the pavilions in Forest Park still standing from the Exposition. They were massive, they had columns, there were steps. And Pantograph had found some impressive costumes left over from a road company *Ben Hur*. Henry decided it was his turn to direct. If they ever did intend to tackle the Passion Play, this would be a good warmup.

What, Anne wondered, did a director actually do? Get the actor within camera range, either a medium shot from the waist up or so, or a long shot, say "Camera... Action..." and when the action was done, shouted "Cut." Not difficult in itself; just a mental leap from seeing the play on a stage to seeing from the inside of a small wooden box.

The actors were fitted up in togas and tights, handed spears and swords, and improvised others from wood and cardboard when there weren't enough weapons to go around.

They motored out to Forest Park, and the actors got into their costumes (men behind one pavilion, women behind another.) Anne didn't dress the part, except to wear the high boots she'd bought at Woolworth's, when she found her small but comfortable shoes inappropriate for location work.

Because of the distances and the largest crowd scene Pantograph had yet assembled, Henry had brought a megaphone, a smaller version of the horn on phonograph players. When he planned a massive charge with the weapons, first up the steps, then down, he surprised Anne by bringing out a larger cousin of the megaphone, big enough for his voice to be heard at the farthest side of the pavilion. The more imposing men were placed at the top of the steps. Henry directed them to brandish swords above their heads and make threatening gestures.

He was so impressed that he told the men to stay where they were and had the cameraman move in for a closer shot. As Anne expected, such posturing and gestures were nothing if not ludicrous when seen in close view.

"It's the face that bothers me the most," she said.

"But Anne, it's fierce! I *want* fierce!"

"I'm sorry, Henry. It just looks silly." She looked at a togaed warrior from a different angle. "Can we try something?"

To her, the fierce part was the sword, suddenly thrust straight up into the air. She told Will to train his lens just above the actor's helmet. They practiced the sword thrust, and on the last try, she had Will crank away.

While Henry rehearsed the crowd for the next big action shot, Anne told Will to shoot all the super-close views he could: a sandal thrust forward, and a clenched fist, both to go with the upraised sword. Then she pulled over one of the crowd extras, one with especially handsome feet, and had him go up and down the same few steps - with the camera, again, trained on a very close view.

When Henry had finished with a group of women standing against the columns in Grecian urn poses, Anne had one stay behind, then filmed her arm draped across the column, a shot of her head, not in a wild or obvious expression, but subtle, with eyes half closed.

On the west side of the park, near the new St. Louis Art Museum, she thought there would be an opportunity to pose with some statuary. But all they found was a crowd of picnicers who, delighted at the arrival of a seemingly lost theatrical company dressed in ancient garb, forced them to turn back to town.

How a story would come from all this Anne had no idea. But she had discovered the sheer thrill of it, the power exerted over not only the most intimate of scenes, but marshaling crowds, controlling their entrances and exits.

It was the megaphone, the little brass and wood cylinder that set her apart from the actors. *Be silent*, it said. *Listen to me.* Man and woman, horse and dog, *pay attention*. The megaphone in her hand reminded her of that moment on the *Sally Ann* when the pilot wheel was between her fingers.

She never would be a captain; she'd come to that conclusion four years ago, as she marched in the parade on a hot Sunday afternoon, her neck itching beneath the uniform's collar. Theatrical life on the river had cured her of the fancies she'd once conjured on the banks of the Missouri, as she watched the wake of a passing steamboat and imagined herself up in the pilothouse.

Theater had delivered a taste, the tiniest taste, of directing. But it was nothing like directing a moving picture. She still dealt with actors, costumes, props and storylines, but the act of directing had little to do with theater as she knew it. It was a process of forgetting all she'd learned about audience and performer.

An entirely different sort of acting was needed. No amount of words could move the story along, for there were no words to hear. The actors didn't learn lines, but expressions and gestures to put across the ideas, the feelings, the story.

She'd started to observe people: around the studio, on the St. Louis streets, at the hotel where she stayed. She watched especially when they weren't speaking, to see how they carried themselves, how they moved and gestured.

Like the people, the pictures *themselves* had to move. By the end of two reels there had to be something big: a shoot out at a covered wagon, a maniac breaking into a house, a speeding train or car, a horse, with or without rider, racing to the rescue.

Back in the studio confines, Anne discovered it was one thing to have the directing clear in your head; it was entirely something else in practice. Shots were too far away; the details were missed. Shots were too close; one couldn't tell what action belonged to who. But, as on the showboat, she began to learn the tricks of the stage.

When Henry asked if she had any good ideas for a story, Anne combed through the notes in her Chautauqua composition books, where a gothic melodrama had been germinating. She named it "Grauerstein," then "Holly House" after a large, forbidding house that figured in the story. Then its title was "Life in the Meadows," and finally, "The Orphan's Revenge."

That night she dreamed of a man, puffing on a cigar, who slipped into a projection booth. He wore a long travel coat and a cap with a visor that concealed the upper part of his face, except for ruddy cheeks that lit up as he struck a match. He peered around, making sure no one was there, then traced a line across the booth with his shoe. He drew deeply on the cigar, so that the cherry was glowing hot, and passed it from one finger to another. He inched it toward the canister of film, which had one trailing piece of cellulose curling from the metal pan. He left the cigar, still burning, on top of the can of films.

*** *** ***

The orphan's name was Lizzie, a girl of sixteen. At first she was pregnant, then Henry reminded Anne that with a baby in the story, and no husband, they'd be unable to exhibit in at least seven states, especially Pennsylvania. So the baby was tossed.

Lizzie made her home on a shanty boat. As a lighthouse keeper would, she tended the lanterns on the riverbank that guided ships along the river. When the Child Welfare Board (who dressed in black) determined Lizzie to be underage they obtained a court order to make her a ward of the state.

Anne still thought there would be a lot more drama and interest with a baby, but there were all those nickelodeons in Pittsburgh and Philadelphia to consider.

The Orphan's Revenge shooting date: May 21, 1907

Scene # 1 Prologue: the death of Lizzie's Mother
EXTERIOR, VILLAGE

A woman in a hooded shawl staggers down a street in the driving rain. She lurches from doorway to doorway, banging on doors, on closed and shuttered windows.

One hand opens a door, an old face peers out. Another hand, thin, bony, reaches around and slams the door firmly shut. The figure continues past more doors, staggering now, seen in low angle.

Closeup, a hand grasping a stairwell, one rung at a time. Fall to the ground, and BLUR.

"*Blur?*" Will asked. "Anne, people will think there's something wrong with the camera."

Anne gripped the megaphone. “The Mother is losing consciousness. When you pass out – from hunger and exhaustion – your vision does blur, your body heads toward the ground. Why can’t the camera do that?”

“Never heard of such a thing,” Will said under his breath as he turned the lens out of focus.

<u>The Orphan’s Revenge</u> shooting date: May 23, 1907

Scene # 4 INTERIOR SHANTYBOAT

View through the window, its glass partly broken. Sunlight reflecting off the water changes to the fall of a leaf, then to blowing snow. Lizzie holds a sheet of newspaper over the broken window. As she spreads it out we see that it's a vaudeville advertisement with a beautiful woman singing at the footlights.

CLOSE SHOT of Lizzie, her awestruck look at the sight of the woman in the newspaper advertisement.

“*Close?*” Will asked.

“Yes, close” Anne's voice was calm. “The emotion isn’t going to register unless we see it in her face.”

"That’s not how it works,” he protested. "There's the nine foot line..."

"An arbitrary measurement."

"It's an industry standard. It's there for a reason, so the action can be seen. What's the good of bringing in an actor if you only show a part of them? If you went to the theater, you wouldn't want to see an actor with no feet, would you?"

There was no arguing with Will. He talked just like the actors; *they* wanted their whole bodies to be seen, too. But the young actress playing Lizzie didn't seem to carry such opinions. She had the look, but not the attitude. If anything, she had the aura of Anne herself about seven years back. Anne had forgotten precisely why the actress was hired in the first place. It might have been for the big, luscious hair that could look even more impressive through artful lighting.

For argument's sake Will moved the camera closer, to show Anne how absurd the shot would look. He was right on one count - it revealed the ghostly white makeup on the actress's face, especially against the shanty boat's dark wood background. Anne told the actress to wipe off the makeup and return to the set.

It wasn't only the makeup that made the close shot so troubling. The bright electric light on the painted set rendered it harsh and artificial looking. The light was so hot that sweat trickled down the actress's cheek.

Anne asked the lighting man if they could shoot in the light of gas lamps.

"Gas lamps?" he protested. "That would remind people of a second rate theatrical."

"That's exactly what it is," Anne replied. "But it might as well be a second rate theatrical with atmosphere."

He pulled some of the lights farther back, creating dramatic shadows. When the actress returned, her face less ghostlike, Anne had the light repositioned to cast a soft glow over her hair, then another light to give her a pale, almost possessed look. She pulled a stool close to the actress. The fidgeting on the set behind her was tangible, but she kept her voice low.

"The audience isn't out in the stalls," Anne said, gesturing over her shoulder to the camera. "They're inside there, on a loop of photographic film. They see you like you see yourself in the mirror. Unless you're *trying* to make a fool of yourself, you don't make grand gestures in the mirror. You lift an eyebrow. You examine a freckle you didn't notice before. It's subtle. That's how it is with close ups. Play just to that camera, as if one person was sitting just a few feet away from you."

Anne cued the violinist sitting on a nearby stool for the mood setting. The camera rolled. This time the lens caught the glint of a tear completely missing from the previous take.

The Orphan's Revenge shooting date: May 29, 1907

Scene # 16 INTERIOR, HOLLY HOUSE

Three ladies from the Child Welfare Board confront Lizzie. They try to wrest from her the handbag belonging to her mother. As they struggle over the bag, a storm outside gathers strength; a curtain in the window flaps wildly. The fight for the bag intensifies.

"All right, stop," said Anne.

Will called backstage. "Jim, turn off the fan." He looked at Anne perched on her high stool, and wearily asked "What is it this time?"

"Everything." For one, the handbag was no prop but her carpetbag; it was very possible they were going to rip it in the course of filming. The fan blowing the curtain was so loud that it distracted both the actors and her own concentration. But, more than anything, it was their movements. It was enough when one person indulged in arm waving and wide-eyed rage; when four people were involved it was beyond belief.

"We need to tone it down," she said. "Remember the intensity is on the *inside.* You can put your whole body into it without being jerked across the stage like a puppet."

"Miss Blackstone, is it?" asked Mrs. Eglantine, one of the women playing the ladies from the Child Welfare Board.

"Yes?"

"I have been active in theater in Saint Louis for over twelve years. I don't know that you've had experience in the theater. I'm quite certain I have not come across your name in all those years."

"Docs that matter at present?"

Mrs. Eglantine took a deep breath. "I was given to understand that Mr. Harrison is the director of this company."

"He is, officially." Anne drew the hand holding the megaphone up ever so slightly. "But I am the director of this picture."

"That she is, Ma'am," said Will, from behind his camera.

Mrs. Eglantine suppressed a look of indignation, and looked away.

"Yes," said Anne. "I've had experience in theater. A member of a stock company, and as I'm sure you know in stock we did everything. Once when I was directing an actress she declared 'Do you expect me to be directed by one of my own sex?'"

Mrs. Eglantine sniffed. "I am not sure what to expect. Pantograph is a new company."

"And maybe acting in moving pictures is new for you?" Anne's question was directed to all of them. Their expressions did not contradict her. "Then perhaps you'll remember what I said about your movements."

"Intensity. From the inside," murmured Will.

Anne walked up to Lizzie and took her hand. "When you first clench your fist, before you strike, make it gradual. And your face – I want you to scowl. No, make it a pout."

"Isn't that a bit subtle to be picked up from over here?" asked Will, as he checked the camera.

Anne looked at the camera from where they stood. "What if…" She took Mrs. Eglantine by the shoulders and planted her a few feet over to the left. "I know. Will, you take the shot from just over her shoulder. The fight will look less like we're watching it on stage and more like we're someplace inside the room. And that curtain won't be flapping so much across the screen."

"You want people to see there's a storm coming, don't you?" asked Will. "Remember where this scene is going."

"All right," said Anne, walking around Mrs. Eglantine and back to her position. "Jim, turn on the fan, but please turn it *down.*"

Scene # 16 INTERIOR, HOLLY HOUSE

Lizzie falls back against a chair. Slowly, she clenches her fists, glowers at the ladies, seizes the chair and flings it against the wall.

TITLE: "Perhaps she is crazed!"

The ladies make a united effort to subdue Lizzie. She seizes an umbrella, breaks its handle in two, and flings it at them. The ladies back off. Lizzie's arm shoots upward.

TITLE: "In the name of God! Heaven will protect the orphan child!"

Scene # 17 EXTERIOR STORM ON THE RIVER

A dark embankment, waves lashing, trees bent over in the howling wind.

INTERIOR SHIP PILOTHOUSE

The pilotwheel can barely be controlled by one man. Chaos among the crew as they scan the river.

EXTERIOR Their view – darkness, waves, driving rain. A crewman's face, seen through the rain-washed pilothouse window. He watches in vain.

TITLE: But Lizzie was not there to tend the lights.

EXTERIOR The ship strikes a submerged obstacle, and begins to sink. Men jump overboard, thrash in the water. The boat swirls inside a whirlpool and sinks.

"Once more," said Anne. "And this time, let the water leak out of the tank just a bit slower."

The properties man sealed up the drain, took a garden hose and refilled the metal basin, which was about the size of a toddler's bath. Anne tapped the model, which bobbed like the toy it was.

"Are you ready, Will? Here we go again…"

As the water in the tank spiraled down she thought of the counterpoint to this scene, a conflagration of Holly House itself, the *real* Orphan's Revenge, as flames burst from the windows, the imprisoned orphans flee, the members of the Child Welfare Board stagger from the burning building, too dazed to chase after the escaping children. *That's* what her dreams about fire had been leading to – a fiery conclusion to the picture!

In the midst of these thoughts there was a loud knock at the studio door.

"Who is it?" she asked.

"Says they're from a General Film Company," called the doorman.

Another film company? The possibility gave her a chill. So maybe they weren't alone in Saint Louis.

Then she noticed Will putting on the lens cap, sealing the camera and folding the tripod legs. "Don't let them in the building!" he said quickly.

"Why not?"

"They're Edison goons! " He lowered his voice. "We pay up or they confiscate the equipment."

There were loud voices at the door; whoever it was had entered the studio.

"Why didn't somebody tell me about this…" Anne muttered.

Five big men, smartly dressed, came onto the set. A couple of them wore leather gloves that were curled into fists.

"I'm looking for Henry Harrison," said a man in front, with a large brown moustache and a bowler hat.

"He's in his office," said Anne. "Can I help you?"

The man looked at Will, who still had the camera in his arms. "You're using unlicensed equipment."

"*Unlicensed?* This camera belongs to us. It's paid for," she said, with a look at Will asking, *isn't it?*

"Paid for or not, you're in violation of camera and projector patents."

"Patent? You're from the General Film Company, aren't you?"

"No. From the Motion Picture Patents Company. We hold the patents on cameras, projectors, and film stock."

"You mean Edison's patents, don't you?" Henry walked onto the set from his office. "You can't threaten us. Edison's in the Bronx, New York. We're in Saint Louis."

The man in the bowler hat smiled and took a paper from his vest pocket. "Mr. Harrison. Thank you for saving us the trouble." He unfolded the paper. "Perhaps you've seen this before."

Henry took the paper and quickly looked it over.

"Oh yes. The lawsuit." Anne gave him a look of *why didn't you tell me?* "Everyone who isn't part of the Patents Company is getting these." He folded the paper and handed it back to the man. "It's a sham."

The man turned to look at his companions. "Violation of patent means we can confiscate your cameras, projectors and film stock."

"I don't see an officer of the law with you," said Henry. "And I don't see a warrant."

By this time actors and crew had heard the commotion. There were quick glances between the man in the bowler hat, his companions, and the growing number of employees on the set. The Patents men were only slightly outnumbered.

Anticipating a fight, broken equipment, and broken noses, Anne spoke up. "What can we do to solve this?"

"Pay up, of course," Henry replied. "So much for the projector, so much for the camera, so much for the film stock per month. Edison's been playing this game for ten years. I still say it's a sham, because Edison doesn't have a leg to stand on."

He walked in a semi-circle in front of the intruders, ticking off names on the fingers of his right hand. “The Lumiere’s in France, the Skladanowsky Brothers in Germany, Friese-Green in England. And Augustin Le Prince, the man who disappeared on the train. Any one of them has just enough claim to a patent as Thomas Alva Edison. Instead of spending $150 to secure the overseas patents on his invention, he passed up the opportunity. He left the field wide open for others to take his idea and improve on it.”

Henry stopped pacing. “I wonder if, for all his genius, Edison has any deeper consideration than how to better line his pocket.”

The man in the bowler hat reached into one vest pocket and pulled out a book of matches. From another pocket he withdrew a slender cigar. He squinted at the corners of the building, where cans of motion picture film lay in stacks. He lit his cigar and tossed the extinguished match on the studio floor not far from Henry’s feet.

“As I said… you’re in violation of patent law. Your film stock belongs to Eastman Kodak. Your movie equipment belongs to Edison. They can be confiscated.” He glanced down at the still-smoking match. “You want to be careful in a place like this. Accidents can happen.”

He gestured to his four companions. One of them handed Anne a little slip of paper.

“Our address,” said the second man. “I think you’ll want to get in touch with us soon.” He gave a little smile and gestured goodbye. The others showed no expression as they turned and went out the studio door.

All the air seemed to go out of Henry Harrison. He barely made it to a nearby canvas chair. A stagehand brought a glass of water. "Thanks. That's a moment I've been expecting a long, long time. I practically had it rehearsed."

"Well," said Will. "What are we going to do about it?"

Henry took a drink and drew a deep breath. "What did they do on the east coast? Smuggle cameras and projectors from Europe behind Edison's back, then assemble them piece by piece. But here *we* are, in the middle of the country. "

Will was livid. "And they could be back tomorrow to bust up my camera." He shook his head. "Not before I bust a jaw or two."

"All right, if you feel that way," said Henry, looking up from the chair. "How many of the guys in the crew know how to use a gun?"

"I don't know." Will shook his head. "A couple of them are from out west, I think."

"Not killers," said Henry. "Just comfortable wearing a gun. Find out. And then a few more who can use their fists; give them fake guns from the props department. And *you* take that busted camera, in case they do play rough with the equipment."

"What about actors?"

"Cowboys," said Henry. "Pretend you're shooting a western." He smiled through a grimace. "I've been wanting to do one of those for a long time."

Anne held up the slip of paper in her hand. "What are we going to do, invite them over to watch us film?"

Henry shook his head. “Get word to them through a third party. Anonymous tip. Will, you and the cowboys go out on location; take the Saint Charles Road north where it meets the Missouri upriver. That’s a fine spot for a western.”

“What about me?” Anne demanded.

“Will and the cowboys are one big fancy decoy for the Patents boys, while you and I finish the picture. I’ll do camera. What’s left to shoot?”

“Just the burning of Holly House, that’s all.”

“Good Lord, when did you cook that up?”

“Today.”

“I thought so.” Henry mopped his forehead. “Well, let’s talk about doing it in miniature.”

So Anne found herself back where she started, watching the boat spiral down the drain while she plotted the burning of Holly House.

The Wild West.... true; the business was like that. The next time she directed she was going to wear a gun, one of the fake ones. Just a little buckskin fringe on the jacket, a gun in a holster, and she’d really look like a cowgirl out of the west. If the Patents Company were going to regard her as an outlaw, then she damn well was going to dress the part.

There, on the floor, the discarded match was now cold. She picked it up.

Funny, she thought. He looked nothing like the man in her dream.

Chapter Nine

Two great stone lions stood watch over the Art Institute's entrance – stern-faced, but welcoming. It was Sunday; and admission was free, part of Chicago's policy to encourage more working families at the museum.

Well, I'm working. Anne smiled as she walked up the steps, reveling in the high arches. *Not on art, but commerce.* She'd arrived in Chicago the day before to keep an eye on the Midwest competition. Both studios – Selig Polyscope and Essanay – made westerns. Essanay was started by a cowboy, Bronco Billy Anderson. He and his partner George Spoor also turned out rapid fire comedy. Like Pantograph, they filmed on city streets, but they also had an all-glass studio Anne wanted to see for herself.

An impulsive trip, but that was in keeping with the Wild West tone of late. A few weeks ago there had been a shootout between Will and the Patents Men. The only casualty was a camera, and a not very good one at that. Shots were fired, but gunplay ceased when hirelings on both sides realized this Patents War was not worth dying or even getting grazed for, so they backed off.

Now, it seemed, they were at a draw. It put her in a mood to develop a western story for the screen, and to get out of Dodge. "Orphan's Revenge" was in the can and all needed a breather, so Anne decided to breathe Chicago air.

A voice echoed through the vestibule. She followed it to its source: a man in a long overcoat, standing at the portal of the Egyptian exhibit, pointing toward the ceiling as he addressed a motley group who could have been his friends, or perhaps students. He sounded like a tour guide, though without an official uniform. Anne tagged behind at a discreet distance.

From Egypt they progressed through the ages, stopping at one marvel and another to hear what lifted them above the commonplace. Anne jotted key words in her Chautauqua notebook. "Color scheme is drama. The art of the High Renaissance is cinematic art. The art of Brueghel, the peasants, the wedding feast, the images of death incarnate - this is a moving picture landscape."

The tour guide had them stare at a Greek sculpture, a head in relief, and imagine it making simple movements, no more than a few inches or a centimeter - a turn of the head, a raised shoulder, a curled lip. As he pointed out the features, his hands drew invisible lines in the air, his own outlines over the work of a master.

"You now see – animation." His words bounced over the marble. "Sculpture in motion." While everyone else stared at the sculpture Anne looked at the tour guide himself. He had an expressive forehead, a strong brow and deeply-set eyes.

He showed them Winslow Homer's "The Herring Net" and Turner's "Fishing Boats," tossed on a seething wave under a black-draped storm at sea. *That* was the sort of seascape she wanted to see on film, real, with full sails billowing. No more fake toys bobbing in a water tank!

For contrast, he introduced them to stillness absolute - Corot's "Interrupted Reading." Were it not for her rather robust, almost French peasant arms, the woman who set her book aside for a moment had a gaze so unfathomable it was worthy of the camera.

"Such intimacy isn't expected from an artist who achieved fame through landscapes," Anne wrote. She saw the limitless possibilities of the scene: the body, even the close-ups, within the frame around the painting.

At the North Wall, the guide pointed to a representation of the Three Muses. "Look at them closely," he said. Some in the tour had to step closer.

"Why, it's Mary Pickford!" someone exclaimed.

"Yes, it's Little Mary, all right!"

That's why she's so popular, Anne thought, as they walked toward the exit. Mary was like one of those Renaissance angels come to life. At some level those rough customers in the nickelodeons, who as a rule never set foot in a museum, recognized that and returned to see her, week after week.

The guide thanked one and all for coming, and for sharing his appreciation. Anne waited for everyone to go, then extended her hand to him.

"Thank you," she said. "And for letting me eavesdrop a little while."

"That's all right." He shook her hand. "I felt amused you wanted to tag along. Vachel's my name. Vachel Lindsay."

"Anne Blackstone." His hand felt large. "Vachel. I've never heard that name before."

“This is one of my Life Classes, where I spread the Gospel of Beauty."

“And what do you do besides preach the gospel?”

“Lately,” he pulled his overcoat forward, “I call myself a cartooning preacher. I used to attend drawing classes here.”

“Oh, you’re an artist?”

“Not if you listen to my teachers.” He smirked. “Or most of my friends. Or especially my father. It all depends on your reaction to my pictures. I’m a perpetual art student, but first I’m a poet.”

“Writing *and* painting - like William Blake?”

“Oh, you know about Blake?”

Anne smiled. “And why not? I’m Chautauqua educated.”

“Chautauqua!” He took her hand suddenly; his eyes had flames kindled in them. “I *love* Chautauqua!” He gave her a quick glance from head to toe. “And what do you do, Miss Blackstone?”

“I work in moving pictures.”

“You mean that quaint box with the small people running around inside it, jumping up and down, hitting each other over the head?”

She looked up at him. “That’s not what you said back there… ‘Art of the High Renaissance… painting in motion.’ And besides, I believe it does much more than people running around and hitting each other.”

“You do?” His large brow furrowed. “Yes. I believe you do.”

Anne looked quickly about the foyer – a bit nervously, she realized. “Was that your last tour of the day?”

“I'm afraid it will have to be.” Vachel glanced at his watch. “It's almost closing time.”

Anne shrugged and looked around the vestibule. Her gaze went towards the stone lions. “Do Life Classes exist only at the Art Institute?”

Vachel leaned closer. “Oh, we'll have a Life Class, Miss Blackstone.”

*** *** ***

On the walk to Essanay Studios Vachel outpaced Anne several times, even in the midst of a conversation. ”A fifteen mile stretch,” he said, “is nothing to me. I can walk for miles and leave almost anyone in the dust. Last year I tramped across the country.”

“Alone?”

“Alone, of course. On my own timetable, far from cities, railroads, automobiles.”

“How did you manage, just by walking?”

“Not by money. For food and lodging I exchange my poem *The Tree of Laughing Bells*, with my own illustrations. And, on request, public performance of any poem I’d committed to memory.”

The gates of the studio lay ahead of them. “Have you thought,” he asked, “how we’ll gain entrance, and see all that you hope to see?” he asked.

"Yes," Anne said. "We're Chautauqua students on a research trip."

"That's part-truth, anyway," he said. "I'm a perpetual student."

But at the door, because she thought it would provide more conviction, Anne let slip that she was studying to be a scenario writer. The receptionist and a man in the front office exchanged looks, then whispered something to a set hand, who motioned for Anne and Vachel to follow him.

She knew what she had to see first – the one outstanding feature of the studio, a roof and walls entirely of prismatic glass. She'd had discussions with Henry on whether to build a glass stage, to take advantage of natural light and still be able to film in cold weather.

It was large enough that from two to five separate productions could photograph at the same time. At the sides were huge windows open for ventilation. "Without that, and without cold air pumped from the basement," the set hand whispered, looking at Vachel, "it would steam up so much the actors would have to perform in the nude."

Vachel let out an elongated breath. Anne sensed his body pressing an inch closer to hers. Her heart beat faster; or was it his heartbeat she felt through her blouse?

"It's cold in winter," the set hand continued, "and like a hothouse in the summer, when it's fine for growing ferns and tulips, but not good acting."

"Where are the actors, then?" she asked.

"Rehearsing." The set hand put a finger to his lips, and quietly opened a door for them to slip through. Anne noticed on this enclosed stage the immense Cooper-Hewitt lights, tubes of mercury vapor hot enough to peel skin. They were suspended at a precarious angle above the players, held in place by a spider web of wires. The combination of heavy equipment, tenuously held, emitting light so powerful that it could scorch the skin and singe the hair, must have been a forbidding sight to any actor who stepped on the stage for the first time.

Back on the street, Vachel was all for finding some relaxation, but Anne was determined to maximize the day and press their luck as Chautauqua students with a visit to the other "major" Chicago studio, Selig Polyscope. She told Vachel he'd probably enjoy it – Selig was known for wild animal specialties and Westerns.

Again, their Chautauqua credentials gained them entrance, though Anne said nothing this time about writing scenarios. "Colonel" Selig, colorful founder of the studio, was not in his office, but in Florida, making production arrangements at their winter headquarters.

From the lobby, they were greeted by a lion's roar and the sight of the most familiar man in the country strolling past, dressed in his distinctive hat, hunting attire and riding boots.

"What is President Roosevelt doing at the studio?" Vachel whispered.

The man at the front desk shook his head. "Fooled you too, has he? He's a vaudeville impersonator."

"Hunting Big Game in Africa" was the day's production. The set was an African jungle beneath mercury vapor lights.The Teddy Roosevelt impersonator strode through the set, taking aim with a fake rifle.

"When does the lion come in?" Anne whispered.

"And is it for real?" asked Vachel.

"You heard that roar, didn't you? He's for real, all right." Behind the desk the man shrugged. "But a bit on the timid side."

And that, Anne thought, fit just perfectly with a vaudeville President.

Close to evening, Vachel's suggestion for relaxation was a section of town called "the Stroll," where the vaudeville houses could be found. Anne wanted to return to her hotel. As they stood in the lobby, she glanced upstairs. "Would you like to...?"

Vachel looked intrigued and surprised in the same moment. The hotel clerk hadn't heard the question. Anne was already walking toward the elevator.

"Of course," he replied. "I'll see you to your room."

When they reached her door, she said, "Boarding houses, hotels... St. Louis, Kansas City, Chicago – it feels like the same hotel, same room, wherever I go." She opened the door. "But I guess you don't know about hotels."

"Yes, it's the open road and the sky above," he said, glancing about Anne's spare but comfortable room. "At least for me."

"Yet we seem to have a lot of the same ideas," she said, pulling down the shade. "In fact, in my line of work, you could be my Idea Man."

"Idea Man?" He pushed his crumpled hat back on his head.

"He's the fellow that works with me, gives a different perspective, something other than what the camera sees. Gives fresh ideas to the story. Gives me ideas."

"Ideas. Yes."

He sat next to her on the bed. She removed his hat. He asked her about directing, but she didn't want to talk about it. She didn't want to talk about anything; research was done for the day. After the hat, she allowed him to remove her shoes, then her jacket.

She had felt this coming ever since he'd pressed close to her when the Essanay man joked about the actors in the nude. But it was no joke now, and it was nothing, absolutely nothing like the hurried fumbling with boys back at the Meadows, whose names she now forgot. It was slow, sinewy, as if they moved to the cadence of a snake charmer's flute.

Vachel worshipped her. His instruments were his tongue, his eyes, his poet's fingers. Were poet's fingers any different? she wondered.

As he was making his way down her shoulders he broke away, fished through his coat pocket, and brought out a pencil and small pad of paper.

"What are you doing?"

"I'm going to write you a poem."

The two minutes while he scribbled seemed the longest of her life. Yet, she considered, perhaps this was part of his worship.

Maybe that was true, for he returned to Anne with new vitality, a sweatier body, and an erection that helped her lose time altogether.

He cradled her for a very long time after, saying he felt moved to share secrets with her, more moved than he'd felt with anyone recently, except in his poetry. He told her he'd lost three sisters to scarlet fever, for which his father, a physician, blamed himself. His dearest friend in the world was his high school English teacher, Miss Susan Wilcox. He admitted to having visions, sometimes in full daylight, wide awake. When she asked, he told her they were of Biblical things, prophets in robes, smoke and clouds.

With that, he bounded from the bed to recite a poem. Whether it was the poem he'd written for her in the midst of lovemaking, or something he'd recited to farmers on the road, she couldn't really tell. It must be, she thought, all part of the Gospel of Beauty. And in his reciting, as he declaimed and waved his arms about, it appeared at that moment that he boxed with God, or at least took punches at Heaven.

*** *** ***

"It's snow, Anne! Real snow!" Vachel said. His boots slid from the chair in front of him and hit the nickelodeon floor. The thud made Anne spill some of her popcorn.

On screen, snow blanketed the Moscow skyline, coating the Kremlin's walls and onion domes. Drifts piled high in the distance, where horse-drawn troikas drove in stately procession across the screen.

"That's Saint Basil's square!"

"Quiet there!" It was a man's voice from two rows in front and across the aisle. It was Vachel's custom to talk out loud in theaters – where, Anne supposed, he took one more advantage to spread the Gospel of Beauty.

The scene changed from the street to a closer view of faces, *real* faces of Russian citizens standing in the marketplace.

"Peasant faces," said Vachel.

"Salt of the earth," said Anne. She turned her head towards him.

"They look desperate."

"You think so?" she whispered into his neck.

"Yes, somehow they do. I think that country will see some trouble."

The travelogue came to an end; the lights came up. The man across the aisle stood up. When he passed Vachel he said, "Hey, friend, why don't you hire your own theater?"

"What, watch the movies all by myself? Are you crazy?" The man turned to give him a glare. Vachel waved. "But thanks for calling me friend."

As they left the theater, Vachel defended his right to speak freely and publicly. “It’s because I’m an American, with the same right as every American to express him or herself in democracy’s theater.” He turned toward the nickelodeon, now five blocks behind them. “The cinema is the newspaper for the working class… a school for those who cannot read.”

“I’d like to believe you,” she said, trying to catch his eye.

Vachel's Life Class continued on foot, until it was time to check out of her hotel and catch the train for St. Louis.

As Anne's train pulled from Chicago, she took a tiny pocket mirror from her handbag. Except for a glance at the mirror in the hotel room, she hadn’t seen her own face in days, and was curious how it looked since meeting Vachel.

Through the train window, the sun struck thc tiny mirror. The burst of light struck her in the face. She moved her wrist the slightest bit, and the reflected sun hit the back of the seat in front of her.

Forgetting her face for the moment, she reached in the satchel again for her notebook. *This Side of the Moon,* she wrote. *A Story of the West.*

EXT. A MOUNTAIN SCENE DAY

A buckskinned figure stands on a bluff overlooking a broad stretch of the Missouri River. He reaches into his satchel, takes out a pocket mirror and looks to the sky.

HIS POV of the SUN emerging from clouds.

Return to the MAN as he slowly holds up the pocket mirror to face the sun.

TITLE: While on the Western Shore...

A PULSE OF LIGHT comes from the bluff across the river. PULL BACK to a man in a cloak who watches, his back to camera. When the pulse of light ceases, the man goes to a horse waiting nearby, mounts it, and RIDES TOWARDS CAMERA.

Will shut the notebook closed. "There you go again, asking the impossible from the cameraman."

"Why, what's impossible?" asked Anne, without looking up from her desk.

He opened the notebook to find the page. "OK… here we are, overlooking the Missouri. Then we're galloping over the plains." He glanced over his shoulder at her, still writing. "I thought you wanted to do a western."

"I do. It is."

"Sounds more like a *Mid*-western. I don't know where we're going to find a stretch of unused highway for this galloping horse – without houses, stores, train tracks, autos. You want to go somewhere in Wyoming. Isn't that where Bronco Billy's packing his cameras off to?"

"Nevada."

Will turned a few pages. "Then there's this 'pulse of light.' I don't know how in hell we're going to do that."

“Special effect? Super-expose the film?” Her voice was impatient. “I don’t know, Will. You’ve got the raw materials there.” She looked at the disassembled cameras strewn across his desk. He’d been taking them apart to make basic modifications, something to show the Edison goons in case they showed up again.

“I don’t see why we can’t just use smoke signals,” he muttered, thumbing through more pages. “But what really gets me is this *sudden* jump to a closeup of the woman’s face just after we introduce her in long shot.”

“Nothing strange about that; we did it right through ‘Orphan’s Revenge.’ They call it the ‘close view’ now. Griffith over at Biograph claimed he was the first to do it, but I’m not so sure.” She turned back to her desk. “Anyway, you’re looking at the first draft. I'm working on the second. But of course, we’ll make it up as we go along, just as we always do.”

Will paced through the workroom, hands in his pockets. “You got enough in second draft for a day’s location shooting?”

“Why, Will,” she smiled. “For the first time today we’re agreeing. I've had it up to here with fake sets and curiosity-seekers.” She closed her notebook. “It’s time to open doors, open windows, and show the real world outside.”

“Hah! Now you sound like that poet friend of yours.”

“Like Vachel? How do you know what he sounds like? You've never met.”

Will held up a copy of *The Tree of Laughing Bells* - poems with illustrations by Vachel Lindsay. “We certainly have. His personality leaks from these pages.”

"I *asked* you to read my script. I didn't ask you to read his book."

Will laughed. "Well, you left it out for one and all to see. So I did."

"Do you think they're any good?"

"Damned if I know. I'm just a mechanical kind of guy."

"Don't sell yourself short. I think you and Vachel have a lot in common."

"And I suppose we'll have the opportunity to find that out… very soon?"

She returned to her notebook. "Yes, you just might."

With a sense of timing that Anne found both admirable and annoying, Vachel arrived at Pantograph Studios one day before the company's location shoot in the neighborhood of St Charles, the state's first capital. He arrived on foot, claiming he was "out for a tramp, a ramble, a pilgrimage into the heartland."

But Vachel was here, on Pantograph's doorstep, visible to enough to the stage crew that Anne addressed him as if he were an employee at his first day on the job.

"I should say, Mister... Lindsay, that stunt work is a good starting level position. Five dollars to start. If it's a horse stunt, we'll pay as much as ten. For tomorrow's shoot we offer five dollars for the day, lunch and transportation. If you land a role in the picture, or came from the stage, highly recommended, pay is fifty dollars a day."

"*I* come from the stage," he whispered.

"I thought you'd say something like that." When they were out of view of the workers she took his arm. "Yes, Vachel. You can join our 'outing.'"

"Naturally. I'm your Idea Man, remember?"

She gave him a nudge in the ribs. "Oh, yes," she said with a wink, "It's going to be a picnic."

From his blank look she realized he hadn't a clue what she meant.

*** *** ***

St. Charles had streets over one hundred years old, paved with brick, free of trolley tracks and telephone wires. It had been the point of departure for Lewis and Clark, and the place Daniel Boone and family called home.

Anne had hoped that in Boone's country she'd find the true Indian actors she couldn't locate in Saint Louis. The extras who smeared themselves with red-brown paint and carried fake bows and arrows were, in her opinion, a plain embarassment.

But even if she had to make do with shellacked Indians they'd look impressive racing through the countryside of Boone's Lick Trail, the Missouri River in the background. Henry had arranged for some real horses and riders in St. Charles; the wagon-pulling nags of downtown Saint Louis weren't adequate for "This Side of the Moon." Cameras, film stock and props were stored in an open-ended truck, while the costumes, actors and provisions piled into a horse wagon pulled by one of those St. Louis nags – in case the truck broke down or fell into a rut.

Will drove the truck, his camera case next to him, Anne in the passenger seat. Vachel perched on a box just a foot behind them. The poet drank in the morning air, his eyes roving over the St. Louis outskirts. "Like players in the Commedia del Arte!" he said. "And here's one lucky poet, tagging along on the High Renaissance of cinematic art!"

Anne shook her head. "No, Vachel. It's the early Dark Ages. We've only just opened our eyes and are beginning to see."

"Eyes?" Will spoke for the first time since the car pulled out of the garage. "You mean one eye, don't you?" He patted the camera case. "A Cyclops."

"Will, I'll write that down." Vachel rummaged through his pockets for a pencil.

Will glanced up. "Hey, Vachel?"

"Yes?"

"You know how to use a gun?"

"Will!" Anne nearly jumped out of her seat.

"What, you didn't tell Vachel about the Edison boys?"

Vachel stopped writing. "You mean those men who tried to wreck your studio?"

Anne crossed her arms. "They're over and done with. Aren't they, Will?"

Will shrugged.

"You didn't have any trouble with them while I was in Chicago, did you?"

“Not exactly. But all the same…” He gripped the wheel until his arms stretched to their full length “…I’m glad we have a few real cowboys waiting for us up at Boone’s Lick. *With* guns.”

“I only shot squirrels back where I grew up in Springfield, Illinois,” said Vachel.

“And he’s been sorry for it ever since,” Anne said, glancing over her shoulder.

The truck approached the bridge to Saint Charles. The paint was still fresh; it had been finished just in time for the World’s Fair.

“What about that horse stunt?” asked Will, after a silence.

“Some local boy,” said Anne. “Name's Junior.”

“Junior, huh?” Will smiled and glanced over his shoulder. “I thought Vachel was your man.”

Anne looked back at Vachel; he was blinking like a turtle. “That was all for show, Will. I thought you knew that.” Her eyes returned to the road. “Junior isn’t like one of your cowboy stunt riders. He and his horse Phoebe practically grew up together. She’ll do anything Junior asks her to. So says Henry.”

“*Junior.*” Will shook his head. “I still ain’t shooting it.”

“But I just told you…”

“Tearing down a narrow trail, jumping over a chasm, falling into the river: alright. But *not* galloping towards the camera. No way.” He patted the case. “Not this baby.”

“Alright, we’ll use the Pathe' camera.”

“Henry isn’t here to make the decision, so I’m making it. End of discussion.”

Anne scrunched lower in her seat. “We’ll see when we get there.”

A confused mix of actors and Missouri cowboys greeted the truck at Boone’s Lick. The morning had been mild enough that some of the actors had set out on bicycles. They were waiting for their costumes, hungry, and not pleased to hear that the food was some ways back in a wagon pulled by a horse.

“Not even a thermos of coffee?” asked the comic, who looked odd out of his baggy pants.

“Or a cup of tea?” asked the character actress.

“Sorry,” said Anne, as she hopped from the truck. “We didn’t have room.”

As Anne passed around copies of the scenario and spoke with the actors, Vachel descended from his box like a spider, taking in the sight of actors, cowboys, and horses gathered in the meadow. Anne was careful to keep them busy until the clop-clop of horse hooves announced the presence of their coffee, tea, mineral water, sandwiches, fruit and costumes.

The comic, once fed, stood up and without a word began to undo his belt. The women looked at each other, some with surprise, some shock. They looked to Anne for some assurance.

"Ladies," she said, "I'm sure the bushes will offer you some comfort," handing them their costumes.

With a great deal of squirming and rustling they changed into their western costumes behind the lilac bushes. A few of the men stripped to the waist and began to apply brown pigment. Anne turned away.

Anne took some of the actors into a local barn, one of several that were in various stages of dilapidation. Beer and wine bottles were scattered over a table inside the barn. An actor with disheveled hair sat in the midst of the bottles.

"I thought this story was about a girl raised among Indian tribes," Vachel whispered to a cowboy with a long moustache.

"So did I." His false moustache drooped further when he spoke. "This must be the background story."

Anne clapped her hands. "Nancy!" A little girl with dirty knees, wearing a frayed brown dress came skipping up to her.

"This is the table where you find your father." Anne sank to one knee, and clasped her hands together. "You look up at him and say…"

"Oh Father, please come Home," Nancy chimed in.

"Good." Anne rose from the barn floor. She stepped behind the camera. "Cue the violin!"

"Marvelous!" whispered Vachel.

"Ready on the set!" She glanced at him. He thought he saw a smile.

Nancy had to go through several entrances and knee-bendings before she got it right. Once she did, the man playing her father stirred awake. Shaking, he recognized his daughter. He swung an arm aside, scattering the table full of bottles to the ground.

Nancy, on cue, began to pray. Her father mouthed the same prayer, looking first to her, then somewhere slightly above, toward the unseen object of her adoration.

"Alright, now the effect," said Anne.

"What effect?" said the cameraman.

Anne planted her fists at her waist. “Look in your script.”

The cameraman bent the script in half. "Hold on. What is this 'camera creeps?' You have it farther, you have it closer, you can't *creep.*"

From a prop bag Anne pulled one small metal rollerskate. She slid it slowly across the table. The cameraman caught it. Anne cued the violinist.

As the scene was finishing Anne saw the Missouri farm boy riding slowly towards her. “Junior.”

The broad-brimmed hat slipped over the boy’s face as he nodded. “Yes, Ma’am. Miss Blackstone?”

She measured the horse’s broad face with her hand. “And you must be Phoebe.” Phoebe snorted. “You didn’t come from the direction of the river, did you?”

“No Ma’am, we rode from the other side of town.”

“Run into any other riders, or a man working a camera?”

“No, Ma’am.”

“I’d be most grateful if you’d steer clear of them, at least for the next hour or so.”

“You have directions for us… Ma’am?”

“I think we’ll be using you very soon.” Anne glanced quickly around, reached in her pocket, took out fifteen dollars and handed it to him.

“Ma’am that’s five dollars more than Mr. Harrison mentioned on the telephone.”

"I know." She leaned in toward the horse. "This is for a *special* stunt." She pointed down the trail. "You see that lone tree there? I want you to ride Phoebe straight for that tree, then give her a quick turn at the last moment."

Junior pushed his hat up on his forehead. "That will take some practice."

Anne glanced for any sign of Will and the other riders. There was a bit of dust in the air towards the river, where his stunt unit was still in full swing.

She patted Phoebe's side. "We're going to break for lunch. Right before we do I want you to take some practice rides with that tree." She pointed to the river. "But soon as anyone walks or rides up to ask what you're doin'… *don't let on.*"

"Not a word, Ma'am." He dug in to Phoebe's ribcage and they were off.

She looked for Vachel. He was waiting for her, pen and notepad in hand. She asked him to instruct the crew to break for lunch, and send a runner to tell Will's stunt riders to get off their horses and eat. While he was away she fished out a picnic box and a large soft bundle, tied with string, from below the truck's front seat.

"What is that, laundry?' asked Vachel when he returned.

"Another surprise." She tossed it to him. "You can carry it for now."

He glanced at the box she carried. "I suppose that's the picnic?"

"Mmmm hmmm."

He planted the parcel on his head, supported by his hands. She giggled at the image of him carrying that on a long trek through the jungle.

"Don't suppose this picnic will be interrupted by rampaging cowboys and Indians?" he asked, from beneath his load.

"Not so long as they're gathered 'round the food."

They took turns feeding each other. Then Anne undid the string on the parcel, folded back the paper, and spread out a fringe leather jacket, skirt and a frontier hat.

"What in the *world?*" he said.

"It's a frontier picture," she said. "Got to dress the part."

He gathered up the picnic. "A horse riding, roping, buckskin-wearing lady.Our Annie Oakley."

"Maybe." She pulled on her boots.

"Instead of a loaded rifle, a megaphone."

"Vachel, when Will asked you about the gun…"

He looked amused. "You still think there's going to be some for-real gunplay here?"

"It isn't about the gun, Vachel. It's about courage." She looked him straight in the eye. "I *need* to pull this off. This shot I've been talking about – it's not just business as usual. You heard how Will feels about it. That's why I want you to give him this."

She took a paper from her jacket's vest pocket and handed it to him. It was an entirely new scene of a group of Indian riders, hotly pursued by a cowboy posse. Her note at the top said "Crucial to the climax of 'This Side of the Moon.'"

Once they emerged from the bushes, Vachel sent a runner to gather all the stunt riders, spruce up their costumes and makeup, and prepare to charge through a canyon pass and up a steep hill. If Will was to ask, he was to be told that Anne had returned to the barn for some re-takes of the scene with Nancy.

Near a downhill stretch of Boone's Lick Trail, Anne quietly set up the Pathe' camera on a tripod and motioned to Junior. "This time," she whispered, "no miniatures."

Phoebe pranced back and forth, Junior reined her toward the camera, and they were off at a gallop. Anne cranked the camera, in fluid, even motions. The approach was too wide, and Junior pulled Phoebe away too soon.

Anne signaled to him to try again. Looking up, she could see the dust of Will's Missouri cowboys charging up the hill. Phoebe paced back and forth in the shade of the trees.

Junior gave a quiet whoop; Phoebe reared.

Phoebe and Junior charged for the camera. Anne cranked, hands steady as the pistons of a steam engine.

At the top of the hill a cowboy waited for his horse to regain strength. Looking through the dust cloud he saw one lone rider charging breakneck for a camera that was worked by a lady clad in buckskin.

"Will, you've got to see this."

"No!" Will hollered, and very nearly on the word Phoebe made a sharp right turn away from Anne and the camera, leaving what appeared to be a scant ten feet of space between.

An actress screamed; some of the local cowboys loped towards Anne, who had slumped to the ground. The Pathe' camera on its tripod still stood.

By the time Vachel arrived Anne was doubled over on the ground, caked with trail dust, a small crowd gathered around her. Vachel brushed her face.

The cowboy who had first seen her came up with Will, cussing under his breath.

"Well," said the cowboy. " If you're lucky that camera got every second of it. Going to look even better up there on the screen."

Will stepped up to peer through the Pathe's eyepiece. It was a good composition, the hills, the trail. If that ride was half as good as it looked from up there…

Anne was finally standing. Vachel shouldered her, and looked at Will with the unspoken question, *All right, what now?*

"I think," said Will, "we'll call it a day."

Chapter Ten

"Will... look at this." Anne had never seen so many people on the avenue, even for a late Friday afternoon.

Will glanced up from his desk. "I think they're heading toward Union Station." He grabbed his hat and jacket from a chair. "Come on; let's find out."

Anne felt the electricity as soon as they stepped onto the avenue. People walked faster than usual, and she heard giggling, as if they were going to the circus rather than the train station.

Will asked what it was all about. "Not what, who," a man replied. "The Biograph Girl's back."

Anne recalled the newspaper headline from the week before. "MOTION PICTURE ACTRESS MEETS TRAGIC END BENEATH WHEELS OF STREET CAR" Her name was Florence Lawrence, known as the Biograph Girl, and she'd been killed here in Saint Louis. A week later the *Post Dispatch* carried an ad as big as the headline: "WE NAIL A LIE" accompanied by a photograph of the supposedly dead "picture personality." The account of Florence's death was blatantly false; she had *not* been run over by a street car, and would make a personal appearance in Saint Louis to prove it.

The crowd pressed tighter as they passed through the train station doors. There were more people on the platform than had turned out for President Taft's appearance two weeks earlier.

Several people held slips of paper. Anne had a closer look at one; judging by its ragged edge it had been torn from a newspaper: "March 25, 1910, Twentieth Street Entrance, Union Station – The bearer is entitled to one personally autographed photograph of Miss Florence Lawrence."

"Hey Will!" A man waved from a spot near the platform's edge.

"Hey, Curtis! I see the press is here." Will pulled Anne through the crowd to the place where Curtis stood with camera and tripod. Other photographers stood close by, jostling for a place at the front.

Anne heard a slow clanging and the toot of a whistle coming from down the tracks. A singular tremor rippled through the crowd as the train from New York approached the station.

"That train's taking its sweet time," said Will.

"Milking it for maximum effect," said Curtis. "For a week these people thought the Biograph Girl was dead." He spat on the station floor.

"But why bring her back to life in St. Louis?" asked Anne.

"Because publicity hatched the idea in New York. So – announce that she was killed in Saint Louis, then follow with a full-page announcement saying, oops, she's not dead, and drop a hint that maybe Biograph, or maybe even the Trust, had planted the story."

"Then who did plant the story?" she asked.

"IMP."

"IMP?"

"Independent Motion Picture Company," said Curtis. "Miss Lawrence just signed a contract with them."

Ankles and feet came uncomfortably close to the camera equipment; Curtis picked it up and motioned for Anne and Will to follow. "Stick close and you'll get front row seats."

With a squeal of brakes. the train from New York pulled up to the platform. Curtis and the other photographers stood ready, eyes to their camera lenses. Among the first to step from the train were a small woman in a well-tailored blue suit, flanked by two tall men.

"Look there, it's the Biograph Girl!"

"Biograph, nothin'!" said a distinguished looking man at the front of the crowd. "She's the IMP Girl now!"

Florence's wide, feathered hat and ample scarf concealed the figure beneath the clothing while at the same time drawing attention to it. To a volley of cheers, she removed the hat and scarf to reveal a handsome young blonde woman in her mid-twenties.

"People of Saint Louis! My name is Florence Lawrence! And I am alive and well!" The applause that greeted her was echoed by the crowd outside the station. The man who'd proclaimed her "The IMP Girl" stepped forward, helped her to the platform, and motioned to the photographers and reporters.

"Who's that?" asked Will.

"Owns a big theater chain in town." Curtis hoisted his tripod on his shoulder. "I'll have to leave you two here."

A group picture was taken in front of the train. While flashbulbs popped there were brief attempts at speeches, though Anne could hear only a few words. Florence introduced her husband, Harry Solter, and co-star King Baggot, "a hometown boy from Saint Louis." Solter announced their new picture, directed by himself.

The theater owner led Florence and the two men toward the station exit. As Florence passed by Anne noticed that she had blue eyes, and seemed smaller and more fragile up close.

When they were halfway between train platform and exit the crowd made a surge. Those with newspaper coupons wanted their promised autograph. Hands reached to grab a feather from Florence's hat, a button, a piece of her clothing, a few strands of hair. Her hat was knocked from her head, trampled underfoot, and torn to pieces. Florence tottered, then crumpled into her husband's arms. King, her co-star, fought off the mob as the IMP Girl was deposited, with some difficulty, into a waiting car.

"They're headed for the Grand Hotel," said Curtis, grabbing his tripod and camera. "Tag along with me if you want to see some action."

Anne declined; she'd seen enough action for one day. Curtis pulled Will in the direction of a streetcar, already packed to capacity.

A crowd still lingered about the station, unsure what to do after witnessing a celebrated woman brought back from the dead. Walking in their midst, Anne felt that she had just experienced something altogether *new.* If the energy of that surging crowd could be harnessed it could drive a steam engine at full throttle for hours.

Of course, she thought, the moving picture personalities would command attention, and would want their names to be known. People had been lining up for blocks to see them without ever knowing who they really were.

Of course they would ask for money, outrageous amounts of money; of course the studio executives were scared to death of that. But after what Anne had witnessed, it seemed as if the power had shifted from the executives to the "personalities." Florence was just the first out of the gate.

*** *** ***

Over the next two days Florence and her entourage turned St. Louis upside down. The police at the Grand Hotel made a gauntlet of linked hands so Florence and company could make it from the street to the hotel doors. Soon after, Florence and her husband appeared at a balcony, as a spotlight from the street – could it have been from a police vehicle? – bathed the couple in theatrical light.

The IMP Girl's next personal appearance was on Saturday afternoon at the Gem Theater, while across town her latest picture would be projected at the Strand. Anne caught up with her on the way to the Gem, as Florence posed for photos aboard a streetcar. She stood like a ship's figurehead, clutching her parasol and looking towards the sea. Apart from an isolated "We love you, Florence dear!" the crowd on this occasion was better behaved than the Union Station mob. There had been a mad, animal passion about that one; Vachel would have loved it.

When a reigning diva of the opera house had a spectacular opening night she would be carried through the streets on the shoulders of cheering young men. Florence's triumph was no less complete. As she was called to the stage at the Gem, Florence was introduced as "the Queen of Moving Picture Actresses."

"Florence, is it true you are the real Biograph Girl?" asked the announcer.

"I *was* the Biograph Girl," she answered. "But now…" her voice rose a few decibels, and she raised her arms to the ceiling, to fervent applause. "I am the IMP Girl!"

Florence introduced her husband and her leading man. King gave an aw-shucks speech about how great it was to be back in his old hometown, and Harry talked at some length about the thrills and romance of Florence's next film, "The Broken Oath," directed by himself. Husband and co-star were greeted warmly, but it was clear from the start who the crowds had come to see: Florence Lawrence, Biograph Girl or IMP Girl, the personality of the hour.

As the announcer said in closing, "Florence Lawrence, Saint Louis has taken you to its heart!!"

At intermission Anne heard her name called in the lobby. It was Will, out of breath. He had spoken to someone in Florence's entourage about Pantograph, and now they had scheduled a studio visit for late that afternoon. He was heading back there to make the studio presentable. First he had to find a phone and give Henry a call to get things rolling.

There was no use, Anne thought, explaining this phenomenon to Henry. He wasn't able to grasp the idea of actors and actresses in films making personal appearances. Moving pictures, to him, were just that – not comedic or dramatic stories with personalities at their center. His sensibilities were of the last century; hers were molded by the World's Fair and Chautauqua, and the chance to tell stories on both a vaster *and* a more intimate scale.

Perhaps, Anne hoped, these New York moving picture people might agree. She took a compact from her purse to check her eyes and hair.

*** *** ***

At Pantograph, the stage hands were busy sweeping and putting a painted canvas backdrop of a mountainside to conceal the inherent disorder of the shooting stage

Anne straightened her desk, rearranging papers for no good reason, and brought out her own props: director's jacket, riding boots, and the megaphone. She asked Henry to put on his good clothes, but he mumbled something about not wanting to appear in any photographs, and if they needed to find him, he'd be in his office.

"All right, stay in your old office," she said, and stuck out her tongue so he'd know she wasn't really upset.

The entourage that did eventually arrive was a smaller group than Anne had pictured, so she took careful note of who came through the door. King Baggot wasn't among them, but there was Florence's husband Harry, on the arm of Florence herself. There was the theater owner who'd been at the train station, and there were a few members of the press, including Curtis with his camera. There was also a short, slightly stocky man in a bowler hat and long travel coat whom Anne didn't recognize, but felt as if she ought to, for he had an important air about him.

"So Miss Blackstone…" Harry Solter approached her, his eyes closed half way. "I understand you're a fellow director."

"Yes, Mr. Solter, I am."

"I do mostly westerns. Flo practically started in westerns."

"All in the family, then." Anne smiled.

"Just so." Solter tilted his head a few inches back, as if trying to size Anne up.

"I filmed a western," said Anne. "Just over a year ago. 'This Side of the Moon.'"

"Sorry, I didn't catch it."

"That doesn't surprise me. It was sort of an Indian Western."

"I see." Harry looked at his watch. He struck Anne as an oafish sort of man who'd decided to try good manners on for size. Perhaps he was a director, perhaps even a *good* director, but he'd never command attention like this without Florence.

Will was keeping the press and theater men preoccupied, so for this moment there was only the hand being extended toward Anne. Any other person within the St. Louis city limits would kiss that hand as if it belonged to royalty. Her uncredited presence on the screen had only succeeded in making her more desirable, until now she'd become the toast of the town, the Herald of a New Age of celebrity.

"Miss Lawrence," said Anne. "I am very pleased to meet you."

Florence glanced sideways at her husband. "Won't you *introduce* us, Harry?"

"Flo, this is Anne Blackstone. She's a director."

"What, like you, Harry?" It was a bit disconcerting that while taking Anne's hand, Florence had yet to acknowledge her.

"Your husband and I were just discussing westerns."

Florence waved a braceleted arm through the air. "That's what I get for knowing how to ride a horse. Making westerns and doing my own stunts."

"Flo, you know the audience loves it when you do that," said Harry.

Florence shrugged.

"Miss Lawrence, I'd like to express my apologies for that incident at the station."

"No need, Miss Blackstone. No need at all." She put a gloved hand over Anne's. "It was nothing a good shot of whiskey couldn't set straight. A good thing my husband had a tight grip on me when we took our bows from that balcony." She turned to her husband. "Isn't that right, Harry?"

Harry nodded vaguely, still looking as if he preferred to be somewhere else. Standing behind him, Anne noticed the man in the bowler hat, acting all friendly with the stage hands and gentlemen of the press.

Something about him looked more and more familiar. Before he left with the entourage Anne felt like she needed to speak with him.

She returned her attention to Florence. “You were on the stage before appearing in motion pictures, weren’t you, Miss Lawrence?”

"Say, not many people remember that. I was practically brought up on the stage.“ She turned so she was in profile, then puckered up her lips. “Ever hear of ‘Baby Flo, the Child Wonder Whistler?’”

Anne remembered the name from an old poster, perhaps in one of the Ohio River towns. “Yes, I believe I do...”

Florence took Anne by the wrist and pulled her closer. “I was lucky to make five dollars a week back then. With this new contract I get a *thousand* a week, and my name on a marquee.” She wagged her head. “Not bad for Florence Annie Bridgwood from Hamilton, Ontario!”

“Hey, Flo!” Harry gestured their way. “We have dinner at the Chamber of Commerce, then a speaking engagement at the Grand Opera House. Time to go.”

“And all in *one day*!” Florence put her hands on her hips, gave Anne a grin and swiveled away. “Nice chatting with you, Miss Blackstone…” She glanced over her shoulder. “… woman to woman.”

The entourage had finished their tour by this time; most were out of the building by now or making their way to the door, ushered along by Will, who was set on a chance to crash the Chamber of Commerce dinner – representing Pantograph, of course. Anne said she would close up shop.

If nothing else, she thought, this visit had been good for studio morale. The hallways were swept, costumes hanging on their hooks, papers in reasonable stacks. Even the carpentry room was clean.

She remembered that Henry was still in his office. On the way there she noticed someone ducking into the projection booth.

From the doorway she could see it was the man in the travel coat and bowler hat, his back to her. There was a hiss, then a small puff of smoke as he lit a match. He turned ever so slightly, and Anne saw that he puffed on a long cigar. He drew deeply on it; in the glowing cherry's light she saw his cheeks turn red.

"Are you mad?" Her fingers groped for the light switch. He caught her arm, giving it a slight twist.

"Not at all…" he whispered. "You never can tell. Accidents will happen." He threw away the match. "These rat trap buildings are always burning down." The cherry glowed hot as he passed the cigar from one hand to the other.

"But we already *met* with your people…" Anne held fast to the door frame, bending, supplicating the tiniest bit. "We're not violating the Patents… we're not using your equipment." She made a move to another part of the booth. "Here, I'll show you."

Holding the lit cigar in his left hand, with his right the man tightened his grip on her. "I'm not with the Patents."

"Not with Edison?" The man shook his head. "Who are you, then?"

He dangled the burning cigar above a basket of coiled nitrate film. "I represent certain business interests in Chicago…. You're not supposed to make pictures here in Saint Louis." There was a sputter and spark of the suddenly-ignited film.

"Henry!" Anne cried as the man pulled her from the booth. At that moment someone else grabbed her from behind, tied a blindfold around her head and a gag across her mouth.

"I'm not going to leave you here." It was the man's voice. "I'm afraid I can't say the same for Mr. Harrison. His time has come." Hands gripped both her arms and pulled her away; she could feel the heat receding at her back. "You've got talent, Miss Blackstone. You should go on making pictures. Just not in this town."

"You can't get away with this..." she murmured beneath the gag.

"But I already have. You know how many fires flare up in this part of town. Poor fellow… he must have dozed off, while holding a lighted cigarette."

"A real shame," said another voice.

"Quiet!" hissed the man. They continued to drag her out of the building, until she felt the brisk night air on her skin. At a distance now, she heard the pops and crash of glass bulbs breaking, then a small explosion that would have been the film in the storage closet. In the midst of it, she thought she heard Henry's voice, crying out "Nicodemus!" Then she felt herself pulled into another building, and up flights of stairs. She tried to count them, thinking the information might come in useful – if she lived.

She was thrust into a room. There was the sound of a metal door slammed shut and a bolt sliding into place.

"I know you'll try and find me." It was the man's voice. "But believe me, it won't do any good. Saint Louis and Chicago are big towns. You'll never see me again."

There was a clanging of bells and a siren that she knew came from Engine Company 26 as it raced down Broadway, but it was too late and far away, at least for Henry. They wouldn't have heard her pounding on the door, and as far as she knew no one would until morning.

***   ***   ***

There was a hole in the window glass the size of a thrown rock. From the window Anne could tell she was in a warehouse, probably abandoned, nine floors above street level. The window faced an alley, but the light coming from one side meant the street itself was about a block away.

Behind her, something darted among the cement dust and concrete rubble on the floor. Anne gasped. It was dark and, she was almost sure, had a tail.

The walls were covered in grime and copper-colored water stains. Her only way out led through the window.

"Help!" she screamed. If the ones who locked her here were in earshot, it was worth the risk.

Anne screamed again, this time sticking her arm through the hole in the glass. She heard muffled voices from the street, and a horse's slow clop on the pavement. **"Up here!"**

Two men stood in the alleyway, a horse-drawn wagon behind them. One pointed toward her window.

From the sound of their heavy boots on the metal stairs she felt every one of the nine floors. While they tried to break the bolt on the door Anne wavered, dropped and hit the ground.

When she awoke, she was slung across a man's broad back like a sack of potatoes. Her right arm dangled below her head, striped with blood. She tried to count the steps: *one... two... three... four...* as they descended the stairwell.

Out on the street a grey cloud still hung above the smoldering ruins of the studio, as a lone fire company engine sprayed a long stream of water into the wreckage.

The local hospital bandaged her cuts, gave tests for smoke inhalation, then released Anne to the district police station to identify the arsonist. With bandaged hand she went through photographs strewn across a desk. None looked enough like the man. At the end of their session the best that could be done was to design a "WANTED FOR ARSON and MURDER" poster with a large question mark over the faceless head at its center. Anne was sent home to convalesce.

Though physically able, she rarely left her bed. She tried to sleep on her right side, then her left, then curled in a ball. First she had to absorb her injuries, then the shock, next the thought of her unfinished films, of the studio itself, no more. There was no use in rebuilding. They couldn't go on without Henry.

With Vachel tramping out west, and for the time being unreachable, Will became her tunnel to the outside. He brought food, gossip, and news of the world. A comet named Halley's was approaching; some feared the earth would pass through its tail.

One morning while Anne sat propped with pillows against her headboard, Will opened a page of the industry paper *Variety* to a bold announcement.

ALICE BLACHÉ OPENS SOLAX STUDIOS IN FORT LEE

Alice Blache, president and director of the Solax Company, has announced the largest moving picture studio in America, the first major independent headed by a woman. Construction of the Solax studios has already begun in Fort Lee, New Jersey.

"That means they'll be hiring." Anne looked up from the article "Will, that would be perfect for you."

"Not me," Will shook his head. "I've got a date three years in the making, and no telling when it's going to end." He tapped the article. "This is for you."

"Solax?" she asked.

Chapter Eleven

"Watch your step, please!" Alice Blaché's words, filtered through a strong French accent, emerged from a wide pith helmet with a long trailing scarf. She strode through the construction site like a ship's captain, helmet set at a jaunty angle, pointing with her cane toward one shooting stage after another that did not yet exist, but would rise from this wooden wreckage.

Her cane tapped at a pile of two by fours planted at dangerous angles, then shoved aside a sawhorse and muttered a French curse beneath her breath. "Herbert! Did you not tell the workers to clean up this mess?"

Anne, tromping over nails and splintered wood, tried to keep pace with the woman. If it had been any other first day on the job she would have been scribbling notes inconspicuously on a pad, but she needed both hands to avoid the many obstacles in their path.

"Yes, Alice, I did." The man's voice was weary.

"Maman?" A little girl's voice came from behind.

"Oui, Simone?"

"Je suis très fatiguee."

"English, please, for Miss Blackstone's sake."

"Please, Mrs. Blaché, call me Anne." Maybe it had to do with Continental manners, but Anne saw no reason for the forced informality. Alice knew perfectly well that Anne was no guest, but a companion, an *au pair* for their daughter Simone. But the five year old had not warmed to her yet; when Anne was first introduced Simone stood frozen in place, then ran to hide in her mother's skirts.

"Anne? Then Anne it is." Left and right her arms pointed. "Wardrobe room. Property room. Finishing room, where prints are approved and sent to theaters."

Anne heard Herbert talking to his daughter in a soothing mix of English and French.

"Offices, dressing rooms, on the ground floor," continued Alice. By now they were standing in the midst of a large building whose sides had been constructed, but still lacked a roof. Alice spread her arms upward. "And here… the *glass* studio." She was beaming. "Prismatic glass."

Herbert, who now stood next to them, shook his head. "Glass," he said. "Very hot." Though he looked very French to Anne, with those two words he betrayed his British origins.

"*No!"* Alice strode to each side of the building. "Here and here, large windows, to open to… le vent…"

"The wind," said Herbert, with a sideways glance toward Anne.

"And air… réfrigérés…" Alice's arms made a pumping motion from the direction of the floor.

"Refrigerated air, piped from the basement," explained Herbert. "But believe me, it will *still* be hot." He shook his head again.

"Shooting, film processing, distribution," Alice emphasized. "Le tout!"

"All in one," said Herbert. He leaned closer, whispering "She gets very excited about this."

“I would be, too.” said Anne. She could understand Alice’s excitement, and relief. After churning out one reel comedies and melodramas in Flushing for the nickelodeon market, to be in charge of her own studio...

Alice paced across the foundation in long, even strides, measuring the distances, muttering to herself in French. At a certain point, she stopped, shook her head, and turned to her husband.

“Herbert! A conference, please."

Herbert shrugged. "And Simone?"

Alice beamed in Anne’s direction. “My dear, would you be so good as to watch Simone for a short while?”

Anne swallowed. She'd come all the way to New Jersey to get back to work, in a grand, modern studio – not babysit a child. Anyway, she thought Simone was terrified of her. What were they supposed to do? Where would they go?

Herbert led Simone by the hand towards Anne. “Simone, show Miss Anne the river, will you?” The child gave her mother a confused look. “You remember the way, yes?”

Simone nodded and stepped away from her father “This way, please.” She walked toward a dirt path that led away from the construction site.

“Certainement.” Anne stepped alongside. “Aprés vous.”

“It’s all right, I’m speaking English now.”

“Good for you.” Anne could think of no more to say, either in English or the very limited French she’d learned at the Chautauqua study circle. She followed the child down the narrow dirt path, winding through brush and hardscrabble farmland, startling an occasional rabbit and, at one point, a noisy grouse.

"And this is the Henry Hudson River," said Simone, with great assurance. It rolled on peaceably below the Highlands where they stood, a smooth and cultured river, so unlike the untamed Missouri that she knew best.

Ahead of them lay the haze, clutter and gray confusion of Manhattan, ringed by barges, paddle boats, and sails of all sizes. Beyond it, some miles just to their south, the sea, beckoning.

Simone was getting close to the edge; Anne put out a cautionary hand.

"I'm all *right*," said Simone. "Father and Mother bring me here lots of times."

"Well thank you, Simone, for bringing me here, too." Not far from them, just below the bluff, geese flew south, making for the open sea. Anne caught her breath.

"I like to watch the birds," said Simone, spreading her tiny arms outward, imitating their flight.

"Do you ever see swans, Simone?"

"What are swans?"

Anne took a deep breath. "Well, they're a bit like a goose, but big, and white."

"Do you eat them?"

Anne was caught off guard. "Ah, no, you don't – "

"We eat goose," said Simone.

Anne felt suddenly dizzy. She didn't know if it was the height, the city view or the thought of cooked swan on a plate. She stepped away from the bluff, and motioned for Simone to do the same. "May we head back now?" It felt odd making a request to a five year-old.

On the return walk Simone grew tired, and asked to be picked up. Anne thought that would be all right for a brief while. Feeling Simone's arms around her neck, Anne's dizziness gradually left. Her own mother must have carried her this way, trekking back and forth along the river shore many, many miles west of here.

She noticed the green ribbons in Simone's hair. Green like the ribbons Ma had tied into her own hair, before the picnic on the river.

"Are you crying?" asked Simone.

"I think the ocean got in my eyes."

"But we didn't even see it."

A tiny river ran the full length of Anne's cheek. "I didn't have to," said Anne. "I could feel it."

*** *** ***

"FOR RENT OR BEST OFFER"

The hand-scrawled sign, propped against a rusty, dented, mud-caked Ford, caught Anne's attention on her way downtown. She could well imagine what this car had been through: driven through clouds of dust, flipped on its side, chased by a horse, braking to a dead stop at the brink of the cliffs above the river.

Everything in Fort Lee seemed up for rent or hire: front porches, farm animals, small children and visiting relatives. The only notable exceptions were the convent and the ladies seminary. If a house was condemned one of the studios bought it outright, only to burn it down or dynamite it the following day. Before the arrival of the picture folks this had been a quiet town of hotels and livery stables; the most frequent visitors came from across the river for a day's stroll in the country and a pint at the tavern in the evening.

Now, like Anne herself, nearly everyone was an outsider. On any given day the town looked as if one of her Chautauqua books had exploded and left all of history on parade. On any afternoon she could see knights in armor, a bare-chested man wearing an enormous turban, Indians and, of course, the cowboys. Trolley stops were named for the studios: Champion, Eclair, Willat's, Peerless... and Solax. Alice and Herbert's studio was still the "new kid" on the block, and at a price tag of $100,000, the most expensive.

Solax had a stable of expensive actors, among them Billy Quirk. Today he was needed on the set; it was Anne's job to bring him back.

She appreciated the irony. It was so much like her old job, gathering up the lost and hungover actors when it was time for the *River Queen* to shove off. She'd come so far just to arrive at the beginnig.

Glad girl, Go-Fetch girl.... Why put up with it? Because sometime, perhaps very soon, Alice, or someone, might call upon her to do something important, and she could return to the work she was meant to do. In the meantime she watched Alice in action, paid attention, cultivated patience.

She said goodbye to the abused Ford and walked down Main Street towards the lunch counter. Main was one long dusty artery, strung with telephone wires, watered twice a day by sprinklers from a horse-drawn water wagon.

A truck loaded with Indians lurched past her. Anne thought the derivative term "redskin" applied more accurately to these bare-chested Caucasian actors covered in Bole Armenia dye than to any true North American Indians. Yet the iron oxide–rich dye looked natural in comparison to the yellow makeup the other actors wore, and the ghostly white on the faces of the actresses. She thought all three colors looked horrid. But all that mattered was what looked good on camera.

The lunch counter was filled with Russian cossacks and Confederate soldiers sitting elbow to elbow with the Union Army. Anne found Billie Quirk, in yellow makeup, seated at the counter, his slight body tucked behind the greatcoat of a Cossack lieutenant. He was dressed for his role as an office boy in Solax's production "The Phantom Paradise."

The proprietor, waving a large spatula, harangued Billie. "You see? They come into my place, eat up everything, charge everything to the studio, and they're gone. Wearing different clothes, too, sometimes." He pointed to a narrow hallway beyond the counter. "They duck into my bathroom to change. Then they take off in their motorcars and tear up and down the streets, or ride on horseback over people's lawns, firing their guns and raising holy hell.

"Next afternoon, they come into my place, slap the table, rub their hands together, and want more food!" He shrugged. "What am I gonna tell them? I tell you what - I tell 'em *no.*" He arm swept the air. *"No."*

"You're absolutely right," said Billie, between mouthfuls of his egg sandwich. He opened his mouth as he caught sight of Anne. "Madame wants me?"

Anne nodded. Everyone at the studio, whether on set or off, had taken to calling Alice *Madame*.

"Then I must be going." Billie slipped from his stool. "Charge to Solax," he said, over his shoulder. The proprietor bared his teeth and raised a huge ladle as if to swing but Anne had already pulled Billie past the Cossack's coattails and through the Civil War regiments.

"Thanks," said Billie, as they emerged on Main Street.

"Only doing my job," said Anne. They headed towards Lemoyne Avenue, not speaking for a while. Anne heard Billie muttering "my job... *my job!...* my job!!"

"What are you saying, Billie?"

"I mean, what *is* my job?" He tugged at his shirtsleeves. "Is playing an office boy anything to be proud of? Am I a character actor? A featured player?"

"Neither one." Anne looked straight down Main Street. "You're part of a stock company. A stable of actors."

"Stable is right! I was a stable-hand in the first picture to come out of Madame's modern, streamlined studio."

"'The Equine Spy.'" Anne smiled. "That was my first, too.

"The star was a horse!" He shot back. "Obviously that picture meant more to you than to me."

They fell silent again. The morning sun glinting from Solax's roof reminded Anne of glass palaces at the World's Fair. On her first day, when Alice had described the wonders of the glass that would rise above their heads, Anne had seen only wood, and thought only of fire. Then the studio took shape – four stories tall, steel, brick, iron and glass, bigger, bolder than any other studio on the block. Her forebodings of fire receded.

"You know, Gem Studio wants me," Billie's voice intruded. "They're planning a whole series of 'Billy' pictures."

Anne turned to him. "You'll be missed, I'm sure."

Billie put a finger to his lips. They were close to the open air shooting stages, draped in muslin. One stage showed sections of a medieval wall, another had columns of antiquity, and a third was stacked high with furniture that would easily fill a modern parlor.

It was a perfectly fine spring morning, and all the outdoor stages were idle. Anne was still puzzled that Alice hadn't given her an opportunity to oversee even one small, insignificant scene. Yet the experience of just over a year told her exactly why. There was no room for anyone else; the stamp of Alice Guy Blaché was firmly on every one of her creations, her "children," as she called them.

They passed a ring of parked automobiles and through the studio door. Above a jumble of mismatched furniture was the sign that greeted everyone who stepped inside: BE NATURAL, in letters eight feet high. The blistering arc lamps that hung just above the actors' heads had thankfully not yet been turned on.

"Bee-lee! There you are!" Alice's cheery tone was as close to American informality as Anne could recall hearing from her, though that could be in part because "Mr. Quirk" sounded bad no matter who said it. Usually Alice was thoughtful, measured, polite but ever so formal. Today she wore a dress coat, her flowing hair tucked beneath a broad-brimmed hat. She took Billie Quirk aside to confer with the other actors, Miss Cornwall and Mr. Karr.

Just what did Billie mean by telling her about his offer from Gem? Did he actually want her to share the news with Alice, so he wouldn't have to?

Anne hated studio politics. Even thinking about it made her uncomfortable. The feeling was heightened by the sense that someone standing nearby, in the shadows, was watching her.

She looked over her shoulder. Herbert was smoothing back his slick dark hair. At the same moment he noticed her, and stepped closer.

"Simone's with the script girl for the moment," he said. His accent still struck her as odd – an Englishman who had become used to speaking French. With his Gallic features and prominent waxed mustache he even looked like a Frenchman.

"Fine, then I'll watch her later," Anne replied.

Alice rehearsed the scene at hand, where Miss Cornwall and Mr. Karr are interrupted by Billie's entrance. As they spoke their lines, Alice placed her hands over her ears.

"Why does she do that?" Anne whispered.

"Testing the authenticity of the emotion, instead of the sound of the voice," he said.

It was so unlike any director's work she'd seen before. At nearly every other studio the directors shouted orders through a megaphone. Alice would only use one if she needed to speak to a crowd while filming out of doors. Through her direct gaze and reassuring tones she created a world of safety and trust between herself and the actors.

Herbert, by contrast, always looked uncomfortable in his role as studio head. Alice, as Artistic Director, was acting head in everything else. Herbert sometimes worked as cameraman, and frequently huddled with Alice over scripts and business matters. Their times "in conference" were punctuated with entreaties, harsh whispers, and curses in English and French.

"I heard you had some experience with the Edison boys." Herbert leaned closer to her.

Anne gave a slight nod. How the Devil did he know about that?

"Received a sock on the jaw from them once, at the studio in Flushing." He moved one side of a well-chiseled chin closer to the light. "But I tell you, I gave them what-for in return!"

Anne tried to smile. "I never saw their unpleasantness out in the open," she said. "But they did give us a rough time on location. I wasn't there."

"Unpleasant fellows!" Herbert smirked. "Patent Goons." He stretched out the vowels as if he were the first to think of the term. "We kept our studio in Flushing as inconspicuous as possible so they wouldn't know what we were up to. Just a big long shed with some wagons parked out on the street, no signs or glass roof."

As he spoke, Alice signaled for the arc lamps. Immediately Anne could feel their pulsing heat. When it came time for the closeups, the hot lights could almost blister the skin.

Herbert began to loosen his collar. "Almost enough to make one want to shed one's clothes, no?" he said in a near-whisper. There was, Anne decided, almost certainly a Frenchman inside him.

"Camera," said Alice. The cameraman set up the box atop a tall, heavy tripod. "Now, Mister Karr, please take Miss Cornwall's hands. And please remember, we have just read the title card that says 'He decides to tell her the truth.' This is very important. The truth!"

Anne inched away from Herbert. The leading man took the leading lady's hands in his.

"Roll film!" said Alice. From where Anne stood there was a perfect view behind the cameraman as he rhythmically turned the crank on the camera box.

“Two revolutions per second,” whispered Herbert.

“Yes, I know,” Anne whispered back. “Will told me many times.”

“Will?”

“My cameraman,” she said, giving Herbert a big, fake smile.

“Quiet on the set, please!” Perhaps Madame had heard them, though she did not turn and look in their direction. “Alright, Bee-lee... ready for your entrance...”

*** *** ***

Anne had heard that the French were easygoing and prone toward their leisure time. But it was all she could do to keep pace with Alice. Fetch cafe´, mail this letter, prepare these scripts, gather the actors, find these props, then the canvas backdrop, and mind Simone. Always mind Simone.

This particular morning it would be impossible to keep up with Alice at all, as she was on horseback, scouting outdoor locations with the star of “The Equine Spy.” Alice had grown quite fond of Don, “the horse that can do anything but talk.”

“Don't be afraid, Simone” Alice reassured her daughter that it was all right to reach up to pat Don's head. “Isn't that right, Don?” The horse nodded twice and bent his head low for the girl to touch. Alice patted Don's neck. “The most intelligent horse in the world.” Don nodded again.

As Alice trotted away with a cheery "au revoir," Anne and Simone headed toward the Palisades, the place they walked to on Anne's first day. The orange and black rock ramparts meant something more now that Anne had seen them from both above and below, when she rode the zigzag trolley that ran from the ferry landing all the way to the top of the cliffs. The rocks were as sheer and solid as the walls of a medieval fortress; it was easy to see how they doubled for the walls of Paris in "The Hunchback of Notre Dame."

"Anne, what are they doing there?" Simone pointed toward a group of people at the very edge of the cliff, gathered so tight that it looked as if they were standing over someone.

"Stay here a moment," Anne said. As she got closer it looked not as if they were standing over someone, but as if that person had fallen from the cliff, and was trapped on a ledge.

Then she saw the woman dangling from a rope.

"That's it Pearl!" A man who must have been the director encouraged her. "Now flail a bit. Hold – hold on to the rope! Kick your legs! Kick and scream!"

Anne was about to fetch Simone, to tell her that it was perfectly all right, it was only a moving picture, but the child was at her side the instant the woman truly did scream – loudly.

The picture's name was chalked on the clapboard at their feet: "The Perils of Pauline" Miss White, Mister Carlyle.

About twenty feet below, a queen sized bed in a makeshift frame was wedged between two granite outcroppings. It didn't look strong enough to hold her if she *did* happen to fall, but Anne was sure the woman on the rope was grateful it was there.

“That's grand, Pearl. Grand!” The director swung a fist in the air as if cheering a touchdown. Pearl continued to swing and kick at the rope. At the moment, however, Anne was more concerned for the cameraman, vertically sprawled on an index finger of rock just opposite the actress, camera aimed to get the best possible angle without having the mattress in view.

“A real cliff-hanger.” said one of the men in the crew.

“Cliff-hanger,” said the director. “Let's remember that.” He returned his attention to the actress, dangling hundreds of feet above the rubble and the river shoreline. “All right, Pearl. That's good. Pull her up, boys.”

Back on solid ground, Pearl was handed a towel and a hot drink. Out of the corner of her eye Anne caught a rather blasé shrug from the child standing next to her. After all, Simone observed this sort of thing almost every day, had even appeared herself in a few of her mother's productions.

They continued their walk along the Palisades. Maybe, Anne wondered, this – what did they just call it? Cliffhanger? – was the nature of the business. She looked across the river, and wondered if the people there had their own cliffhangers, even if they weren't dangling from the windows of their own skyscrapers.

*** *** ***

“Bring in your washing right quick; there's going to be a picture show!” an Irish matron’s voice called from a window. Pulleys squeaked as long lines of washing strung across the courtyard were hauled inside. As the linens and the sheets gave way to an unobstructed view, Anne saw people leaning from their windows, seated like so many fine fancy folk in their box seats at the opera, while children perched on the steps of the fire escapes, all seeking the best possible view of the huge canvas sheet that stretched across the courtyard of this tenement on the lower East Side .

Alice liked to have one great cause to devote herself to on her occasional visits to Manhattan. She'd been to "the Tombs," the prison at the East River, an opium den in Chinatown, a madhouse, each time to visit those she called *les malheureux* – the unfortunates.

Tonight, it was an outdoor screening at a tenement in Hell's Kitchen. When the nights were too warm and theaters and nickelodeons closed, the people in the poor parts of the city enjoyed, courtesy of the New York Department of Health, motion pictures outdoors.

In the courtyard below long rows of benches rapidly filled with entire families, pushcart peddlers, and some, Anne guessed, who had no home whatsoever, but were given a seat alongside everyone else on this fine spring evening.

One long bench, in the very first row, stayed empty. Anne glanced at Alice, asking, "Is that for special guests?"

Alice nodded. "The most special of all. You'll see."

A hush came over the crowd as a line of young boys and girls on crutches, or riding in small boxes on wheels, made their entrance and, with some assistance, took their places in the first row.

There were some words of welcome from a man in a tailored suit, very likely a representative from the Health Department. Anne leaned from the window that was her watching place to hear, but with all the voices saying "Shush! Quiet!" she could barely hear a word.

Her first day in Manhattan had unraveled in an unreal fashion from the moment she, Alice, Herbert and Simone caught the early morning trolley at the Palisades headland. The dark granite rocks seemed a fitting gateway to the underworld, so it was no great surprise that the waiting ferry, from Fort Lee to 125th Street, seemed as if it had just crossed the River Styx. The toll was ten cents.

"All aboard!" Alice declared, as if she were the ferryman himself. And off they sailed, from ferry to elevated train, which delivered them to 57th Street, where they found row upon row, massing on the corners, the Army of Women's Suffrage, in broad sashes and bright festive hats.

Herbert took Simone uptown, to make preparations at Columbia College, where Alice would deliver a lecture the following day. Alice instructed Anne to stay close, and the two of the fell into the symphony of purple, white and green. These were the colors, Alice explained, of the British suffragettes, to which their American sisters added gold, as she pointed to the gold ribbon on her own lapel.

There must have been thousands of them. Each spring, Alice told her, they marched five abreast down Fifth Avenue, and would keep marching until women had the vote. Block by block they went, singing and saluting the crowd.

To the Women Give the Vote... For the hand that Rocks the Cradle.... Will Never Rock the Boat!

Anne had never known the feeling of many voices joined, not just in harmony, but in Cause. The chant continued, echoing from the sturdy gray walls of Fifth Avenue.

To the Women Give the Vote!

To the Women Give the Vote!

TO THE WOMEN GIVE THE VOTE!

The marchers and banners unwound close to Union Square, none too soon for Anne's feet in their imperfect shoes. After refreshment at an outdoor restaurant, when daylight faded they made their way further downtown, to the place called Hell's Kitchen.

Because the city Health Department were sponsors, Anne expected a film with a message. “But tonight,” said Alice, “it will be something about a little boy, produced by Edison.”

Anne felt a punch to her stomach. Out of principle she hadn’t seen a single film by Edison since the day his goons invaded her studio and threatened to wreck it. Surely Alice remembered the evil wrought by that unspeakable inventor.

Anne caught the final words from the man in the tailored suit, declaimed in a voice three times as loud as anything previous: “And now, we present to you, produced by Mister Thomas Edison and Company, *The Land Beyond the Sunset!”*

The title flashed on the giant canvas sheet. At the sight of the first image, a newspaper boy in pants torn above the knee, plaintively holding out a newspaper, Anne heard a subdued but palpable gasp from the crowd.

Hadn't these people seen a photodrama before? she asked herself. Were they really like that backwater crowd up the Kanawha River, who'd never seen a play in their lives?

But this was New York! After Pittsburgh, the virtual home ground of the nickelodeons. Doing steady business for over ten years, in fact! She didn't understand it.

Her attention returned to the story. Jack, the newsboy, lived with his unforgiving mother in absolute squalor, with nothing to sleep on but a dilapidated chair, and nothing to wear but the same rags he'd worn yesterday.

Then it occurred to her: *They all knew this boy. He could have been any one of them.*

Enter the church ladies, the Minister and the Fresh Air Fund. But rather than sending the boy to a workhouse, *these* church ladies chartered a boat for the slum children.

Jack stepped onto their boat just as it was about to sail. They were going on a trip that for many of them was their "first sight of the world beyond the slums," a boat trip to, of all places, a flower-strewn riverbank, where they would picnic, tell stories and play.

Anne had to look away for a moment. It was too much like an early page from her own story – not so much the world she grew up in, but the one she wished she could remember. Only she lived in squalor beside the river, not away from it, and their mothers had nothing in common.

For a few moments, she leaned from the open window to watch the audience below here, out in the strangely quiet tenement stillness. Many fanned themselves, and, taking a cue from the picnic on the screen, passed around a bottle of wine, a salami, a loaf of bread.

When Anne looked back at the screen the picnic was over. The minister, the church ladies and the children held a moment of prayer and thanksgiving. Then the children ran off to play ring-around-the-rosy and leapfrog, the newsboy with them.

The chaperone told Jack and a few other children the story of a young prince escaping from a wicked old witch, rescued by fairies. They set him out into a boat, bedecked with flowers, and guided it to sea "along the Path of Shining Light, to the 'Land Beyond the Sunset'" where he lived happily ever after. Behind the minister, a boat was seen on the horizon.

The story finished, Jack looked up and had a sudden, shocking memory of his mother striking him to the floor. When the other children returned to the boat, he stayed behind, drawn by the dim boat on the horizon. On the shore he found a small rowboat. Clutching a book, he got in, and drifted from shore, to that land beyond. The boat went gradually out of frame.

There was applause at the finish, but it was slow in coming, as the many bodies gathered at the windows, on fire escapes and on long benches considered what they had just seen.

"Did the boy die, Ma-Ma?" It was a young girl's voice from a nearby window.

Anne heard no reply. If she were the girl's mother what would she have said?

"Yes, but he's found peace in the land beyond?... No, for he's found a better life beyond the sunset?"

Alice stood from her seat by the window. "So, what do you say about your Mister Edison now?"

The truth was that she had a great deal to say, but Mister Edison's production – whether or not he'd had a personal hand in it – had affected her to the point where she couldn't utter a coherent word. In fact, she couldn't budge from her window seat.

Down in the courtyard, the man who had introduced the film made some closing remarks, but Anne couldn't hear them. The other people in the room greeted Alice and shook her hand, but Anne couldn't grasp what they were saying. The families at their windows, the children on the fire escapes, the crippled children in the front row – all were looking around, stretching, talking with one another. But Anne felt as if part of her was still up there, suspended on that great canvas sheet stretched across the tenement. It wasn't so much the picture itself; but her *experience* of watching it.

Vachel had been absolutely right. This *was* "democracy's theater." They were no longer divided into Pole, Irish, Italian, Catholic, Jew. They were simply mothers, fathers, sisters, sweethearts, sons, and laborers.

The working class, the tramp on the street, the unshaven miner, the bartender who'd heard every story in the book, *they* were her cast and audience too, not the swelled-up, smarty-pants society crowd. She wanted to make films for people who hadn't the time or the education to read a classic novel, and didn't live within a hundred miles of a legitimate theatre, even if they could afford it. But they did have the time and ten cents to see a picture show.

If she had felt a fire before, it had been re-ignited. When she was finally able to stand up, walk, speak, and be present in the world again, Anne longed to share all of this, even some of it, with Alice, peer to peer, one film maker to another. But Alice had her speech to prepare.

As she walked to the podium the following day Alice wore her marching outfit – the purple, white and green dress with the gold lapel. In those colors she was not alone, for a number of her sisters-in-arms sat proudly in the front rows of the university hall. Even seated they seemed to sit up at attention. The march down Fifth Avenue continued still in the halls of Columbia University.

Anne and Herbert, with Simone between them, sat in a special reserved section at the side. Were it not for the particular angle of the floor Anne might have missed the sight of one man. His naked body was more familiar to her than the elegant clothes he now wore, finer even than those he had worn when they first met at the Chicago Art Institute.

It was the worst possible moment to notice him. For Alice had just been introduced from the podium, and at the same time, Vachel noticed Anne.

From the first words out of her mouth, in her charmingly-accented voice, Alice cut no corners.

"It has been a source of wonder to me that many women have not seized upon the wonderful opportunity offered to them by the motion picture art to make their way to fame and fortune as producers of photodramas. Of all the arts there is probably none in which they can make such splendid use of talents, so much more natural to a woman than to a man, and so necessary to its perfection."

Vachel kept his eyes on Anne, then moved them to Simone. With a slight tip of his head and an expression in his eyes, he telegraphed *Who's the little girl?*

"In the arts of acting, music, painting and literature," Alice continued, "woman has long held her place among the most successful workers, and when it is considered how vitally all of these arts enter into the production of motion pictures one wonders why the names of scores of women are not found among the successful creators of photodrama offerings."

With the utmost care, Anne raised two fingers, one toward Herbert, the other toward Alice.

"There is nothing," said Alice, "connected with the staging of a motion picture that a woman cannot do as easily as a man, and there is no reason why she cannot completely master every technicality of the art."

Simone noticed the interplay, then looked at Vachel. He looked right back at the child.

"The technique of the drama has been mastered by so many women that it is considered as much her field as a man's, and its adaptation to picture work in no way removes it from her sphere. The technique of motion picture photography, like the technique of the drama, is fitted to a woman's activities."

Anne tried to see who was sitting next to him, but the woman looked unfamiliar, and a bit older. She reasoned that he had probably come alone.

"A woman has a keener instinct, especially when it comes to the emotions. Men are apt to rein in their emotions. When they attempt to express them, or, when directing, encourage others to express them, the result often rings false, even misjudged."

Now Herbert noticed the interplay, quickly glancing from Simone, to Anne, to Vachel. He leaned slightly just above Simone's head, toward Anne.

"Women's eyes are more attuned to details - the backdrops, sets and props, furniture. But most of all, she knows what other women want, and it is usually the woman who decides what will or will not be seen when they go into town for the picture show. Women, mothers, children are the ones buying the tickets and going to the nickelodeons. So it makes sense that a woman would have the best insight into what this audience wants to see. It should be no surprise, then, that half of the stories for the moving picture are written by women."

"Is this a friend of yours?" Herbert whispered, but before Anne could whisper a reply, there was a quiet *ssssh!* from the row behind them. He made a brief apologetic smile, and leaned back to his own seat.

Alice's talk – her performance, Anne thought – continued: an account of her early days at the Lumiere Brothers, taking up directing because there were few others who seemed as interested in it as she, and her joy at discovering moving picture technique, which was a much, much different thing from the cameras and tripods that she had been selling.

She spoke of trying her fortune in a new world, tapping into the root of a brand new medium, her early efforts in directing, learning that before she could direct even one scene she had to be able to direct herself. If she wanted a naturalistic performance from the actors, she had to first tone *herself* down. How difficult she found it to cut the film down to a standard number of feet, to wind around a spool. How difficult – she struggled for the right word – to *let go.* She even compared it to letting go of her own children, and she did not say this lightly, as she had a child of her own, a young girl whom she loved very much.

Without looking at her directly, Anne could feel Simone beaming, positively glowing, as Alice described the world she wanted to leave for her daughter, and for her grandchildren.

Some in the audience began to applaud. Alice held up a gloved hand.

"I cannot leave the subject of women's place in the 20th Century without a mention of the three great forces of this age that are helping to liberate women."

She leaned forward on the podium, taking a long dramatic pause. "They are…" she held up one finger, "the automobile." A second finger. "The moving picture." A third finger. "And the Vote! Thank you, and God bless you all!"

Before she had even finished the words, the suffragettes in the first rows stood up as one, positively shrieking their approval. Compared to this demonstration, the reaction from the remainder of the audience was polite, if not restrained. Anne did notice that Vachel was the one person in his row standing, and applauding lustily.

In the "informal" reception afterward, which still had the formal trappings that dripped with Easter lilies, finger sandwiches and a huge punchbowl with fine crystal cups, Vachel orbited the far parts of the room. Of course he was deep in conversation, as was she, but at least she could try to catch his eye again.

"Miss Blackstone!"

A woman under a large hat, which camouflaged part of her face, came forward. Anne recognized the man standing next to her, for his hat carried no such mystery.

"Harry Solter?" Then she recognized the woman, from the way she extended her hand. "Florence?"

A star's smile glowed beneath the large hat. "I heard you were working with Alice. My dear, so sorry to hear about that terrible fire back in Saint Louis! And so soon after we paid you a call!"

"We're glad you're back on your feet again," Harry cut in.

"We were in Fort Lee, too, don't you know." Florence countered.

No I didn't, Anne thought, as her eyes searched for Vachel. He was still at the back, talking to the woman he'd sat next to. As Anne was about to catch his eye, an Army officer in full dress uniform strode up to her.

"Miss Blackstone?"

Anne glanced at Florence and Harry, unsure whether to introduce them first, or to wait and see if she were being placed under arrest.

"Yes?"

The officer offered his hand. "Captain Stanhope, U.S. Army Signal Corps. Mrs. Blaché pointed you out. And you are the director of my favorite western, 'This Side of the Moon.'"

Both Florence and Harry stepped back a bit, appearing to see Anne in a new light.

"Good, honest storytelling," said the Captain. "A woman's point of view, but not... sentimental."

Anne was at a relative loss for words. 'Uhh… thank you."

"May I inquire, are you in production now?" Both Florence and Harry looked interested in the answer as well.

"Well, you see, I'm presently assisting Alice – Mrs. Blaché. I haven't had the resources to direct my own pictures for several years."

"Is that a fact?" The Captain was visibly disappointed. "Something should be done about that."

"Ah!" Alice cried out. "I see you have found each other. I must say, after my talk it was a bit of a shock when such an impressive looking member of the armed forces walks right up to me…"

The Captain shifted on his feet uncomfortably.

"But after all, *ma chère* , it was you he was looking for." At this moment Anne noticed the sun-burnished young man who was at Alice's side, lightly touching her arm. "And here's a young man who's not afraid to speak the words 'poetry' and 'moving pictures' in the same sentence. He's just returned from a most amazing journey –

"We've met," Anne said.

"It was at the museum, wasn't it?" asked Vachel. "Art history as I recall."

Anne took Vachel's free arm. "Thank you for your kind words, Captain. Would you excuse us?" She smiled at Alice. "Until I see you at dinner?"

"Take your time, *ma chère.*"

She led Vachel away, not looking at him. "I must thank you for your book," she said.

His face looked blank. "The book…"

"The one you sent me, about six months ago? 'Rhymes to be Traded for Bread,' or something like that."

"Of course." He stuck his hands in his pockets. "And…?"

"If *that's* your rate of exchange, I wonder how highly you value your poetry."

"Can you explain…?"

"I find some of it very highfalutin'."

"You do?"

"Yes. Especially those odes to Springfield, home of Lincoln – and Vachel Lindsay."

He gave her a contrite smile. “And what did you think of the illustrations?”

“Well… detailed. Craftsmanlike. Ornate. But confused.”

“Really.”

She nodded. “They reminded me of incense censers. The ornateness almost obliterates the buildings in the background.”

“Now you’re thinking like a director.” He smiled.

“I can’t help it.” Of course she couldn’t. She hadn’t directed a picture in three years. Nor had she a camera, an actor, or a crew to her name.

“I know what it is.” He stopped walking. “You’re upset that you haven’t seen me all this time.”

“A book! Not a note, not a postcard. You send me a Goddamned book, Vachel!”

The curse was just a tad too loud, and the acoustics of the auditorium a bit too good. Some conversations nearby ceased.

There was a slight cough, and Herbert appeared. “Is this man annoying you, Miss Blackstone?”

Her mind flashed on the consequences of answering yes or no. For both were true.

“Yes,” she said, giving Vachel a very private wink. “But at this particular moment I don’t mind.”

*** *** ***

Sunlight from Anne's window fell across the bed and onto the man asleep beside her. It highlighted the traces of sun and open sky written in the small cracks and furrows on his face. To all appearances Vachel had, indeed, been tramping the countryside, trading rhymes for bread.

For months she'd imagined him lying there next to her. Now that he was, she took time to observe every inch.

His forehead still glistened. *Good,* she thought. *Let him sweat.* For hours he'd moved over and around and through her, cool and sleek as a panther, breaking a sweat only before sleep.

Anne peeled back a corner of the top sheet. His shoulders and torso were sun- bronzed as well. She pictured him with his shirt off, splitting wood like Lincoln, his hero, as some cream-complexioned farmer's daughter admired him from the porch.

His body flinched in the cold; his hand clutched for the sheet.

"Good morning," she whispered.

He smiled. "You're still mad at me."

She shook her head. "No. I'm too glad to be mad."

"Why's that?"

"You kept your mouth shut this time."

"You mean no poems." He smiled and curled the sheet around his body. "Were you watching me sleep?"

"No."

"That's funny; I felt your eyes on me."

She looked toward the window. “I was watching you spread your Gospel of Beauty. In my mind, that is.”

“How was I doing?

Her hands played with the bedsheet. “Well, you were tramping down the road… singing one of your songs, or maybe it was a poem. Then you came to a house. You walked up the porch steps, knocked on the door, and...”

Vachel sat straight up in bed. “Dear Lady.” He cleared his throat. “I come to you penniless and afoot, to bring a message. I am starting a new religious idea, the church of beauty… The church of the open sky." He took her hand, spreading out the fingers. “It has two sides. The love of beauty…” He turned her hand over. “… And the love of God.” He kissed her palm.

“Kiss and all?” She smiled.

“No, that’s for a special member of the church.”

“Did you just make that up?”

“It’s printed on my handbill, in words not quite so…”

“Poetic?” She smiled at his touch. “Yes, I *was* watching you. I could have watched longer.”

“And I ask...” he peered into her eyes. “Who is this Anne Blackstone? Sounds like a magician. And she could be. There is the hypnotic gaze of eyes dark as her name. They glisten frequently, though she does not even come close to crying, even when we talk of things which touch her heart.”

She noticed the bedside clock. "Christ, I need to get to Solax. Alice has a special guest at the studio; I have to keep Simone out of her hair."

"I'm going with you."

"You... what?"

His arms caught her waist. "I'll follow along, like… a Solax employee on his first day of work. That's me." He pressed his bare thighs against her cotton dress. "Just another working guy."

"Then stay out of the way." She shrugged her way out of his arms. "And don't walk in front of any cameras. Especially if Madame is directing."

"Is that what they call her? Madame?"

"Why not? She's earned their respect." Anne put on her floppy hat with the big black bow. "Not one person in the three years I've worked there has seen her lose her temper. Except Herbert, perhaps."

"That cold fish who tried to rescue you after the lecture?"

She nodded. "Her husband."

He pulled his own clothes from the chair where they'd been dropped early that morning. "Madame talks all about how women should make moving pictures, and here *you've* made them, and you're put to work as a nanny."

She snapped her purse shut. "Thanks, Vachel."

"I know…" He reached for her. "I'm sure you've been thinking about it, too."

"And it sticks in my craw." Her hand was on the door. "Let's go."

Halfway down the brownstone's steps, Anne realized it wasn't just being the *au pair* girl, it was this dirty rooming house in the factory belt of Fort Lee, its thin wallpapered rooms magnifying arguments, laughter and screams. She had to get out of there.

"I think the actors are getting to me," she said. "They come in howling drunk, at all hours. Some of them pay by the week, so I guess it doesn't matter to them."

"Like the actors on that showboat you told me about? The *River Queen?"*

"You remember!" She felt an inward smile. They hadn't talked of those times since Chicago.

Down the block a trolley came to a stop. "Come on!" She tugged at his coat. The studio-bound actors were already filling up the seats when they climbed aboard. She offered him a window seat. If he wanted a tour, it began right here. He had shown her Chicago; she would show him Fort Lee – from the inside.

"Remember what I said." Anne took her seat. "Things could get a bit tense if Herbert's around. They're still together, but Herbert's moved out business-wise. He has his own company, Blaché Features. Now he and Alice have a distribution agreement."

"Sounds more like a disagreement," Vachel said.

The nearer they came to the bustling heart of town and the long rectangular studios, the more actors and studio workers stepped aboard. A man with sawdust caked overalls stood in the aisle next to Anne's seat.

Vachel pulled her closer to him. "Tell me about this dream project of yours," he said softly.

"Dream project?"

“That lady captain. On the Missouri.”

“Oh, Delia.” Anne looked at her lap. “That’s where she stays, in a dream.”

In fact, Delia had taken shape in Anne's Chautauqua notebook, written on a sleepless night in the tiny Columbia University dormitory room the night before Alice's lecture.

Delia Cartwright is her name. She stands on a bluff high above the muddy Missouri, watching through a spyglass the ships plying upriver and down. The mid-day sun reflects from the buttons on her coat. Her Captain's cap is set at a jaunty angle. When she moves her stride is that of a woman who has walked a tightrope...

On Delia’s last voyage up the river, the men play cards and roll dice below decks as they pass a bottle around. They keep their distance at first, since she is the most qualified crewman on ship. But when one of their worst element tries to take her by force, she sends a warning blast through the ship's whistle. A keelboat comes to the rescue. Paddles and blackjacks and knives clash by night...

Vachel settled back in his seat, closing his eyes. “And why does she stay in a dream?”

“I had a name in Saint Louis. Not in Fort Lee.” Anne looked at the trolley's roof. “Here I’m a Go-Fetch Girl, a nanny.”

He touched her shoulders lightly. “If I had my way, you’d have a floating studio on the Hudson, with a fleet of boats at your command.”

“If only.”

They passed a throng of costumed actors, some riding in a creaking, shaking replica of a Conestoga wagon, and some on foot, the bedraggled remnants of an army, with wooden guns perched on their shoulders. A pioneer woman's long skirts dragged in Main Street's dust.

"You could go to Hollywood."

"What, flit about the citrus groves? Not me."

"Why, what do you know about Hollywood?"

"I know what I've seen," she said dismissively. "Footage of automobiles tearing down long straight roads alongside the citrus groves. And postcards of giant oranges and lemons riding on railroad cars. It doesn't look a bit real; I don't trust it."

Among the crowd they saw the outfits of prospectors, mountain men, cavalry officers, and the nearly ever-present Indian war bonnet.

"Some say it's the next Gold Rush," he said. "There's a steady pool of cheap labor, cheap land, and best of all, they can shoot year round. And there's the whole of the country between them and the Trust."

She didn't have a response, as she hadn't had one when she'd considered the possibility herself. California, the West, the Golden Gate. Places to start over, begin again.

The trolley stop signs, recently named for the studios, flickered past: Peerless, Thanhauser, Éclair. Solax was coming up.

"Get ready," she said, nudging him toward the aisle.

They walked through the back entrance, where the trucks rolled in to unload their cargoes of canvas flats, furniture and carpets, which were dropped aboard a line of rolling carts pushed by stagehands toward a dark, narrow corridor.

"Keep your eyes open," she told him. "And your hands at your sides."

They walked behind one of the carts and just in front of a studio grip carrying a chair above his head. At either side of the narrow aisle the shooting stages were partitioned off row upon row, separated by an ever-changing wall of flimsy flats, painted as fireplaces, bookcases, stairways, even outdoor scenes.

From a distance Anne could tell which stage Alice was shooting on – Herbert paced in front of it. Simone stood next to him, wearing what looked like a blue Sunday dress trimmed in white, fancier than Anne was used to seeing on the child.

Herbert noticed the two of them and stopped pacing. He quickly gave Anne the child's hand, and shot a darting glance at Vachel, punctuated by a slight raise of his upper lip to show a glint of teeth. Then he hurried in the direction of another shooting stage.

Anne eased Vachel to a corner behind the camera so they could watch unobserved. Alice, dressed in her customary working outfit, a smartly tailored jacket, long dress and broad-brimmed hat, was speaking to the actors softly, too softly to hear. Two of Solax's younger stock actors were playing a scene of a boy and girl saying goodbye, trying to convey all in a clasp of hands that gradually separated.

"Camera!" Alice said. The piano and violin changed tone swiftly, from background waltz music to a more heartfelt tune. "Now, Marie. You look at him. Gerald, you feel conflicted. Yes, more of that feeling! Marie, chin up there! Look away!"

Alice's megaphone sat upended alongside her canvas chair; not once did she pick it up. A tall, striking woman sat in a canvas chair alongside Alice. Anne recognized her from the Columbia University talk, seated in the front row among the suffragettes.

"Now, lower your eyes, Marie," Alice continued, "Gerald, you look her up and down. Marie, now raise you eyes… ah! Your eyes meet!" She glanced to the cameraman. "Cut!"

"Well done," she thanked the actors. ""Merci, we will take your close-ups later."

The seated woman applauded. "Bravo, Mademoiselle Directeur! And bravo, Marie and Gerald." The actors received the thanks in about as shy a manner as they had played the scene, then exited the set. Grips appeared from all sides to rearrange furniture, backdrops, and roll up the carpet.

Alice glanced about, her eyes landing on Anne and Simone. "Ah, there you are! I see Herbert found you." Then she noticed Vachel. "Ah, quel suprise!" She put a hand over the arm of the woman seated beside her. "Lois, this is the young man I was telling you about, the one writing a *book* about moving pictures."

The woman stood, every bit as imposing as she had appeared sitting down. She offered her hand to Vachel, and beneath her lace cuffs, squeezed his hand tightly.

"Anne, please introduce your friend again?"

“Yes, of course. This is Vachel Lindsay.”

Alice took his hand. “I was so looking forward to continuing our most interesting discussion from Columbia University. And may I introduce Miss Lois Weber. She is the first *American* woman of note to direct the motion picture.”

Though it was imperceptible to the two other women, Anne could feel Vachel’s eyes glance quickly at her. There were two seconds of awkward silence.

Alice took Anne’s hand and began to pat it. “But of course, I did forget. Miss Anne Blackstone directed some fine pictures of her own at a studio in Saint Louis.”

“I'm pleased to meet you, Director," said Lois Weber.

“And you… Director.”

Their eyes were locked on each other as Alice spoke. In that fraction of a moment Anne felt a palpable charge among the three women, as if someone had just flipped an electrical switch.

“Herbert and I met Lois almost ten years ago,” said Alice. “Soon after we came to America. She applied for an acting job at Gaumont Studios.”

“All I needed to do was watch,” Lois said, with a sideways glance. “I learned from a master. I was on the set when Alice directed her first American films. So it’s like old times, yes? And you, Mister Lindsay, how did you become interested in pictures?”

He smiled; Anne knew it was for her. “That’s Miss Blackstone’s doing. When we met at the Chicago Art Institute I was a perpetual student of art, painting little pictures that I sold to magazines.”

"And your book…?" Alice inquired.

He cleared his throat. "Yes, in fact I'm writing a book about the *art* of moving pictures. I want to chart the growth of something grand and exciting while the film is still fresh, as it goes from achievement to achievement."

As he noticed their interest, Anne could feel him growing bolder by the second, speaking with the confidence of one who could trade rhymes for bread.

"I believe the motion picture art is a great High Art, not a process of commercial manufacture. In fact, I see pictures as something more like architecture, hieroglyphics, even mathematics. They are time and space measured without sound. You don't need sound as long as there is motion and feeling."

Alice and Lois looked at each other and seemed to take a deep breath together. Alice's eyebrows, in fact, gave a slight arch.

"That sounds wonderful, my young friend," said Alice. "But I am afraid that sort of talk will not make you friends with those so dedicated to its commercial *manufacture*."

Lois put up a hand. "One does not need to live at the expense of the other. I am currently at work on a project titled 'Hypocrites.' And in it I intend to portray the Naked Truth." She looked at Vachel. "Quite literally."

Alice pulled back, regarding Anne. "Well, now that the directors have met… Simone has her first day at a new school. Anne, I would appreciate if you would chaperone. She is already late for class."

So that was why Herbert was pacing…

"Fortunately, it is walking distance. Mister Lindsay, if you wish to stay…"

"My sincere thanks for allowing time for me." He appeared to doff an invisible hat. "I will accompany your daughter and Miss Blackstone to this school. " He bowed slightly. "I plan to be around for a few more days, I trust we will discuss the motion picture art at some future time."

"It will *need* to be within the next few days, Mister Lindsay. Miss Weber will be taking the train to Hollywood after that."

Anne felt a rush of gratitude that Vachel chose to accompany her rather than stay and revel in the studio's excitement. At the same time it occurred to her how convenient an announcement that was, letting her know that he would be leaving town.

Vachel stepped up to Simone at the studio gates. "Well, Simone, I like to walk across the country. What do you like?"

The girl squinted at him. "I like to watch the lady dangling from a cliff."

"Oh." Vachel began to walk. "Do you like poetry, too?"

"If it's good," said the girl.

"That's for you to say. Anyway, it's about a magic lamp."

Anne, struggling to keep up with him, had to smile. He'd recited this poem to her in Chicago. Using it on a seven year old, really.

"I asked her," he began. '*Is Aladdin's lamp hidden anywhere?*' He bent part ways toward Simone, as if waiting for an answer.

"'Look into your heart,' she said. 'Aladdin's lamp is there.'"

She took my heart with glowing hands.

It burned to dust and air "

He gestured towards the river.

"And smoke and rolling thistledown blowing everywhere.

'Follow the thistledown,' she said,

'Till doomsday, if you dare,

Over the hills and far away.

Aladdin's lamp is there.'"

Simone looked at the horizon, silent for a moment. "What's the poem's name?"

"The Sorceress," he said, with a glance toward Anne.

Clouds of dust hovered above the hills to the West. The morning breeze carried the sounds of distant shouting and horse's hooves.

"That must be the cavalry," said Vachel, still walking in the lead.

Anne looked toward the hills. Yes, for certain, that's where the army of costumed extras, the pioneers, Indians and cavalry had been heading on their march through downtown Fort Lee.

"Why all the noise?" he asked. "No one will hear it."

Simone spoke up. "Mother says it doesn't matter how it sounds, it's got to *look* good."

"All that smoke and dust," said Anne, squinting at the hills.

Simone glanced up at Vachel. "Do you always walk so fast?"

"I'm in training; in a few days I begin my big Ramble." He paused, as if waiting for a reaction. "It's a fact. A ten or fifteen mile stretch is nothing to me. I can go for miles, leaving anyone walking beside me in the dust in a… matter of hours."

So he continued his gait, Simone's small legs struggling a bit harder to keep up with him, as he tossed off several more of his stories from the Road, familiar tales that lulled Anne into a half-stupor, so that she came close to missing the path to Fort Lee Primary, Simone's new school.

Following the sound of the teacher's voice, the three of them approached the modest-sized schoolhouse, walked up the porch steps and took their places quietly at the rear of the one large room.

What Anne saw, before the students at the back of the room discovered their presence, was a panorama of quiet disobedience. Two girls whispered behind a large open book. Another had her hair pulled by a boy sitting just behind her, who immediately folded his arms and looked away. A girl swung her legs beneath her chair, while another boy took a shot with his eraser at something on the ceiling, perhaps a fly.

When enough children became aware of the new girl and two adults standing at the back, a roomful of heads swiveled over shoulders. Simone kept a tight hold of Anne's hand.

The teacher looked up. "And you must be Simone?" she asked.

Vachel slipped a hand behind Simone's back, inching her forward. "Yes, this is Simone Blaché."

The teacher clasped her hands in satisfaction. "And I understand Simone's first language is French, is that right?"

Simone looked beseechingly at Anne.

"Oui," said Anne.

"Yes," said Simone.

"Isn't that *wonderful*," said the teacher. "Perhaps Simone can help us with some basic French lessons. She may be with us for some time. I'm sure at recess you'll all make her feel welcome, won't you, class?"

"Yes, Miss Daisy," the class murmured collectively.

Simone took her seat with the other third graders. Unable to find any free seats, Anne and Vachel propped themselves in a back corner of the classroom.

As Miss Daisy resumed the lesson in Turkish geography, Anne noticed how the children's hands, now that other adults were present, were folded properly on their desks, their eyes fixed on the teacher. But their minds, Anne imagined, were engaged elsewhere, running, perhaps, in their pinafores and knickers along the Palisades, to watch Pearl White struggle against some new peril, until a nasal-toned assistant director ambles over to tell them to shoo. Then they awake, back at their desks, as the molasses tone of Miss Daisy drips on about the Bosphorus.

Anne glanced at the teacher's desk. There was a polished wooden stick there, perhaps for pointing; perhaps, also, for rapping knuckles.

Her imaginings came to a halt when Miss Daisy declared recess. The children, in a semi-orderly stampede, ran past the corner where Anne and Vachel stood. Simone was soon surrounded on the porch by mostly girls and a few boys her age. Anne hovered nearby, in case the child needed some sort of intervention. But Simone, much like her mother, appeared absolutely capable of handling the situation.

The questions turned quickly from who Simone was to where she came from; in other words, what did her parents do?

“My Mama’s a Director.”

“You mean your Papa,” said a boy.

“My Papa’s a Director too, but so’s Mama,” Simone replied confidently. “And she runs the studio.”

Although most of the children surrounding Simone on the porch probably had at least one parent working at the studios, apparently none of them could so much as *imagine* one of their mothers actually directing a moving picture. As they realized Simone was not bragging, but stating an established fact (for most of them had heard of the Solax, the grandest of Fort Lee’s studios) Simone appeared to expand from within, determined to prove to every child there that not only did her mother direct, but that she, Simone Blaché, knew how to direct as well.

Simone told a few of the children to form a line. One child she told to come running up the porch steps, to announce the battle that could still be heard in the western distance.

Anne felt unnerved to watch a miniature version of Alice in action, giving orders, telling the assembled children where to stand, how to move, gesture, react. Then Anne realized that Miss Daisy watched from the doorway.

"She's not what I expected." The teacher shook her head. "I was told her mother was French, her father English. I imagined she might teach the other children a few words of French. I had no idea."

On the porch steps below, one child shot another with a pretend rifle; the victim grappled with the porch banister, then fell to the dust, dead.

"Maybe teaching French isn't exactly what Simone does best," said Anne.

Miss Daisy wiped a moist strand of hair from her forehead. Anne noticed how truly weary the woman looked.

"To tell the truth, I wish I had an ounce of what she's got," said Miss Daisy. "Sometimes, about this time of day, I wonder if I'll be able to make it through the rest."

She lowered her voice. "You see, their regular teacher's been out with tuberculosis, I'm really a substitute. And I don't mind telling you they've worn me down after three weeks, just worn me down."

"I'm sure you're doing a marvelous job," said Anne, lying as she recalled her first sight of the classroom.

"No, I'm not." Miss Daisy shook her head again. "You must have seen that when you walked in. But I got tired of shouting and telling them to stand in the corner, so now I just," she shrugged, "I don't know, let it wash over me."

Anne looked over at Vachel, acting as Simone's assistant director at the moment, keeping the children from getting too filthy. "I've got an idea."

She thought the opportunity for Vachel to spin a few of his stories before a young audience would fit him like a comfortable shoe. But no, the students were too engrossed in playacting; he wanted Anne herself to be up there at the head of the class. He had plenty of chances ahead to spread his Gospel of Beauty, and this was his day off.

So the map of Turkey was rolled up, and Anne took the stage. For a moment that stretched like an impossibly long piece of taffy, she walked to the front, thinking of all the things about the moving picture business that she should not, *must not* say – how it rose from the milieu of bare-fisted boxing matches and cockfights, vaudeville and burlesque houses, that all the stories essentially played by the same rules: fighting, sex and chases. That, in a nutshell, was what she'd learned about the business, and that was how she'd been talking about it lately.

But not today.

"I'm going to tell you," she cleared her throat, "about a young prince, a boy, about the age of some of you, who took a boat out to sea, alone, following the Path of Shining Light, to the Land Beyond the Sunset…"

And in telling them the story of the prince, she also told the two other layers of the story, about the newsboy from the slums, his first day in the country, and about the tenement audience who watched both stories, the neighbors with their washing, the large families that filled each step of their fire escape, the handicapped children in the first row of seats …

She took the students there as surely as if they'd stood beside her at the tenement window. And when the story was done they wanted more, more, including, as she expected, if she'd personally met Pearl White.

"Not exactly," Anne replied, "but after class, I'm sure if you ask Simone, she can tell you more about Pearl."

The heads that swiveled towards Simone had one look now: wide-eyed.

On the road back to town, Simone skipped ahead, bolstered with confidence and a determination that her legs could carry her faster than Vachel's.

"The cavalry is gone," Vachel said.

Anne glanced towards the hills. "I still think that should have been you up there. You're the one writing the book, not me."

He squeezed her hand. "Don't sell yourself short. Did you see Miss Daisy behind her desk, dabbing her eyes? That proved how well you can do."

"That was when you sang 'Beautiful Isle of Somewhere!'"

"So?" Vachel shrugged. "Every good story needs music to go with it."

She squeezed his hand in return. "Thanks all the same."

"That Miss Daisy… she seemed remarkably plain-speaking for someone you'd just met."

"That's women; we just cut to the quick."

"Yes. But *you* inspire that kind of confidence in people." He leaned over to see her face. "Did you know that?"

She did not answer, though her casual smile gave its answer. It was a beautiful late afternoon in May; he would leave tomorrow.

At the station, he took one trolley in the direction of her brownstone apartment to wait for her, while she and Simone took another that led to Solax.

The relative lack of hustle and bustle on the shooting stages told Anne something was amiss. On the way to the suite of offices shared by Alice and Herbert she put Simone in the care of an actress, an older woman who could be counted on for *au pair* duties.

When Anne reached the office door painted "Mme. Blaché" she heard harsh whispers. Alice and Herbert were at it again, having called a halt to the day's filming so no one at the studio would sense anything was wrong.

It was far from the first time she'd found them arguing. Though on the surface it appeared to be about expenditure, a shooting script, even Herbert's philandering (although nothing was said explicitly) Anne knew that it usually had something to do with the distribution agreement between their two companies, Solax and Blaché Features.

Anne considered turning on her heels and returning when things had calmed a bit, for she did need to give her report about the school.

"Come in!" It was too late; they'd seen her through the glass at the top of the door. She opened it.

"I'm sorry. I've come at the wrong time."

"Wrong time?" Herbert looked incensed. His upraised arms, one grasping a newspaper, beseeched a vengeful God. "*This* was the wrong time!"

Anne skimmed the first few lines of the story: a German torpedo had sunk the unarmed British passenger ship *Lusitania* thirteen miles southwest of Cork, Ireland.

"Nearly 1200 lives lost, nearly 130 of them American, if that matters." Herbert stalked about the cramped office. "Believe me, this… outrage will be in every moving picture house and nickelodeon within two weeks. I don't want to go on…" he waved his arm toward a pile of scripts and costume sketches on the desk, "…making frivolous things!" He slapped the newspaper with its screaming headline. "I want to make something of *this* magnitude!" His right hand crumpled the newspaper. "Beware of the Junkers, the Kaiser, the Bosch!

"*Calme*, Herbert dear, *calme*." Alice soothed. "We must honor our commitments to the distributor, to the theaters."

"Com-mit-ments…!" Herbert growled. He fled the office, tossing the newspaper on the desk.

Alice went to the desk to straighten the creased edges of the paper. "Please forgive him. His British roots run deep. And he is very, very proud." She appeared to shake off something, brightened, and looked again at Anne. "And how was Simone's first day of school?"

"Quite well..." Anne stared at the paper. "Oh Madame, do you really wish to hear about that now?"

"Perhaps not."

"Or –" Anne added quickly, "perhaps you should ask her yourself. She's just down the hall, in the library. I think."

"Ah." Alice looked about the room. "You remind me. You are so good with the costumes. Your experience, yes?" She removed the newspaper and straightened the papers on the desk into two formidable piles. "These are the new sketches for the pictures with Madame Petrova, *The Vampire* and *The Heart of a Painted Woman.* You will please examine them for accuracy?"

"Madame, now?"

Alice seemed to smell Anne's resistance. "Now. Of course. We begin taking publicity photographs with Madame Petrova in the morning." She left abruptly.

Would it have made any difference, Anne wondered, if she'd told Alice that this work, which would certainly take most of an evening, would keep her from the arms and attentions of that young man Alice had been so taken with, the one writing the book?

The sketches for Olga Petrova's costumes were, as she thought, insipid creations of what a second-rate illustrator thought a society woman should wear. Neither the Painted Woman or the Vampire were distinct; in fact, they were practically interchangeable. No attempt had been made to connect them to the stories.

It would be a longer night than she imagined. Vachel, his feet already itching for the road, would probably leave the apartment. Why should he stay, anyway?

Looking over her shoulder, she picked up the office phone and called the brownstone apartment. The landlady answered; Anne promptly hung up. The last thing she'd ask the woman to do was find out if Mister Lindsay was in her room. In any event, Alice did not approve of her using the telephone.

Anne glanced again at the newspaper with its alarming headline. Herbert was right, absolutely right; the deliberate sinking of a ship, the loss of British *and* American lives was infinitely more important than these society dramas, this absolute drivel, bread and butter though they might be for the upper middle class audiences Solax appealed to.

Piles of paper and pages of notes later, she heard the office door open and close, quietly. She looked over her shoulder; Herbert was standing there, hat in hand.

"Please… accept my apologies, Miss... Anne." He glanced at the newspaper. "My feelings for…"

"I understand." She could see him struggling to find the words.

He looked down. "The shock of it, yes. It was the shock – "

"You don't need to explain."

"You say you understand, then?" His hand reached for the newspaper. "Did you read it?"

"I would have liked to, but Madame…"

"She left you with work, of course." His nose wrinkled at the sight of the costume sketches. "Madame Petrova's society ball."

"She arrives tomorrow," Anne said, with a firm undertone.

"Now, Miss Blackstone." He leaned over her work. "I'm sure, I'm almost certain you feel as I do." He placed one hand, then the other, on the desk at either side of her. "You're an artist. You want to create something big, something important…"

Anne spread her elbows wider, intending to brush his hands away.

"I've been walking, gathering ideas. Let's talk about it in my office."

"Mister Blaché, I need to finish with this and then I am expected back – "

She could see in his eyes it made no difference. She twisted in her chair and stood, causing him to step away from the table.

"Madame could return at any moment," she said, trying not to betray the fear beneath her words.

"Madame and Simone have left the studio."

You wouldn't dare be here otherwise, would you? she thought.

"They were talking about her day at school. It sounded like you made quite an impression."

Anne stepped gingerly around the desk. The office door was still slightly ajar. If she moved quickly –

"I'm not sure Alice entirely approves, though, this being Simone's first day…"

Anne took one more step back.

"But I'm sure you must know; I approve. I've always approved of you…"

Her mind flashed for an instant on Mister Bolting, chasing the heroine about the stage, playing a scene of smiling villainy on the showboat. But that was third rate melodrama. This –

The sputter of a flame in a small, dark room.

"No!" Her arm swept one of the piles across the desk and into the air.

"Anne, let me explain!"

She slammed the office door behind her.

Chapter Twelve

Hypocrites

The red-inked letters floated above a naked woman in recline, her body wrapped by an enormous question mark, and the words *Do you* ***dare*** *to see the Naked Truth?*

"Move along you kids, this is no place for you!"

At the sight of the cop's nightstick, three boys stepped away from the Ritz Theater's poster and ran down Main Street.

Anne turned her head as they breezed past. In their sporty caps, knickers and Buster Browns they could be any Fort Lee kids, but it was possible that one of them could be a student of hers. If so there would be questions.

"Miss Blackstone, did you see 'Hypocrites?' Do they really show the Naked Truth? Is she really…"

Yes, she really was naked, she would be bound to say, for after seeing Lois Weber's new film one was compelled not to lie, especially to a child, especially to *her* children, even if they still called her the substitute teacher. From Anne's very first day she'd provided an object lesson in honesty by admitting to the class that she was a fugitive from the Children's Home, an orphan.

These three boys, however – if they were her students – would be more drawn to the film's pageantry: lords and ladies, soldiers, monks, nuns, villagers, peasants, together in one gigantic tracking shot, which aroused both Anne's awe and a twinge of professional jealousy. *That* Anne could talk about, as an introduction to Europe in the Middle Ages.

She pulled her collar around her throat, turned from the cop and the Ritz Theater and walked in the direction of the dry goods store. She needed new curtains, something in the blue spectrum, perhaps teal. Her cottage needed color, in part to compensate for the look of the town. Fort Lee seemed drained of color now that the myriad studios had packed up bag, baggage and actors and gone west to California, toward the setting sun.

It was Solax's logo, a sun rising over mountains, that had first drawn her to Fort Lee. But six months ago, when she'd slammed the door on Herbert and Solax, she discovered that sun, after all, was setting.

Back at her apartment, Vachel had made her tea, declaimed a few poems, and for the next several days gave every good reason why Anne ought to return to Fort Lee Primary. The regular teacher still had TB. Miss Daisy was at loose ends. A steady, though "substitute" teacher in name was needed.

It was her pride, Vachel declared, in her Chautauqua education that had convinced him. He delayed his most ambitious tramp yet, from his birthplace of Springfield to New Mexico, to buck her up, reassure her, and help her claim her rightful place as official Substitute Teacher of Fort Lee Primary.

Once it became a fact, Anne moved out of the crowded brownstone's two dingy rooms. As consolation for a modest teacher's salary, the School District had arranged, as "temporary quarters," a cottage.

It had a garden, perched on a hillside in full view of the Hudson. In the center of the garden, where normally a sundial would be found, there was a telescope. From that spot she could see that the river truly flowed both ways, upriver *and* down, smooth and rippling, not turbulent, muddy, and strewn with sunken boats, like the river that had claimed her father.

The cottage came with a bed, a sturdy dresser, drawers full of tarnished silverware and hand-carved wooden spoons, an old chess set and a hurricane lamp. If she fancied the life of a teacher, and progressed from substitute to full time, she could picture herself living out her days in this cottage, keeping the hedges trimmed, watching the river through the telescope, unpetaling young minds by day, grading homework by night. When work was done, playing chess with a friend by the light of the hurricane lamp. She hadn't had much chance to play since she'd learned the game at Chautauqua.

The cottage did not, however, have curtains.

Half a block from the dry goods store she passed a magazine stand, littered with the latest news of the Balkans, the Belgians, and the advancing Hun. Headlines from Europe had taken a new turn since the *Lusitania's* plunge to the ocean floor. Early in the war she'd thrilled to the news that the American Red Cross sent a Mercy Ship with nurses, surgeons and tons of medical supplies to help injured soldiers on both sides. But since then it felt as if she and every other American watched offstage while the cannons boomed, bayonets clashed and aerial bombs fell at a respectful distance, across the ocean.

Anne paid a nickel for a paper with the headlines **BRITS ARRIVE IN FORCE: Swear to Stick It Out Until the Hun Retreats to Berlin**.

She had a difficult enough time making sense of the loyalties, the shifting alliances, the insanity; she couldn't begin to present it in any convincing fashion to her students.

She taught – when she could get away with it – as she had been taught, in Chautauqua fashion. On her first full day, she chalked the word *Chautauqua* large on the blackboard. None of them had heard of it; to her knowledge the great canvas tents had not been pitched in the vicinity of Fort Lee.

The girls were captivated by Chautauqua from the start. But then, as she well remembered from her own school days, girls grasped things quicker than the boys. Possibly it was because the boys had to leave school to help with chores and the family farm – or, it was simply nature's way.

It had not been that long ago, she learned, that the girls & boys had to sit at separate sides of the room. It only seemed to make sense for punishment's sake, as when a boy was made to sit with the girls, or vice-versa, which was considered more effective than being made to sit in a corner or write a humiliating sentence one hundred times or more on the blackboard.

"There will be no such punishments in my classroom," she'd told them, although what punishments she had up her sleeves she did not say. Fortunately, in the six months that she'd been teaching she'd not been compelled to mete them out.

The bolt of blue cloth from the dry goods store was tucked into her big canvas bag, and she retraced her steps to the trolley stop on Main Street. Someday, she told herself, with whatever savings she had, she might acquire an automobile. Until then, she could make do by trolley, and by foot. At times she thought she walked in solidarity with Vachel, now tramping somewhere out west.

As to where he *really* was, what did she know, outside of his hastily-scratched postcards? The last one she'd received was postmarked Santa Monica, California, a photograph of "bathing beauties" displaying lots of ankle and not much else on a beach. "To prove that there is more than just citrus fruit in California," he quipped on the reverse side, adding only "No, I did not walk all this way..." with a hastily-drawn picture of a smoke-puffing train.

Vachel, she thought, would probably accept the offer of a beach picnic with thosc bathing beauties, if only for research purposes.

Two cars barreled down the street just in front of her, their bumpers perilously close to one other.

"Struggle!" a man in the rear car shouted through the megaphone. "Let me see fear! Fear!" As the two cars whizzed past, the second one bearing the camera and director, she could see just enough of the woman's face to know that California had not yet claimed Pearl White.

God bless her, Anne thought. She smiles and moves well; she struggles *very* well. But then Pearl had plenty of opportunity – captured by gypsies, trapped in a balloon, dangled from the Palisades cliff, clinging to a floating target for long range cannons, and nearly drowned in a sinking submarine. Now that Pauline's perils were done, Pearl had been reborn as Elaine Dodge. This struggle in the car would be the sequel, the "New Exploits of Elaine."

Would there ever be a "New Exploits of Delia"? Anne thought, ruefully. Would there ever be a Delia at all?

As consolation, she had this cottage with its quaint telescope in the tidy garden with a peerless view of the Hudson. It was the cottage that reminded her of boiling potatoes, fresh baking powder and the heady aroma of jarred mincemeat. All hers... as long as she stayed her course as a teacher.

The trolley came to a stop. Anne stepped down and began her walk down the long, tree-lined lane leading to her cottage. For as far ahead as Anne could see she was alone.

The bolt of cloth suddenly felt like lead in her canvas bag. Her arm began to swing the bag in slow semi-circles, remembering how it helped when her old carpetbag pulled her arm towards the ground.

Somewhere over her shoulder she heard the clopping of hooves.

She turned; no horse and rider appeared on the road behind. Just imaginings, she thought. More of her daydreams. Or was this how the Headless Horseman first appeared to Ichabod Crane?

When she reached her cottage, a brown envelope was wedged into the door. The very official-looking return address said "U.S. Army Barracks, Fort Jay, Governor's Island." She'd seen Fort Jay from the Hudson Ferry; an impressive but almost grim castle-like structure. What would anyone in the armed services want with her?

She opened the envelope before stepping inside. 'Miss Blackstone..." it began. "You may not recall my name, but we met after Madame Alice Blache's lecture at Columbia University. I was the officer who liked your western picture..."

Indeed she did recall him; Captain Stanhope. He wished to speak with her, at her convenience, though hopefully soon, at his office at Fort Jay.

Whatever for? Anne wondered. She folded the paper carefully and put it in her pocket. Well, he'd made the effort to find her; she would probably have to return the favor.

The next morning Anne was up early, measuring the blue cloth for her window curtains. The sun had risen over Manhattan, filling the cottage with a warm light. Humming, she took up scissors to cut the cloth.

From downriver came a sound that seemed almost an echo of her humming. As it drew closer, it sounded mechanical, almost nasal.

She looked outside. Though the morning was warm, Anne felt a chill that ran from the back of her neck down to her arms.

A squadron of airplanes was flying up river – six, eight, ten, she couldn't be sure – as they were almost on a level with the sun. They flew in close formation, displaying themselves in not so much skill as a show of force.

She ran to the garden and watched them through the telescope until they were no more than a cluster of black dots hovering above the river.

*** *** ***

By the look and smell of it, Captain Stanhope's office came encased in leather: padded chairs, oversized books, even the desk. It must have been comfortable enough, for on a corner of it the Captain perched, part of his attempt at informality. The Captain himself – tall, close-cropped blonde hair, trimmed moustache – appeared awkward, even in the confines of his own office.

"Tell me about your latest," he said. "Moving picture, story, whatever you're working on."

Her arms on the smooth leather armrests relaxed a bit. "Captain, I haven't made a picture since Pantograph was torched."

He closed his eyes, nodding. "I am deeply sorry," he said, his mouth a sudden frown. "I did forget about that."

Anne tried for a lighter note. "Before I was teaching, I had something in mind. A nautical story, about a lady captain."

"Sounds wonderful." The Captain rose from the desk. "And not a western?"

Though she did not recall stepping down at the entrance, Anne noticed that Captain Stanhope's office sat, like an elaborate, leather-clad foxhole, partially below ground. Just enough afternoon light poured in from the windows to illuminate President Wilson's thin lipped countenance glaring from the wall.

"The President signed that – somewhere in the corner." The Captain paced the room. "Miss Blackstone, I imagine you know that Mister Wilson has exhausted his diplomatic options, and the United States government will not remain neutral."

The baldfaced admission struck Anne by surprise. “I wasn't aware that the President had made a Declaration of War – yet.”

“Think about it.” He turned to face her. “How can the President declare war if the public remains stuck in our official position of neutrality?”

The light from the window was broken intermittently by shadows of recruits marching single file on the gravel walkway.

“The public,” he continued, “needs to know that this crusade is not for conquest, or to re-draw some lines on a map. This is for an Idea.”

Stanhope's left hand slowly clenched into a fist. “And when the public does know, knows the facts, then man, woman and child, *we* are *in* this war If we weren't, mothers wouldn't have the strength to let go of their sons, who would not find the strength themselves to sail across that dark ocean, riddled with German U-Boats.” His fist unclenched, and his arm shook slightly, pointing toward the sunlit window and the marching recruits. “This is a mobilization of not just the Army and Navy, but the whole blessed nation.”

Anne cleared her throat. “May I ask, Captain, where I fit in? I mean, which branch of the service – ”

“Officially,” he smiled, “the U.S. Army Signal Corps. But *our* relationship is through the Committee for Public Information. A civilian organization.”

“Public information.” Anne glanced up. “Or public opinion?”

"Miss Blackstone." He smiled. "I have the impression you may be as confused as some of our members of Congress. This is not censorship or 'propaganda,' as Germany calls it. This is free, open, accurate information, spread through advertising, newspaper columns, the comic pages, and – here is why I went looking for you – through the moving pictures."

The Captain slid one hand across a row of leather-bound maps behind his desk. "There will be no involvement by moving picture studios, at the Front or otherwise. They've done enough damage with their Hollywood – and Fort Lee – re-creations of the battlefield."

He stopped beside a bronze sculpture of a bucking horse about to throw its rider. "At the moment, taking a picture at the Allied Front is punishable by death. No war correspondents allowed at the Front, period. So..." he shrugged. "There will *most definitely* be no war coverage by film companies or studios. The last thing we want are green cameramen losing their heads, bungling military operations *or* getting themselves killed in the process." His look was almost pleading. "Can you imagine what the papers would make of that?"

The Captain paced. "But I'm glad you mentioned the studios. What pictures of American life have they given so far to the screens of America, to Mexico, Asia, Europe? Gangsters, drunkards, outlaws. The Germans hold these up as real pictures of American life. We need to correct that."

He stopped at a row of what appeared to be cans of film, stacked on the shelves beside the leather-cased maps. "Ah.... and here it is." Each had a label, which, she was surprised, he could read aloud in the darkened room. "A kaleidoscope of American life, from Ford Motor Company, United Steelworkers, International Harvesters. Also coal companies, lumber, the Bureau of Education, Public Health Service. And the great out of doors, from the National Park Service. Every kind of educational film imaginable."

"That's quite a collection, Captain."

"Not mine. This is from Mr. Jules Brulatour. This is only a small part; Mr. Brulatour has thousands of such reels, all available for use; for your use, if you wish."

Anne remembered him, gray-haired, patrician, motoring about Fort Lee in his super-sized Ford motor car, his money behind half the studios in town – Eclair, Peerless, and that new one, Universal. Around Fort Lee he was best known for throwing his mistress, a real-life survivor of the *Titanic,* into a movie version of the disaster, rushed into theaters within a month of the sinking.

"I think you have the idea now." Stanhope's voice brought her back to the room. "To give the world an unvarnished view of American life: work, play..."

"And going to war." There, again, she couldn't help it. But if she was going to work for the man, for the government, there had to be honesty. "Will there be an... unvarnished view of military life, of the Front, to go with it?"

With one finger, the Captain drew invisible lines from one place to another atop his leather desk. “Here, footage taken by cameramen of the Army Signal Corps, from the troops' first arrival in France, and all the way to the Front. And here...” His arm drew another line – “...to the Chief of Staff at the War College, who scrutinizes it for anything improper for public showings, from there to the Kalem studios in Manhattan for editing & processing. The finished product will be the Division of Picture's 'Official Bulletin.'”

“Is that when *I* would be involved?”

Captain Stanhope smiled evasively. “Not precisely. There are details still to work out.” He picked up a compass, and played with it, end over end, where the invisible lines of distribution had been drawn on his desk. “Our information tells us theater owners won't be interested in purely government films, because their audiences won't be interested. That must change.” He nodded casually in her direction. “Someone, like yourself, could inject the essential elements of storytelling, edit according to taste, let your creative imagination fly, within reason, and return the completed footage to the Division of Pictures.”

She heard the unmistakable sounds of a mass of airplanes, closer, more ominous than the hornet-like sounds she'd heard above the Hudson. An aviation training school had been pointed out to her when she first arrived at Fort Jay, a small airstrip at the southern tip of the island. Suddenly she imagined a rookie pilot on his first solo flight, heading out over the white-capped waters, the towers of Manhattan over his shoulder, taunting him.

“So.... you wish to enlist my services.”

“Indeed I... indeed *we* do, Miss Blackstone.”

The certainty, the finality of the war hit her at last. For a long moment she was only aware of a loud clock ticking away.

“Well,” she exhaled. “It won't be the first time. I am a veteran of the Patents War.”

“That business with Edison? You'd really call that a war?”

She nodded her head, slowly. “There were guns, though personally, I never saw them.”

What could she lose by this arrangement? Distribution to Europe was at a halt; the studios had been doing badly for the past couple of years. Here was a new avenue that, remarkably, had just opened up to her, perhaps her alone.

How else could she gain access to the great conflict of the day? Deal with red tape, delays, permits, blockades and bureaucracy, or work with Stanhope, the Signal Corps and the CPI, with access to more quality footage than she'd ever known. In return, all she'd need to do was dance to their tune.

"Will you at least give me closeups?" she asked.

“Of course, you'll be provided with all the necessary footage. There will be scenes of marching and battleships, to be sure, but I also expect to have some bang-up footage shot on the front lines by the men of the Signal Corps. The last thing I want is troops and ships and legions of faceless men. I want the *face* on the screen. Something that will appeal to women and mothers.”

"Mothers *are* women, Captain."

"Of course." He rubbed at his chin, partially concealing a blush. "We'll do our level best. But don't expect ready-made human interest. War cannot be staged."

Silently, she wished that it were nothing *but* that – actors and uniforms, props and stage guns.

"There are some conditions," continued Stanhope, "that I must, in absolute honesty, get onto the table. There can be no mention of troop movements, locations of the fleet, arrival and departure times of military ships. There is to be nothing unflattering to the United States Army, its officers or enlisted men. Is that clear?"

"I'm sure it will become more clear as we proceed."

"Two words I would like to stress: nobility, and self-sacrifice. Not vengeance, not battle courage, not even hatred for the German nation. Ultimately, we have one aim, and one aim only. Keep up the morale of the public. Aside from that, you can do practically anything you want."

"Practically," she replied. Her eyes went up beyond President Wilson's portrait to a framed picture of the U.S. Capitol. It, too, seemed encased in leather, and in need of polishing.

The Captain slapped his desk lightly. "Splendid. I see that you've come round, as they say, to our way of looking at things. But if you still need to think it over, consider this: here you can do with striking, moving images what words and paper, even eloquently delivered speeches, can never do. You can be part of a great influence."

As he paced from the desk, he looked quickly over his shoulder at her. “And who knows? This could turn out to be a fine opportunity for you... War brings a lot of powerful energies together. I should not be surprised if you're able to meet some of the people who, after all this is over, could help bring that nautical story of yours to life. Time to rebuild then, hmmm? Perhaps another studio...?”

Careful, she thought. I am already sold on it; do not make the temptation too great, or it will seem too far beyond belief, and I will withdraw. The students – *her* students – still needed her, especially at a time like this.

“I see you may still need a bit of convincing.” *He must be a mind reader,* she thought. “It would be most instructive if you saw one of the Four Minute Men.”

“Who are they?”

“You'll find out. Let's call it your first assignment.”

*** *** ***

It was spring, and war was in the air; in fact it left room for nothing else. Headlines – WAR DECLARED and WE'RE IN IT NOW – papered the news stand on Main Street, and the advance guard of the Committee for Public Information were launched to the theaters, churches and grange halls of the nation. They were known as the Four Minute Men, and the first one to appear in the area was coming to the Lyric Theater in Hoboken.

She'd wanted to see the feature film, "Joan the Woman," that the Four Minute Man would precede. If the United States government would pay the cost of a ticket for a motion picture she planned to see anyway, and in a palace compared to the theater she had been used to, then she and the government were off to a good start, and she could manage the train fare to Hoboken.

When she found her seat, half way back in the crowded auditorium, a glass slide was already projected on the screen: **4 Minute Men 4** As the audience quieted down, the slide slowly dissolved to:

Mister James Eason will speak four minutes on a subject of national importance. He speaks under the authority of THE COMMITTEE FOR PUBLIC INFORMATION George Creel, Chairman, Washington, DC

Young Mister Eason took the stage. He wore a business suit and tie, but in every other respect looked like he was ready to jump into uniform and sail across the waves for Uncle Sam. For most people in the audience he would be the first fresh face of the war, appealing to their better patriotic nature for Liberty Bonds. Yet he started with a note of foreign history.

"The people of Belgium have cried out, **cried out,** I say, and Britain, ***Brittania!*** has come to their aid. Britain has **rallied**, as she did when Napoleon stood ready to swarm across their island, she charged against the foe in the Crimea, in the Sudan, and now, in the Balkans. Now it is **our turn to rally!"**

With the applause, his introductory slide dissolved to one of the American Eagle, its talons gripping a sheaf of arrows. The image was plastered across his entire figure, which made the impact of his words all the more startling.

"Just as we rallied in our hour of greatest need, at Lexington, Concord, at Gettysburg and Bull Run..." With each mention of a battlefield, he faced a different corner of the auditorium. "Now we embark on a **new crusade**, to make the world safe for **liberty, democracy**, for the rule of law and justice applied to ***all humanity!***"

There was even greater applause, which Mr. Eason acknowledged with a smile. "Now I believe I can save half of my pitch." He pretended to rip up a piece of paper. "For I see that you are with me!" Continued applause. "Now I have but two words to say...**Liberty...Bonds!**"

At his words, a group of ushers, young men and women, their uniforms striped in red, white, and blue, came bearing baskets down the aisles. Anne was startled by one young woman who appeared right at her elbow. Mr. Eason's words were nearly lost among the sounds of people rifling their coats, purses and handbags for money.

She saw him point to someone near the front of the audience. "May I ask the Lieutenant to stand?" As the soldier stood, looking even younger than the young speaker, Mister Eason asked "And who will buy a hundred dollar Liberty Bond for *this* soldier?"

There was an awkward, coughing silence. Then one older couple offered up fifty dollars each, to a round of applause and cheers.

Prepared speech swept aside by an unforeseen but best possible outcome, the Four Minute Man concluded his talk with a song with projected titles, “What Kind of American are You?” The song, new to Anne, was performed with gusto by the audience.

She wondered if anyone in this same audience, in this same theater, perhaps, had sung along to the hit of only last year, “I Didn't Raise My Boy to be a Soldier...”

The patriotic slides dimmed, replaced by newsreel footage “Fresh from the Scenes of Conflict,” yet containing the sort of material staged as far from those conflicted scenes as possible: cavalry parades in Russia and Montenegro, white haired dignitaries in silk hats, heads of state in unflattering national costumes, helmets topped by absurd fountains of white feathers. All the typical fodder, all good examples of what she would not find acceptable on screen.

The theater organ burst into a marching tune, simulated trumpets heralding the Maid of Orleans, “Joan, the Woman.” But unexpectedly, and without apparent reason, the scene opened not in medieval France but at the European Front, in the only manner in which it could legally be portrayed – simulated in Hollywood, with dressed-up actors carrying prop guns, dodging studio explosives.

“In the war-torn land she loves so well, her spirit fights today.”

Even when the story went to fifteenth century France the current situation was everywhere. The departure for Orleans reminded Anne of the newsreels she'd just seen of the Balkan cavalry; even confetti was falling in the street behind them. The raid of the Burgundian troops, breaking open houses and scattering pigs and chickens, was like the German Army trampling a Belgian village.

Geraldine Farrar, better known on the Metropolitan Opera stage, may not have been the Joan of Anne's imagination, but she was a Joan of the earth, a sturdy country maiden from Domremy, driving her sheep down a sunny country road. Denied her voice, she communicated with every inch of her upper body, especially her hands. She used them to implore, command, pray, and extend heavenward, Christ-like.

“Men of France, will ye follow me to battle?”

A spontaneous *“Yes!”* burst from the lips of several men in the audience. Generous applause followed the oath of the battle-hardened French general, "Joan of Arc, I'll follow thee to Victory, or to Hell!"

There was enough armor on display to coat several battleships. The direction made unparalleled use of huge crowds, whether in the street, on a cavalry charge, writhing in a Roman-type orgy or fighting at the top of a parapet. Anne had never seen more convincing battle scenes, the desperation absolutely real. The combatants within the frame, Joan included, looked at any moment like they were in real physical danger.

A number of women shrieked when Joan's hair was pulled by her English captors, and some covered their eyes when she was threatened with torture by hot irons, watched by hooded phantoms who looked like members of the Klan. Anne kept her eyes open, and noticed that the terror was all psychological, for in reality Joan's flesh was untouched.

Then the fire! The smoke and orange-tinted flames seemed so real that Anne felt her eyes burn. Joan's arms were swimming through the smoke, breaking through the screen, grabbing for Anne's very soul. For moments Anne could barely see the screen for the tears that flowed down her cheeks.

"Joan, the Woman," on a big screen in a first class theater, was the best American - made spectacle Anne had witnessed, Griffith included. The director, DeMille, showed promise. But Anne wasn't the least surprised that a woman, Jeanie Macpherson, had written it.

On the way out, half-listening to comments that filled the lobby, Anne wondered about the title. Why "Joan the Woman"? Miss Farrar didn't portray her as the sort of woman one was used to seeing on the screen. And her ultimate crime, the reason given for her burning at the stake, was that she dared to wear a man's clothing!

All the more surreal, then, to emerge from the Lyric Theater and come face to face with the Howard Chandler Christy poster, a brunette apple-cheeked young woman in nautical uniform: "Gee, I Wish I Were a MAN - I'd join the Navy."

And there, on a signboard just a few feet away, was a companion poster of the Maid herself, sword held high.

JOAN OF ARC SAVED FRANCE.

Women of America, Save Your Country

Buy War Savings Stamps.

Anne paused before the poster. "Yes, Joan," she whispered. "I'll follow you."

*** *** ***

The Kalem Studios on West 24th Street had been vacated with remarkable haste. Props were strewn about, unboxed; bits of broken glass from an arc lamp that hadn't made it as far as the packing crate were left on the stairs. The studio had followed the exodus to Hollywood. Thus its facilities, in particular the editing rooms, were available to the Signal Corps – and to Anne.

So here she sat with the tools of her solitary trade – gloves, magnifying glass, tape and adhesive – surrounded by strips of curling cellulose, so many sleeping caterpillars dangling before her. There was a story in them somewhere, if by some miracle of editing she could conjure it.

The working space was larger than Anne had been accustomed to, but in no time she had every available inch stacked with tin reels bearing labels such as "King of England," "German Troops," "Naval Battle," "Smoking Ships," "Explosions on Hills," "Nurses on the Battlefront," and "Airplanes Taking Off and Landing."

The footage in front of her was of ships arriving in France, mobs rushing to greet them, Red Cross nurses handing out roses, the Yankees marching, bayonets affixed, beneath the Arc de Triomphe. The suggestion given to her for a title was "Berlin or Bust."

Anne didn't succumb to suggestions like that. She'd already left out footage of school children throwing out books by German writers. Some newsreel would include it, but not hers.

For the dozenth time she held the strips in her white gloved hands, moving them in a series of quick jerks in front of a light box. More frames of men marching, marching, she wasn't sure where from or where they marched to. Once her eye caught a place to edit, out came the magnifying glass and sharp scissors, the cut was made, then pasted over with rubber cement.

Her vision blurred. The footage could go anywhere and nowhere, perhaps because every sort of activity engaged in by the fresh crops of uniformed Yankees on French soil was preceded and followed by marching, marching everywhere.

The first footage she'd received from the Front was appalling. Cameras were bulky, lenses ineffective, and God help the cameraman, for no one else could, if some part of the equipment was missing or damaged. The Signal Corps had been caught almost completely unprepared for the demands put on them by the CPI. They could never have taught the intricacies of camera exposure, temperature, and focus in enough time before the troops arrived in France.

The most she could see of the German lines were clouds of smoke blowing across No-Man's Land and bursts of shrapnel in the air. No wonder scenes had been faked for the newsreels.

Through some blink of the Army censors she'd come across images of the dead waiting for burial. And there might have even been a death captured on camera, as one moment there was a gunner seated on the ground, the next moment an explosion, and one great chunk of what looked like a torso suspended in mid-air. Footage like that made her queasy, and went right to the waste bin.

It was simpler in the heady days of mobilization, when the first troops to sail the Atlantic massed in the streets of Hoboken. As confetti and streamers fell from the sky she and a cameraman fought their way through a crowd to get in striking distance of General Pershing.

When they found him, reporters were trying to get the General to say something worth printing. He curled his fist into a ball and made a stuck-out-jaw gesture of "We're going to give them **Hell!"** That said, the General caught Anne's eye, and quickly tipped his hat.

The rest of her day was a blur, though it did somewhat prepare her for her second assignment, days later, still in Hoboken, to cover the launching of the troop ship *USS Dauntless,* bound for France.

It was not the ship's first voyage; German passengers once strolled where the Yanks now crammed her decks. The ship had been quarantined in the harbor since 1914, when it had taken refuge in Hoboken to escape the British Navy. Since then it had been reconditioned and reborn as a Liberty Ship.

The crowds for the launching were not as vast as the ones at General Pershing's arrival, but they were more compact, especially around the docks, where cameras and equipment had to get through lines of blue-coated, gold-buttoned policemen.

The troops filed up the gangplanks, not in smooth rows, but in a sort of staged informality, patting each other on the back, waving to the crowd, doffing their hats and twirling them in the air. It looked like the start to a great picnic, with 1500 more guests than usual.

The cameras were invited aboard the *Dauntless* before it sailed. When Anne and the crew were taken inside the bridge her fingers were almost irresistibly drawn to the pilot wheel. She had to content herself with two minutes in which to photograph the pilot at the wheel, back-lit by the sun.

They dutifully filmed posed shots of the owners, lieutenants, and all the dignitaries that could be convinced to attend. Perhaps word that "the newsreels will be there" had drawn them out. A smart-looking young woman in a uniform spoke through a huge megaphone mounted on a swivel. There was respectful quiet from over a thousand people when she spoke, but it made absolutely no sense for the camera; in fact, it would leave the audience only hungering to hear her words, so Anne left it out altogether.

When the boat was about to steam away, Anne positioned a camera at each side. Her own camera stayed on the pier, directly facing the bow. The young woman at the megaphone cracked champagne across the bow, and the ship, with its still-waving boys in uniform, slid into the harbor, tugboats at its side. The slick yet gargantuan immersion into the harbor was covered from three different angles.

Anne realized then it was all one great stage show. Apart from the training camps, the marching in formation, Black Jack Pershing and the first Expeditionary Forces, what the C.P.I. really wanted was a complete record, a movie made from departure, to the crossing at sea, the landing, greeted by enthusiastic citizens, the preparedness for assault, the battle, and victory.

Victory? she wondered. Would that be staged, too? Or didn't Stanhope himself assure her "nothing will be staged."

It was all artifice, even when real subjects were photographed. All staged in some way, unless, by some happy accident, the subjects forgot for a moment that the cameras were there, and followed along with the advice written large on the wall at Solax Studio: BE NATURAL.

With scissors, Anne snipped away the more gratuitous marching footage. She rubbed her tired eyes, put down Pershing's arrival in Hoboken, stood up and headed towards the little corner of this drafty studio that provided solace and a bit of inspiration.

There it was, in lurid color, the poster of *A Fiend at the Throttle,* Chapter 27 of "The Hazards of Helen," Kalem's claim to fame apart from the Christ film. Beneath the serial queen's poster were artifacts from her adventures, a riding jacket,and crop, rescued by Anne from the properties rooms on her first day at the studio.

Pearl White, swooning in the face of peril, was a piker compared to Helen Holmes. Helen leapt from buildings, sped around mountain curves in a motorcar and jumped from a galloping horse to a train. And though she occasionally was rescued by a handsome male hero, it was Helen who single-handedly collared the bad guys and brought them to justice.

Get outside, Helen's voice whispered in her ears. *Go find adventure.*

Anne had barely opened the door to the mid-town daylight when she was confronted with the command, "I Want You." James Montgomery Flagg's Uncle Sam poster seemed to be pasted on every block in the city.

Anne smiled as she walked past. Uncle Sam was new on the block; the Maid of Orleans, even when she sold Liberty Bonds, was already an icon of the War in three countries.

Across the street were a group of nurses, headscarves bobbing as they stepped briskly down the sidewalk. Anne had seen, quite possibly, more raw footage of nurses in action than of fighting men: wrapping bandages, sewing uniforms, marching down city streets, an echo of the Doughboys' arrival only months before.

If it were up to Anne she'd give cameras to the nurses. They saw things bluntly, no nonsense, with a woman's perspective. That's what Stanhope wanted, didn't he? The nurses *saw* war, not as parades and officers and guns, but up close. They knew its face.

She followed the nurses downtown, into a great stream of motorcars, carriages and people pouring south on Broadway. Anne felt a distinct buzz in the air, an anticipation, like the day Florence Lawrence arrived in Saint Louis.

As she got closer, past Trinity Church, coming up toward Wall Street, the crowds became thicker, denser, the tingle in the air more palpable. Something, some*one* quite special was ahead. Echoes reverberated from the tall old buildings around her.

Cheers resounded when she turned the corner and came up to the side of the Stock Exchange. There was a small fellow, waving his arms wildly, sitting on the shoulders of another man. Then the small fellow pressed his hands to his face in an almost girlish way, and the crowd roared.

Anne knew that pose; she'd seen it before, in a Chaplin short. That was Charlie, right there, on Doug Fairbank's shoulders!

"And what will you pledge for a handstand?" a woman's voice called, amplified through a megaphone. The woman who asked the question was standing nearby, very short, almost diminutive.

"Is that Mary Pickford?" she asked the woman standing next to her.

"That's Little Mary, all right!" was the reply.

Chaplin, Fairbanks, Pickford, here in New York for a Bond Drive! She knew Helen Holmes had called her from the building for good reason.

"Sold!" cried Mary, as someone had obviously agreed to her request. Charlie jumped from Doug's shoulders, and the latter kicked his legs in the air, and "walked" a few paces on his hands. The crowd roared.

Anne pulled in her stomach and tried to squeeze through the crowd. Ever since that day at the Chicago Art Institute when Vachel compared Mary to a Renaissance angel Anne wanted to see for herself.

Mary was petite, that was obvious at first glance. Her fabled curls were tucked demurely beneath a hat. Here, smartly dressed in a military-style tunic, like a member of some Honor Guard, she looked nothing like the girl-woman she portrayed on screen.

In fact, the attire made perfect sense; Anne had heard that back in Hollywood, Cecil B. De Mille commanded his own infantry unit that staged weekly marches down Hollywood Boulevard, and Mary led the parade.

Anne imagined C.B. giving her a pep talk: "Sure, we can get Doug and Charlie to do the stunts, make the speeches, wave the flag, but only *you* can lead the parade. Only you can rally them, Mary. In a smart looking little uniform and hat, with that chipper little smile..."

Yes, it *was* all a show. Those Hollywood soldiers on parade were almost certainly extras and bit players who carried prop rifles, and whose uniforms came from the costume shop. They marched through Hollywood for the same reason that Anne and the crew of the *River Queen* marched through the riverboat towns: to win the populace. This particular show by Fairbanks, Pickford and Chaplin was the East Coast effort.

This would have been a plum moment for Vachel. Anne remembered his wild ideas about the moving picture stars as the new gods and goddesses, bestowing not godly gifts or ambrosia, but an autographed picture, a smile, a wave of the hand...

And where the hell was Vachel? On a train, no doubt, speeding towards his next whistle-stop, proclaiming his hit poems "The Congo" and "General William Booth Enters Heaven" to some Friends of Poetry society or other. Lord knows, he could skip the little towns by now; he'd already proclaimed before President Wilson and his Cabinet, and where could he go from there?

Vachel hadn't spent even one full night at her cottage. He rushed out early one morning, eager to promote his new book. *The Art of the Moving Picture* had made a new person of him – a prophet of sorts. She felt both overjoyed for his new-found fame and resentful, as it pushed her away.

"Edison is the new Gutenberg," wrote Vachel. "He has invented the new printing." Despite its inaccuracy, reading this had given Anne an electric thrill. "The state that realizes this may lead the soul of America, day after tomorrow."

Back on the Stock Exchange steps Fairbanks had possession of the megaphone. From the sound if it he'd nearly shouted himself hoarse. No wonder he had been reduced to walking on his hands. Perhaps the public did not want, or expect, their gods and goddesses to speak.

*** *** ***

One work day, after four hours and hundreds of feet of solid military footage, Helen Holmes staring at her from wall all the while, Anne hungered to see just one episode of "The Hazards of Helen." She looked for the one person at the studio who might know its whereabouts, and found him, small and hunched, in a stained blue shirt, sweeping the hallway.

"Ma'am, you'll have to ask the U.S. Army," the janitor said. "They came here one day with a flatbed truck and loaded it up with every film can they could find."

"Why?"

"The nitrate; Ma'am. They take the film and melt it down for boot heels."

Nitrate! Will had told her it could be as explosive as a hand grenade. Now it was the very thing to keep the troops marching through France.

The janitor returned to his sweeping. “Films just stacked on the shelves,” he said, “and Kalem moving to California... They needed the space.”

What of Helen, then? Wouldn't the boys in France get a thrill from Helen Holmes, projected against the side of a village barn, dashing about in last minute rescues with trains and motorcars?

Not really, she thought. Like the people of that village, the troops wanted Chaplin, Fairbanks and Pickford. The Gods.

The janitor hauled his mop and bucket up the stairway to the second floor, and Anne with a shrug, returned to her editing room.

Helen was gone, but Anne had cupboards stacked with film cans: *Bombs Exploding... Soldiers on Crutches... Going Over the Top... Wounded at Dressing Stations... Stretchers on Gangplank.*

Today she faced a pile of crumpled editing notes. But laying on top, muscling the others aside, was stationary with the seal of the U.S. Army Corps of Engineers. Though signed by Stanhope, it had the appearance of a summons – to the Gala Premiere of “America's Answer,” at Fort Lee's Ritz Theater.

It could turn out to be an important evening. “America's Answer” was the most prestigious project she'd worked on at the CPI. This was the first occasion in months, exiled to the studio as she'd been, to put attention towards her personal appearance.

In the polished surface of one of the film canisters she caught a reflection of herself in her work clothes: a nondescript olive-colored blouse atop a pleated skirt.

A Gala Premiere... Anne closed her eyes, and imagined something in yellow or white taffeta, with satin ribbons, a Newmarket coat, a fine long skirt, and, strictly for her own pleasure, underskirts of white silk.

$ from Stanhope. She added a hasty note to the already thick pile. He had given her access to the footage; he could damn well give her a small advance so she could wear something decent to her own premiere. And he would have to bring a car around.

***   ***   ***

"So who is this person we're going to pick up?" Stanhope shouted above the noise of the touring car. A small sliding window stood between them and his driver, Jeffrey.

"An old friend..." Anne spoke almost as loudly. "You may remember her as the Biograph Girl."

The Captain squinted. "That... Lawrence woman?"

Anne nodded. "You met briefly, after Alice Blache's speech at Columbia."

"Yes, yes. Unpleasant-looking husband as I recall."

Anne folded her hands in her lap. Her deerskin gloves looked a bit frayed.

"Unpleasant only scratches the surface," she said. "Her husband directed her last picture. When it came time to film the big climax, a fire, he wouldn't accept a stunt double. 'Florence Lawrence does her own stunts,' he said. So on she goes, into a burning building. A wall practically collapsed on her."

Anne looked again at her lap. “She's been in chronic pain since, and hasn't released a film for a year.”

The Captain shook his head.

“But,” Anne continued, “she'll probably shrug it off when we see her, and say that she's 'convalescing between engagements.'”

The Captain looked out the window. “Then that's exactly how we shall regard it.”

Florence's thick makeup was the first thing Anne noticed when the door was opened to her modest-sized home just outside of town.

“Scars from that accident four years ago,” said Florence, touching her face.

“I don't notice anything,” said Anne, only a half truth. For she now realized that she and Florence were bonded, as Sisters of the Fire. One fire had destroyed Anne's past and present; the other, Florence had rushed into, at the request of her husband. Both had just been doing their jobs.

“You might not, but the camera's unforgiving.”

Florence was propped up by a cane in her left hand. A large urn filled with walking sticks and canes stood next to the door. The one in her hand appeared fancier, more polished than the rest, obviously meant for a night on the town.

“I'm ready,” said Florence. Anne took her arm, and helped her from the door to the waiting car.

The Ritz Theater had undergone its own transformation since Anne had last been there, which by her recollection had been the showing of Lois Weber's "Hypocrites" during her final semester at the school. On that occasion there had been a salacious billboard on the sidewalk; tonight it was replaced by giant letters on the marquee, draped in red, white and blue at the edges: "AMERICA'S ANSWER and Other Accompanying Newsreels of Current Interest."

Anne kept a tight grip on Florence's arm as they stepped from the sidewalk to the theater. Ushers dressed as Doughboys stood at attention on either side of the lobby doors, mock rifles across their shoulders. To walk past them and through those doors gave all the impression of entering yet another recruitment rally for Uncle Sam, or at least another appearance by one of the Four Minute Men.

Florence had seemed almost regal when she entered the lobby; once inside the theater she walked less steadily, so progress down the aisle was slow. A military band played in the orchestra pit. The room was sprinkled with men in uniform, but for the most part it was a sea of fancy dress, at least the fanciest Fort Lee could muster.

"Look at them," whispered Florence. "They used to love me."

"I'm sure they still love you; they just haven't seen you on the screen for a while."

"You know, I'm coming back from two deaths, not just one. The first was in Saint Louis."

"I was there," Anne reminded her.

"The next one was that fire."

Anne stopped. "This is our row." They took their seats.

The red curtains parted to reveal an image of a spinning earth, gunfire and cannons. The camera closed in on a cartoon map of Europe. What followed was all cartoon, with a raving, drooling Kaiser and a simulated encounter between a British plane and a German zeppelin. In quick succession came the newsreels, "The Spirit of 1917," "American Ambulances," and one Anne had contributed to, "Women's Part in the War."

Newsreels concluded, a woman dressed as Lady Liberty took to the stage, and as the military band tried to sound not quite so brassy, held her orange-tipped torch aloft to sing "Keep the Home Fires Burning." The audience was encouraged to sing along.

The lights dimmed again; Anne took a deep breath in preparation. "America's Answer" flashed across the screen, to applause and cheers from the full house.

Anne gave herself an invisible pat on the back when the real thing, the barbed wire, clouds of gas and showers of dirt, flashed up on the screen. There was a foxhole, and there in the distance a shell exploding, accompanied by a bass rumble from the pit.

Yet even when heavy artillery pounded away, there was no fear of death. The audience would see no bodies or parts of them thrown into the air. The mercy of the editor's scissors had whisked them away before that point. Cut to a title, or a reassuring shot of an officer. The result was to keep the war deathless, and very far away.

Anne shifted her peripheral attention from Florence to an older couple seated in front of her. She noticed their uncomfortable shifting *and* their rapt attention. At one point the woman grabbed the man's wrist and seemed to pray to God it wasn't so, it couldn't ever happen here, we *mustn't* let it.

At the conclusion, soldiers marched towards the camera, their ranks stretching to the horizon. Their lines parted just before they reached the camera, probably mounted on a platform.

"You did that, too?" Florence whispered, quite in awe of the onrushing sea of men.

"No." Anne shook her head. "I had nothing to do with it."

A hushed "Ssssh!" came from the row behind, but it was no matter, as the closing credits flashed, and the military band built to a flag-waving crescendo.

"Good job," Florence said into Anne's ear during the applause. "I had no idea it all looked like that. I mostly read about it in the papers."

"Do you get out to the pictures once in a while?" asked Anne as she helped Florence up the carpeted aisle.

"Well, keep this to yourself," whispered Florence. "But I have a soft spot for 'The Hazards of Helen.'" There was a quaver in her smile. "She did her own stunts, too."

A woman in the next aisle waved. Florence waved back.

"Someone you know?"

"I haven't a clue." The Biograph Girl smiled. "But they know me!"

*** *** ***

Florence left the touring car and hobbled along the stone path to her front door. Despite the cane, she walked with the same confidence she had displayed in the Ritz Theater's lobby – once more the Biograph Girl, the assured young woman who had arrived on the Illinois Central to announce that she was not, after all, dead.

"Interesting friend you have," said the Captain, as the car pulled away.

"Friend?" Anne replied. "Not really. But I believe she's one of the bravest people I've ever met."

"Why?" he asked. "Government work?"

Anne shook her head. "Moving pictures. Florence was the first, the very first star. And because she did her own stunts she has injuries that will make her the first to face retirement." The car rolled down the gravel driveway. "I keep thinking she's like some lucky survivor of the Triangle Fire."

"Wretched business," Stanhope muttered. "I can't believe the owners get off with only a fine."

Anne put a hand to her forehead; the conversation practically made her head throb. "Anyway, it's behind us. 'What's next?' is the real question."

He shrugged. "You won't like the answer."

Anne turned to look at him.

Stanhope took a deep breath. "Influenza."

His answer only partly surprised her. She'd seen the headline from the place where it began: ***Fort Reilly, Kansas: Army Corps Struck Hard By Influenza.*** The afflicted suffered nosebleeds, spat blood, and, at the end, their lungs filled with fluid and they drowned.

"I'd say by now..." He looked quickly out the car's window. "...the Army's taken it across the Atlantic several times. Just in time for the end of the war."

For a moment she felt as if they were back in his leather-bound office on Governor's Island, only this time instead of the war he was speaking of the Plague.

"I.... think we're going to have our hands full," he said, "once this business in France is over and done with. We could see a medical mobilization to rival the big push Over There."

Anne put her hand to her forehead again.

"Yes, talk about something else," he muttered. "What... what about that nautical story of yours?"

"Delia?"

"That's right."

Anne shifted in her seat. "I was supposed to meet people who might help to produce it."

"Did I say that?"

"Your words."

He shook his head. "Miss Blackstone, we need to look at the situation in the light of the present day. Except to see newsreels, perhaps, people aren't going out to picture shows like they used to."

She looked at him, incredulous. "After the Liberty Loans, Bond Drives, Savings Stamps and the war tax, people are left with nothing for leisure."

"Captain, you sound like a socialist."

Stanhope tapped a stick by the driver's front seat. “Jeffrey, please disregard what I just said.”

The driver touched his cap. “Didn't hear a word, Captain.”

Stanhope sat back in his seat.

“But since you asked,” she said. “I've put some thought into it. Some sketches. There's enough on paper, anyway, to make a start.”

He turned in his seat, without looking directly at her. “What about that poet friend of yours?”

“Vachel?”

“That book of his on moving pictures, surely that's brought him some important connections.”

“Surely, yes. But that hasn't stopped him from living like a tramp, 'trading rhymes for bread.'”

“So you still don't know where he is.”

“On tour.” She smiled, unfolding her fingers as if they contained a sheaf of cards. “All I have are postcards. Or he turns up some day, on my doorstep.”

The touring car reached the ferry station at the Hudson. City lights shone across the water, with the greatest blaze to the south, the theater district, where her doorstep – for now – could be found. Vachel could find it if he wished to; he was as much a Child of Manhattan as a Child of Springfield.

“In the meantime,” said Captain Stanhope, “We aren't out of it yet. There will still be work for you.”

*** *** ***

Anne's next trunkload of footage from the Signal Corps was filled with Yanks parading towards the waiting ships, waving to the camera, cramming the ships to the bulwarks, clustered against the rail, swinging their legs, waving and winking at the girls.

After thirty million lives, ten million in battle, twenty million more from dislocation, illness, famine and ethnic purging, the Fires of Hell had been put out.

On that November day Anne joined the crowds, linked arm in arm, walking eight abreast, clutching little American flags, waving them as they welcomed the soldiers home. Lines of autos and columns of infantry marched up Fifth Avenue, while cascades of flowers and confetti fell from above.

For the first time, at least in public, she noticed the presence of the masks, strips of white cloth covering the nose and mouth, tied with delicate strings behind the neck. She first saw them on the policemen, then on a number of well-tailored people.

A woman in that well-dressed group, not wearing a mask, stood out in her military-style riding outfit, two tiny American flags jutting from her wide-brimmed hat. As she waved to the columns of marching doughboys, her cries of "Hoorah!!" had a distinct *tone Francaise.*

"Alice!"

Their hands clasped by the lampost, where Alice had a premium view of the parade. Alice gestured to the well-heeled, mask-wearing citizens nearby. "I was sick with the flu myself. *Tres Mal*." She waved the small flag in her hands.

"Is Herbert with you?" Anne had to shout.

His very name provoked a furious glance. “Herbert is in Hollywood. An offer to direct – he said. But there is an actress.”

“I heard you were in Florida!” Anne shouted, eager to change the subject.

“Ah, the Everglades!” Alice beamed. “What locations! I believe the film will be a success.” She waved the little flag above her head. “And what of your own story, my dear?”

Anne turned to look at the parade. “I'm just picking it up again. Not much time, since...” she gestured to the procession of khaki and silver buttons. “I did write a scene of how Delia first goes to sea.”

Alice, who had kept her attention on the parade, turned to Anne and smiled softly. “I am glad. And... I apologize if my English is not adequate to say... “ She put one hand on Anne's shoulder. “... I am sorry if I could not help you fulfill your dreams.”

Anne returned her mothering gaze. “That wasn't your responsibility, Alice. *Mes rêves sont ma propre.”*

“Indeed,” said Alice. “They are your own.”

Chapter Thirteen

EXT. NEW BEDFORD HARBOR, ABOARD A FRIGATE DAY

The year is 1838. DELIA, dressed in a male sailor's uniform, is on deck, helping to gather up the topsail.

CLOSER ANGLE of Delia as a part of her sailor's jacket slips aside, revealing a corset.

TWO SAILORS One sailor nudges his companion, gesturing towards Delia.

DELIA turns sharply. Her eyes reveal that she's been discovered. Looking about cautiously, she approaches the two sailors. Slowly, she shakes her head.

FIRST SAILOR: “Give us a reason, then. Why shouldn't we tell the Captain?”

DELIA: “Just this...”

CLOSE SHOT, DELIA'S HAND She passes it above the glistening water as she narrates the tale:

DELIA: “It was almost five years ago:”

Brief scenes superimposed above the water:

- Delia and a handsome young man, stealing away from her small cottage. He carries a bundle over his shoulder.

- Delia sitting beside a pier in a South American country. People walk past her; she is alone.

- Delia, looking at herself in the mirror, puts on man's clothing.

DELIA: "He abandoned me for another; left me with nothing. So I took passage on a merchant ship."

LONG SHOT The Merchant Ship, sailing out to sea.

RETURN TO THE FRIGATE'S DECK Delia concludes her tale to the two sailors.

DELIA: "So you see, there is no rest for me, until I find him."

SECOND SAILOR: "And when you do?"

Delia picks up a marlinspike from a coil of rope. She hefts it for a moment in her hands, then throws it at the mast.

CLOSE ON THE MARLINSPIKE It quivers in place as it strikes the mast.

DELIA: “I'd kill him.”

*** *** ***

A body was curled up on the doorstoop of Anne's lower Manhattan apartment. A tramp, she reasoned, had found it a good place to sleep off his rotgut gin. If not for the rise and fall of his dusty jacket she'd have thought him dead. She considered stepping over him.

His face was concealed by a crumpled hat, but his hands, lit by the late afternoon, were visible. Dust was seared into the knuckles and sunburned wrists, and there was the long thumb to summon the milk truck and hay wagon.

He rolled over and groaned as if nudged. His dislodged hat and the glisten of one sleepy eye told Anne her hunch was right.

“Vachel, how long have you been there?”

“Since my recital.” He stretched like a lazy cat. “At the Salmagundi Club. Whenever that was.”

She fussed in her pocketbook for the keys. “Just because you did this sort of thing in Fort Lee doesn't mean it's acceptable in Manhattan.”

Wobbling, Vachel rose to his feet. “Acceptable to the neighborhood?” He leaned one elbow against the door as she opened it. “Or to you?”

Anne took a deep breath and opened her apartment door. Once inside she fed Vachel crusty bread, hardened cheese and celery at her small kitchen table. He told of the big splash he'd made with the young artists at the Salmagundi, then asked how things were with Delia.

“Awful.” Her shoulders drooped. “It's the finale. I'm stuck.”

Vachel pushed his chair closer. “Tell me about it.”

“This is where I'm at.” Anne raised her hands, palms face down. “Delia's crew is below deck, ready to mutiny. Step by step” – her hands contracted – “they climb, up the ladder and onto the deck, armed to the teeth.” She put one hand to her hip. “Delia has one flintlock pistol. She stares them down....” Anne sagged in her chair a bit. “Then she's rescued. But whether by one keel boat, or a whole river town, I still don't know.”

“Why can't Delia bring them down herself? One by one?”

Anne stood and moved toward the kitchen sink. “This isn't an epic poem, you know. And she isn't God. Or even the instrument of God.” As she scraped the dishes she looked through the tiny kitchen window to the brick facade of the adjoining building. “And the town *would* come to her rescue... because that's what river folks do.”

“It sounds like a corker.” He reached for a stray piece of celery.“However you end it.” He crunched loudly. “But what makes this one different?”

"Different?"

"From 'Orphan's Revenge' or 'This Side of the Moon.'"

"Vachel..." She glared. "This is the picture I've wanted to make all along. Remember?" She wiped her hands, and reached for a sheet of paper with the U.S. Army logo at the top. "Two more short subjects I owe them. *Two.* I'm going to make *three,* and hold Stanhope to his word. My bonus will just about cover production costs for a week or two."

"And what will two weeks get you?"

"Stanhope's promised me a boat."

Vachel looked incredulous. "A real boat?"

"Authentic paddle-wheel sloop, in drydock at the Brooklyn Naval Yard. I'm going to look her over tomorrow."

"You mean *we're* going to. What about interiors?"

"At Kalem Studios; what's left of it."

He shook his head. "Would be a lot easier across the river, you know... locations, actors..."

Anne wiped her hands on a towel. "I'm *done* with Fort Lee." In truth, she could not imagine herself there at all. If anyone – those who hadn't packed off to Hollywood – remembered her, it was as Madame Blache's assistant, the Go-Fetch Girl. The one who used to be a director.

Vachel rose from his chair, went to the closet, pulled out Anne's hat and coat, and handed them to her. "I have just the thing for you."

"What are you talking about?"

"We're going to Union City."

Anne folded her arms. "You sound mighty sure of that. What on earth for?"

"To see the Girl from God's Country. She's giving a talk at the Fifteenth Street Library."

"*God's* Country?"

"Northern Alberta." Vachel pulled her, two steps behind him, down the apartment stoop. "Snow covered mountains. The tundra. Fur parkas and mukluks."

"And *who's* this Girl?"

"Nell. Nell Shipman."

"*Nell?*" Anne scoffed. "Whenever I hear that name all I can think of are the heroines named Nell in the melodramas." She shook his hand free. "Vachel, I can't. I told you: the boat... the Brooklyn docks... tomorrow morning?"

"Exactly why you need to see Nell tonight. She has the spark, Anne." He gave that look that told her even if his words weren't true, he sincerely believed they were. "The divine spark. And wait till you see her."

All the way to Union City, from streetcar, to ferry, to trolley, Vachel told Anne about Nell's latest film, "Back to God's Country."

"It's like the climax of your story – well, in a way. The boat's near the Arctic Circle, but there's a crew of thieves and cutthroats. And the villain chases her and her invalid husband by sled across the frozen tundra. But the real selling point of the film is the nude scene."

"*What?*"

"Oh, it's perfectly innocent and idyllic; just Nell in a spring-fed pool with raccoons and squirrels for company. But the way they played it up..." He shook his head.

"*Well?*"

"There was this cartoon in *Moving Picture World,* a naked female, seen from behind, with the message "Don't Book 'Back to God's Country' unless You want to prove that the Nude is NOT Rude."

As they walked through the library entrance, Anne pointed to the auditorium. "And that's... her? The naked woman? God's Country?"

For the first time since they'd left the trolley, Vachel paused. "Silly. That wasn't her; it's advertising. And this is her East Coast tour to address the question of whether the Nude *is* actually Rude." He smiled. "I'd like to find out. Besides, I hear she's got lots of animals."

They found two seats in the auditorium's second row. On the back wall was a canvas backdrop of snowy mountains.

The auditorium lights went down. In the dark, a man's voice intoned: "Out of the North she comes, on a bobsled, head back, defiant, with the speed of a pack of wolves and the fresh bite of an arctic gale! Ladies and gentlemen, I give you... Nell Shipman!"

In a slow fade the lights returned. From the back of the room, as if from the snowy mountains themselves, a woman emerged. Contrary to the Lady Godiva image Anne was expecting, Nell wore a long dress and a cardigan sweater. Her cascade of dark curls was barely covered by a white Tam O'Shanter. She had dark, piercing eyes and a slightly turned-up nose.

"Ladies and gentlemen," Nell announced, "the true hero of the picture, Rex!"

At that moment Anne noticed the giant dog at Nell's feet. This must have been "Back to God's Country" dog-hero Wapi, the fiercest dog in the north. He didn't have enough fur for a Saint Bernard, but there was the same massive skull, the great drippy tongue and big dark eyes that looked beseechingly up at Nell.

The last thing Anne expected were dog tricks, especially in the confines of a library auditorium: count to three, bark, sit up, roll over, go up to the nice lady in the first row, extend a paw. She glanced at Vachel; what *had* he been thinking, dragging her to an animal show....

"Ever since I was a child, in Victoria, B.C..." Nell's voice returned Anne to the auditorium. "...I dreamed of being on the stage. At thirteen, I left home to join a small touring company. Eventually, my Mother joined, to make sure I was fed and properly cared for. We did everything: stage crew, costumes, promotion..."

Here we go, Anne mused. *A story I know too well.* At sixteen Nell played character parts, the heroine's younger sister, then graduated to playing the heroine herself. At eighteen, she discovered motion pictures, and became a junior star at Vitagraph. In her first big picture, "God's Country and the Woman," she was actor, director and producer.

Like Alice, Nell had nearly nearly succumbed to the flu epidemic. It was only when her long dark hair grew back that she went north to film "Back to God's Country." For pure drama the location filming in Alberta rivaled the events of the finished picture. Forget the fictional pirate crew and sled chase across the ice; in real life the leading man died from over-exposure, and had to be replaced.

Her narrative done, Nell asked if there were any questions. "This is the time." Vachel whispered in Anne's ear.

"What?" Anne whispered back.

"You know, about the nude not being rude..." He began to raise his hand. Anne grabbed it and held it at her side like a vise; she was prepared to clap her other hand over his mouth.

"Miss Shipman!" Anne said loudly. Nell turned towards her, as did nearly every other eye in the room.

It was, Anne realized later, one of the high-wire moments in her life, up there with her first recitation to the drunken patrons at Fantine's, the first appearance on the *River Queen's* stage, or her first attempt at directing on the streets of St. Louis. The question she asked – something about the way Nell had managed the scene in "Back to God's Country" between her character and the cutthroats on the ice-bound ship – was not important. Because she'd been obsessing how Delia could handle a similar situation it was the first thing that came to mind. What *was* important was that as a result of the question Nell learned just who Anne was.

"I *loved* 'Orphan's Revenge!'" Nell gushed as they stood together by the podium after the talk. Nell had brushed aside the well-wishers and autograph seekers just to speak with Anne. Off to one side, Nell's companion, Bert Van Tuyle, assisted by Vachel – always at home in the company of star-struck strangers – dealt with the public crush.

"You'll have to excuse me," said Anne. "You see, I've always wanted to meet someone actually named Nell. Just the name brings back memories of wolf calls and drifts of paper snow. Back on the showboat that was how we referred to any heroine of the melodramas, no matter what her character's name actually was."

"Well, it's my given name, for Heaven's sake!" Nell's eyes appeared to flash anger, but her lips broke into a smile. "And what of it? I played those parts, too."

Nell, Bert and Rex were scheduled for Baltimore, the next stop on their publicity tour. But they had the evening free, and perhaps tomorrow.

Vachel offered Anne's apartment. Anne gave a quick, disapproving glance, but he returned it with that look of sincerity that she could not completely resist. They piled into the studio-owned touring car provided for Nell's tour, complete with a rear compartment sleeping area and water bowl for Rex. Throughout the drive,Van Tuyle expounded on the limitless possibilities of the Canadian north as outdoor location for epic moving picture versions of best-selling novels.

When they stood in her kitchen, Anne gave Vachel a glance, and he guided Bert, accompanied by a bottle of brandy, toward the equally tiny parlor. Rex found a spot beneath the table.

“I'm not sure that was such a good idea,” said Nell, once the men had retired. “Bert has been at the bottle since he caught a bad case of frostbite in Alberta.”

Anne looked nervously toward the parlor. “I'm so sorry... I'm sure Vachel wouldn't have suggested such a thing if he'd known.”

“Well, what of it!” Nell slapped the table. “They're grown men.”

“In a manner of speaking,” Anne muttered.

“It's the publicity angle!” Van Tuyle poured a glass first for himself, then for Vachel. “We get the Calgary businessmen together, convince them Alberta will be the next major destination for outdoor filming.”

“Filming what, for instance!”

“Ah!” With his free hand, Bert swept the air. “The writers of the great northern wilderness – as popular in their own way as your western writer Zane Grey. Jack London, B.W. Sinclair, Robert Service, and in particular, James Oliver Curwood.” He raised his glass, and drank. “Our benefactor. Screw him.”

Vachel gave a little shake of his head. “Really?”

“Curwood was pissed because Nell got more footage than the dog. All he cared about was the dog. I mean, it's from a *Good Housekeeping* short story, for God's sake...” Bert picked up the bottle. “Have another?”

“So about this Nude not being Rude...” Anne said.

“Well, I wasn't about to bring *that* up at the library.”

"You're darn lucky nobody asked you about it..." Anne had no intention to let on that Vachel was all set to.

"It was my husband's idea, that slogan."

"Bert?"

"Hah!" Nell scoffed. "Bert isn't my husband. Just likes to create the impression he is. I mean Ernest, Ernest Shipman. I was his fourth wife. He was my first."

"Did you always love animals?" Anne shifted in her seat. "Grow up with them?"

"Of course," Nell gave an almost sad little smile. "I've always loved them. But I knew it, *really* knew it, on the set of one of my very first pictures, when I was a junior star at Vitagraph. A bobcat was supposed to frighten me. They gave it electric shocks to make it snarl, and then doped it so it would lie still. It died in my arms." Nell clenched a fist. "Over its body I swore an oath to protect all the moving picture animals from abuse – but especially, and above all, the wild ones." She stretched a hand below the table to rub Rex's ears. "Dogs and horses, you see, are protected by the ASPCA. But not the wild ones."

"Well, *I* have a new idea." Vachel pulled his chair closer. "It's how the motion picture camera is a stealer of souls. Like mirrors."

"Old superstition," said Bert, with a dismissive wave.

"Of course." Vachel refilled his glass. "But at the heart of every superstition there's a seed of truth. Think about it: after a loved one died, the Victorians covered all the mirrors in the house, so the departed's soul wouldn't be captured in the mirror."

"Terrifying."

"Perhaps to us. But think of the old time photographers who covered their camera lens – an enhanced mirror! – with a black cloth, only to *uncover* it to imprint the subject's image – the reflection of their soul – onto the metal plate."

Bert's eyes grew larger.

"Then picture this." Vachel swirled his hands in a circle. "The panopticon. The flickering mirrors on the carousel. Finally..." his hands twirled like a magician's... "the motion picture lens. Duplicating the photographer's plate, only many times faster, many more frames, more images, then projects those images – *magnified* – onto a screen, for the entertainment of those sitting in the dark."

"Devilish!" Bert was practically drooling. "But... haven't you discussed this with your lady friend?"

Vachel scowled. "She won't hear of it. Too caught up in her own story." He glanced toward the kitchen. "I should say, Delia's story."

Bert rolled his eyes. "Oh, I know about that one. When Nell starred in 'God's Country' she couldn't turn it off. I was *sleeping* with the Girl from God's Country."

Vachel leaned closer. "Exactly. I knew you'd understand." He raised his glass. "We're in the same boat."

"Please." Bert winced. "Don't mention boats."

"I think I know what you mean," said Anne. "With me, it's the swans."

"Birds?" Nell's look was quizzical.

"Not all birds. Water birds, mostly. Swans especially."

Nell's left hand sunk into the fur around Rex's neck. "I guess I'm partial to fur."

Rex lay patiently, big head between his paws, just as he'd posed at Nell's feet in the library's multi-purpose room. At that time Anne thought that Nell and the dog shared a psychic connection. Now she was convinced of it. This Nell, sitting before her, *was* the Girl from God's Country, in fact as well as name.

"Dogs can hear me a half mile away," said Nell. "And even farther." For a second, Anne was sure she caught a glance, such as a friend would give another friend, between Nell and Rex. "When I discovered the *fact* of direct communication, species to species, with *all* of life... that's when I decided to get my own wild animal cast and make actors of them without whips and electric prods. Just one big family, humans and critters."

Anne felt like shaking her, like Alice shook the Red Queen, to pry loose some of the pixie dust that had settled over her. How did she come by it? The woman was not only at ease with dangerous animals, but in the way she spoke, and stood, and carried herself, was as comfortable as an animal itself in her own skin.

In her own dreams Anne had seen herself as Queen of the Rivers and Seas; and here came Nell, Queen of Ice and Snow, the person most like Captain Callie Anne had encountered. This woman could captain a boat, and Anne bet that if she had to she'd walk a tightrope. Even naked.

“What did you say you did before you met Nell?” Vachel refilled Bert's glass. “Race cars?”

“Cars!” Bert picked up an empty cigar box from the table. *“That's* the other thing I wanted to tell you!” Bert spun the cigar box in the space between his chair and Vachel's. “The great racing car story for the pictures!” He spun the box faster. “And they're off! Around the wide curve of the highway! Cars chasing each other... racing to the rescue!”

“I see. It's all about speed. And the leading character? Not a person, but an automobile.”

“That's it!” Bert's watery eyes gleamed. “Nobody else gets it, but you do!”

“I get it, all right.” Vachel looked down at the thin carpet. “Maybe Delia gets rescued by a racing car.”

“What's that?”

“Long story, Bert. Too long.”

“So about that Orphan's Revenge...” Nell put a hand on Anne's knee. “I think you should re-do it. But make it an outdoors picture.”

Thank you, Nell. Anne beamed inwardly. “'Orphan's Revenge is the past,” she replied. “Someone very different's in the now.”

Delia was the now. Anne described the story that grew from snippets and sketches in her journal to the full-fledged script, the subsidy courtesy of Stanhope and the Signal Corps, the visit to the sloop tomorrow, and a little of her terror at filming – perhaps this week – without an ending.

"Is that what's worrying you?" Nell chuckled. "Going to shoot without a script happened all the time in the early days."

"I know," said Anne. It happened all the time in St. Louis, then Fort Lee. Now they were "the early days."

"Then tell me...." Bert looked up from his recline on the little divan. "How do you make a moving picture about a mirror? Break it? Seven years bad luck?"

"It *isn't* a moving picture." Vachel said decisively. "It's a poem."

"Hurrah!" Bert elbowed his way to a sitting pose. "Let's have a poem."

Vachel leapt to his feet. "I have it!" He tossed down the last of his brandy. "The battle cry I gave today, at the Salmagundi. Full of righteous indignation."

"Let's hear it!" cried Bert. "What's the name?"

"'The Black Hawk War of the Artists!'" Vachel cleared his throat. "In the manner of the Indian Oration and the Indian War-Cry. Though not all of it." He fumbled a bit on his feet, then caught himself on the edge of the divan. "Not because it's too long, mind you."

He scowled, stretching his right hand toward the heavens.

"Wolves of the West at bay.

Power, power for war

Comes from these trees divine;

Power from the boughs,

Boughs where the dew-beads shine,

Power from the cones

Yea, from the breath of the pine!

Power to restore

All that the white hand mars.

See the dead east

Crushed with the iron cars—

Chimneys black

Blinding the sun and stars!"

"Vachel!" Anne called from the next room. His gestures had been enough to make the glass dishes on the mantlepiece rattle. When he looked up, Nell and Anne stood in the doorway. Anne's arms were folded.

"Vachel was just giving a recitation," said the now-upright Bert.

"For the whole block, apparently," said Anne. "It's late. Nell and I have discussed it. They're staying over – we'll make space on the floor – and tomorrow they'll join us for a look at the boat."

"Baltimore..." Bert mumbled. "We're supposed to be in Baltimore."

"We'll delay Baltimore a day," said Nell. "Maybe two. I'll let the studio know."

"Then all hail the studio." Bert raised his glass to toast his sodden reflection in the mirror. "For they can afford it."

Chapter 14

"Oh, *come* on, Bert!" Nell was halfway up the plank, one hand held out. "Let's have a look at this wreck."

"Yes, please do." Anne tried to sound cheerful. "I'd like your opinion."

Bert stayed frozen to the pier. "Nell knows. I haven't set foot on a boat since Alberta."

"Why *Bert*." Vachel chided. "You said Alberta was the next Gold Rush."

Bert pulled a leash from his coat pocket. "It's OK; Rex and I will take a walk."

"Where?" asked Nell.

"Wherever he takes me." Rex strained at the leash. "It's all right; you all go ahead and locate your movie. "

"Very well." Nell led the way up the plank. "Poor dear. I should have remembered boats aren't his cup of tea." She stopped, and gave a sour look. "Anne, *why* in God's name a paddle-wheel sloop?"

"The power of steam and the majesty of sail," Anne glanced from bow to stern, and beamed "Iron, wood and sail. That's a clue to Delia."

"I don't know... " From her thumbs and forefingers Nell formed a square, which she pointed at different sections of the boat. "It looks neither fish nor fowl. But closeups will tell the real story."

"They will indeed," said Anne.

"Lifeboats," Nell pointed to four lifeboats, two fore and two aft. "You can hide mutineers in them, then throw off the covers as a surprise."

"I'll remember that," said Anne, though she wished Nell hadn't mentioned it. The mutineers' climb from below decks was one scene Anne was quite sure of.

"Where does the mutiny occur?" Nell asked "At sea?"

Reflected sunlight pierced Anne's eyes. Things had been somewhat bleary since she'd opened them. She'd shared her bed with Nell, who tossed and mumbled in her sleep. Anne put a hand up to the sun. "No. I never pictured her out at sea."

"Well, *I* did when you told me the story. Maybe it's too big for the river." Nell's eyes narrowed. "I have it: the Great Lakes."

"Which one?"

"Superior," Nell said, confidently. "It's big, and it sounds the best." Her foot tapped the hatchway doors. "Is this where the mutineers come on deck?"

"Let's have a look," said Anne, and they carefully descended the stairs. The floor of the hold looked as if it had been recently swept, but wherever they glanced the dust of ages still clung to the cracks and seams.

"You really want to film down here?" asked Nell.

"There's room enough for lights," said Anne. "I think if we gave it, you know... a woman's touch, a carpet, sofa, a table." She stood by the wall. "And maybe a grandfather clock. A small one."

Nell spread her hands wide in the center of the hold. "And on the table, maps. A big sea trunk, and a large globe on a wooden stand. And how about a pile of barrels in the corner?" She put her hands on her hips. "Now *that* would spell Captain." She frowned. "But what would mutineers be doing in the Captain's quarters?"

Vachel would know about the mutineers. But where was he? Anne was used to his wandering off, but now it was getting so the minute her back was turned... she climbed the stairs, Nell close behind her.

He was standing all the way toward the bow. his back to her, one leg propped against the rail in a way that brought Zachariah Wilkes to mind.

Why think of that now? This dusty relic had almost nothing in common with the candy-striped showboat. Then she remembered: except for the Hudson ferry and the launching of the troop ship in Hoboken this was the first time since the *River Queen* that she'd been on a boat. That could explain an apparition like Mr. Wilkes. Now she understood why Bert didn't wish to board.

Nell brushed past Anne, practically pushing her aside. Then she stood, ramrod straight, back firmly planted against the mast, dark eyes looking soulfully heavenward.

"I have it!" she cried, in a voice that caught the ear of everyone on the boat, and two docks to either side. "*Lashed* to the mast... " Her head, still planted against the mast, turned sharply toward Anne. "There's your climax."

"Yes!" said Vachel, with a loud snap of his fingers. He sounded surprisingly chipper for a man who'd spent a cramped night on the sofa while his new friend made a pillow of a dog's undulating stomach on the floor.

"So?" Anne looked blankly from one to the other – the woman at the mast, the man at her side – as if they were crazy. "How does she get out of it?"

Vachel scratched the back of his head. "She sends up a signal flare?"

"*While* lashed to the mast?"

Nell's eyes narrowed. "No. Delia stares them down."

"She's not a hypnotist." Anne said, almost beneath her breath.

"Very well!" With a flourish Nell threw off her pretend ropes and stepped from the mast. "I'm sure you'll think of something within the week." She glanced toward the pier. "Ah! Here come Bert and Rex."

The man and dog still went no closer to the boat than the gangplank, but both looked out of breath – and happy.

"Rex and I had the same idea," said Bert. "No boats, no piers, no dry docks. So he followed a trail of cats, and we ended up at the Parade Ground. No marching cadets, so we romped. And what a place for race cars! Gave me all sorts of new ideas."

"Oh you darling," Nell scurried down the plank, hugged Bert and patted his cheek. "I'm glad you both had a good time."

Anne had to fight her mouth from opening wide. How could the woman act this way after all the frustrations she'd confided to Anne last night? Anne would never have greeted Vachel in that manner, not even after one of his cross-country tours, much less a walk with a dog.

And for God's sake, what was she doing comparing herself and her relationship, with Nell, anyway? What she had with Vachel was a world apart from this. Vachel was a carefree wanderer, a will-o-the-wisp. Bert was an anchor, part of a framework of smiles, nice clothes and agreements. He was to Nell as Herbert had been for Alice, or as Harry had been for Florence.

Would Nell and Bert follow the same pattern of deceit, of betrayal? Florence paid the price, and Alice was now on her own.

"So where to now, my love?" Nell asked.

"I'd say Rex and I are just about ready to go to Baltimore, then on to Philly," said Bert.

"We're off to the train!" Nell called out to the boat. "But we'll be back for your first day of shooting; you can be sure of that!"

Vachel eased next to Anne, and put an arm around her. "So until then, what will you do?

"Film what I can, at the other shooting stage the Captain's made available to me."

"And where's that?"

"A horse barn with a rather large water trough. Come on, I'll show you."

*** *** ***

EXT. A BROAD STRETCH OF THE RIVER

Two steamboats are in the final stretch of a race. Black smoke pours from the funnels as more coal is shoveled on.

CLOSER ON THE LEAD BOAT

The large paddlewheel becomes unhinged; the boat has lost control!

BACK TO A DISTANT VIEW as the lead boat crashes into the wharf, setting it ablaze!

“Cut!” Anne yelled.

The properties man snuffed out the three inch blaze, just enough to leave a black smudge on the barn's ceiling.

"I'm sorry," said Anne. "It doesn't look *real* enough."

"Of course it doesn't," The cameraman coughed. "What do you expect from toy boats and a pier made of popsicle sticks?”

Anne stepped for a better look at her boat race: postcard photographs of steamboats, pasted to pieces of wood floating in a trough filled with greasy water.

"'Remember *The Battle of Manila Bay*?' she asked.

“Nope.”

“A Vitagraph picture, from the Panamerican War. It was in all the nickelodeons. Do you remember Vitagraph?”

The camerman shook his head.

“Amazing.” Anne rummaged through a bin. “Any scraps of black cardboard here?”

The properties man stepped up to lend a hand.

"Vitagraph faked the entire battle at sea," she said, over her shoulder, to the cameraman. "They used a water tank, cardboard model ships...and smoke from the director's cigar."

Anne glanced up at the properties man. "Scissors, do we have any scissors?" He rifled through a tool drawer and handed her a pair. Out of black cardboard she cut the outline of a smokestack, and then another. Satisfied that the cardboard fit properly atop the floating pieces of wood, she placed the models at the water's edge.

"You," she said to the properties man. "Set the incendiaries *behind* the boat – just enough to light it from one side only." She turned toward the camera. "And *you*, bring the camera closer to the tank."

The two men occupied themselves with tripod and Roman Candles.

"Action!" said Anne.

The boat lurched forward, its innate falsity concealed in near-darkness, as impressive spouts of flame leapt from the popsicle pier.

"Cut!" Anne smiled. "That's more like it. Now let's make the fire even bigger."

*** *** ***

One thing could be said for the extras Captain Stanhope provided: they did look authentic. The moment they gathered on the sloop's deck Anne felt unsafe, even though Vachel and the camera crew stood close by. Stanhope must have scoured the prisons and military brigs of three boroughs to find them. Their sailor's costumes – soiled, ripped, holes at the knees and elbows – looked as if they'd been slept in for weeks. She knew at least one of the faces from the back of a police wagon, an anarchist she and Vachel had seen on these very docks, sent down for deportation.

The question now was whether they could act.

It was time to take charge. Anne picked up the megaphone. "All right, may I have your attention!"

She began with the basics, as much for her benefit as theirs; it had, after all, been eight years since she'd actually directed people; "actors" was a real stretch for this crew.

"Don't look at the camera when you hear 'Action!'" she said. "And don't look at it when the cameraman stops cranking or you hear 'Cut.' Now, I need just four of you by the lifeboats."

She decided to try Nell's idea of having them crawl from beneath the canvas covers of the lifeboats. Two attempts at it and she decided the effect was more silly than threatening. Then she had them crawling from the hatchway; it wasn't much better but at least an improvement.

"Anne," said Vachel. "I think they're here." A big touring car had just pulled up to the pier. From it stepped a woman and a man, both wearing long traveling coats, and a big furry dog.

"Quick, the costume." Anne said. Vachel went to fetch the dark blue coat, trousers and cap, carefully wrapped in brown paper.

Over a series of telephone calls and cablegrams from Philadelphia and Baltimore, Nell had expressed keen interest in Delia's character. She'd even asked for a few pages of the script, then canceled the request later that day. She didn't have time to read, but did have a solid grasp of the character; if no actress had already committed to the role, could Nell herself play Delia?

By late in the week no other option seemed possible.

Before they were within ten feet of the gangplank, Bert and Rex took off in another direction. Anne was quite relieved Bert was not sticking around; he'd only be a distraction.

"He wanted to head straight for that parade ground," Nell announced upon boarding. "To work out some ideas for his car racing story."

With the crew waiting there was no time for social niceties. Anne handed the coat to Nell. It didn't fit, and the sleeves were too long. For a moment Anne was sure Nell would tear the thing off and throw it to the ground. But no, uncomfortable as she was she would carry on.

"So?" Nell asked. "Where should we begin?"

"Closeups." *Well, she's a trouper,* Anne thought.

"We'll try the stare." Nell's eyes slowly widened. "The one that brings them to their knees."

"Camera!" Anne called, over her shoulder. The cameraman fumbled with the lens, the tripod, the whole apparatus. Anne shook her head. Will would have been on this within seconds.

"My eyes," Nell said, between clenched teeth. "Closer on my eyes."

"In this light?" Anne shielded her eyes and looked to the sun. "You'll be in shadow. It won't look like anything."

"We won't shoot it here. It will be closeup with special effects. Special filters." The left side of Nell's mouth curled up in a smile. "Or something done with mirrors. We'll ask Vachel."

Anne nudged the cameraman. "Nell, look up, quick!"

"Where?" But Nell did look up; she couldn't help looking upward.

"That's what I want!" Anne came close to clapping her hands. "Delia looks *up,* to the crow's nest. To the wind."

"Perhaps," said Nell. "But better look around you first."

Something in Nell's voice brought Anne's attention back to the extras, waiting behind her. In small huddles, they stood close enough for Anne to see that their eyes, if not their body language. betrayed thoughts of imminent mutiny.

"Keep the camera on me," Nell said firmly to the cameraman. Her eyes blazed. "Closer!" The cameraman obliged. "How dare you!" Nell waved one arm defiantly at the mutineers. "What do you think you're doing? I'm still captain here!"

The mutineers were as surprised as Anne at Nell's outburst. Some reached for the prop knives and guns at their belts. Nell stepped towards them; instinctively, they stepped back.

"Get the crew!" Anne hissed, and the cameraman pulled back just enough to get the standoff between Nell and the mutineers in one frame. Now it didn't matter that her coat was ill-fitting, or that the captain's hat had slipped over one eye. Nell had been absolutely right: she *did* have a solid grasp of Delia, probably better than Anne herself. What had taken Anne years Nell had achieved in just over a week.

“A gun!” Nell snarled out of the side of her mouth. “Aren't I supposed to have a gun?”

Vachel looked helpless. “There wasn't one in the bag,” he whispered. One of the nearby extras offered his prop gun. The cameraman stopped cranking for an instant.

“Keep rolling!” Nell commanded. “Is the gun supposed to have bullets, or am I pretending?”

Anne's mouth hung open. The haziest, least-defined part of the script, and Nell needed an answer as if her life depended on it.

“Well?” Nell practically shouted.

“Ah... No bullets!” Anne was close to shouting herself.

“Then it's only a threat!” Nell pointed the prop gun wildly at one mutineer, then another. They kept their distance as it it were actually loaded. “There's only one place to go from here!” She looked quickly at Vachel. “Give them a rope!”

“A rope.” Vachel mouthed the words. When a sufficient rope had been found on deck, Nell stood with her back to the mainmast, allowing the mutineers to practice winding the rope around her torso.

“Cut,” said Anne.

“That's good,” said Nell. “We'll need another take where they overpower me and drag me to the mast.”

“Nell,” Anne purposefully made her voice calm. “I've been thinking about that.” She looked over her shoulder, to Vachel. “Lunch for the crew. Or breakfast, anything. Just take them over there.” She pointed across the deck. When all had gone, she faced Nell.

"No mast. Delia walks a tightrope."

"A what?

"Tightrope."

"In the middle of Lake Superior?"

"Then maybe we're *not* on Lake Superior!" Despite their talks, their understandings, all the things they'd shared, now that they were working together, with actors and a crew, there was something dismayingly Constance Margaret about Nell.

Anne pitched her voice softer. "It's my story. The tightrope's stretched between two boats; if Delia can walk it without falling the mutineers will set her free. It's been done, that's why it's in. Callie French – I told you this story, remember? – did it in her younger days on the river. And of course I wouldn't ask you to walk it, we'll get a stunt double. Someone from a traveling circus. That shouldn't be hard to find."

Nell looked down at the deck. "Traveling circus." Her shoulders flinched, as if she were about to sob. "That's marvelous." She turned her deep, soulful, actress eyes towards Anne. "Of course it's your story. You wrote it. And because you wrote her so well I *understand* her."

Perhaps Nell was on to something that Anne, in her trail of revisions and crumpled script pages, had been missing all this time. Something visceral, untamed; more "God's Country" than Callie French, for sure. Maybe Nell was cutting to the heart of what Anne had been skating around ever since she began this story.

"Do you have a sword?" asked Nell. One was put in her hand, and Nell scampered across the deck with any mutineer who'd cross swords with her. She began with one, then took on two, three, four at a time. She slipped one particularly surly mutineer a ten dollar bill, then put a boot in his gut and gave a shove that sent him toppling downstairs. She had two men tug at the arms of her coat, holding her fast. Like a whisper she slipped out of the coat and ran.

Now the coat was gone. Nell ran up and down the deck in her white blouse, chased by sword and pistol-waving mutineers. The men appeared to enjoy it immensely.

Anne folded her arms and, for the first time that day, relaxed. It was more Nell's production than hers, anyway. And for that she was almost thankful. It gave her an uncanny opportunity to observe someone like herself, a director in action. Vachel had come closest to describing it to her, but she'd never really seen it before.

"Wasn't she supposed to have a gun?" Vachel, his arms likewise crossed, stood next to Anne.

"A flintlock pistol." Anne craned her neck to see if Nell had actually pushed one of the mutineers in the water. "What was that you once asked me?" she asked, almost dispassionately. *"Why can't Delia bring them down herself? One by one?"*

"Delia isn't," Vachel replied. "Nell is."

As they watched, now from a distance, the rope lines, then the uppermost mast became obscured. Late afternoon fog was rolling in. The mutineers, most of them exhausted from their exertions, looked spent. The fog only provided a good excuse to close up shop for the day.

Through the fog, now thick across the pier, Bert and Rex returned, moving as slow-paced as those on the boat. But Bert was beaming, flushed from their vigorous walk.

"I thought you'd be wrapping up once the fog rolled in." He smiled at Nell, toweling the sweat from her face and hair now that the cap was off. "How'd it go, Nellie darlin?"

"Great stuff, Bert. Lots of action!"

"That's what we like!" Bert offered a hand to help her down the gangplank. "Speaking of action, did I ever get some ideas!" He raised an outstretched hand. "How's this sound for a catchline: *The Super Spectacle of Speed*. Do you have one, Anne?"

"Have what?" Anne felt like she had to shake her head to understand him.

"You know, a catchline. The big words above the title on the poster. In the magazine ads. The thing that catches the eye and the ear."

"My department," Vachel offered, as he joined the three of them on the pier. "Anne's on another tack right now."

Bert tousled Rex's ears. "Hey, I've an idea... let's go celebrate. Soak up the local color." He stood between Anne and Vachel, putting an arm around each. "Your first day of location shooting. The launch of my racing picture." He hugged tighter. Anne gave him a weak smile. "Let's celebrate like old times! Like a week ago!" He laughed.

"Oh, and listen..." Nell leaned toward Anne. "Another idea; it came to me out there on the deck. We'll work in a scene where Delia wrestles a bear."

Anne looked confused. Yet at this moment, everything in her world was confused.

"Remember Brownie, the bear? I told you about him last week. We wrestle all the time. It will look terrific!"

"Terrific. Yes." Anne closed her eyes, slowly. She felt like slamming a boot down on the pier, or, even better, right on Nell's foot. *You think it's possible to have two captains on the same ship? Do you?* she thought to say.

"I think," she said at last, "that's enough for one day."

*** *** ***

Anne stared at her kitchen wall. It was blank, blank as a nickelodeon screen before the customers arrived. Still, she preferred to look at the wall than anywhere else in her apartment.

Dishes and drinking glasses from last night's celebration filled the sink behind her. The four of them had been up late toasting their various successes, but since it had been Bert's idea, it really felt like *his* celebration.

Vachel was perched on the edge of the couch in the living room. It would be out of character for Vachel Lindsay to sit back comfortably.

"I've got it!" he said.

"Got what?" She'd forgotten he'd been speaking.

"The end of the picture. Forget the swordplay footage, the town coming to her rescue. Forget tied to the mast, the tightrope walk, the stare." He slapped the scribbled pages in his hand. "I've solved it. An unstoppable force of nature."

"A storm?"

"That's one."

"What else?"

"A shipwreck."

Anne's shoulders sagged. "Vachel, the whole damn picture's a shipwreck."

"Take your pick! Why not shoot two endings? See which one the audience likes best."

What have we come to? she thought. Film making by approval? The people in the theater seats to dictate the outcome of stories?

"Vachel!" It took effort to turn in her chair and face him. "I spend my days in an abandoned studio with miniatures and a storm in a bathtub. Special effects; that's what I'm good for, goddamned special effects! My exterior is one derelict boat at the Brooklyn Naval Yards, where we've had, so far, one shooting day. From which we have great footage of someone else's movie."

A tear dripped from her right eye down the length of her nose. "I'm shooting *around* Delia's story, not inside it. So far I don't have one decent scene of *her* on film."

Vachel rose from his perch. "Are you crying?"

Anne shook her head. "No. I'm just finished. Done. Through."

The clatter of horse hooves from the street distracted her. How rare, she thought, to hear the sound at all these days. It had been replaced by the automobile's roar and the cable car's electrical hiss... much as the furniture in storefront windows had given way to washing machines and the latest phenomenon, radio. She had seen the new merchandise, glowing behind the windows, illuminations worthy of a museum.

Anne finished wiping her eyes. The sound was a welcome distraction; she could breathe better now. “It sounds crazy,” she said. “But I'm tempted to go into filmed advertising.”

Vachel stopped pacing. “Advertising what?”

“Oh, luxury items. Perfumes, toilette water.”

“You mean piss.”

“Listen to the one who's spent half his adult life in barns. Piss on you.” For the first time that day, Anne gave him a smile. “Seriously. It's a chance to be creative with titles, dissolves, maybe animation. And professional models are a lot easier to manage than actors.”

He left his perch. “I think you just need a change of pace. You should go in for romantic comedies.”

“I don't do romantic comedies,” she said definitively. “Sometimes I have trouble remembering what it was that I did so well, before the war.”

“Not just a change of pace; you need this.” He went back to the living room for a newspaper. “Talk about advertising? Here it is; the wave of the future.” Front and center was a display ad for the Palace Uptown, *Five Acts of Vaudeville plus Feature*.

“Vachel. I don't think five acts of vaudeville is the answer for me.”

“I'm not talking about the show.” He slowly folded the newspaper. “I might be able to arrange a private tour of the Palace Uptown. Before show times, in fact. No moviegoers in the way.”

Anne sighed. “Last time you took me out for inspiration we met Nell.”

“Then let's not say it's for inspiration,” said Vachel. “How about consolation?”

“I'll settle for distraction.” She got out of her chair, and walked to him. “And you can arrange this on your credentials as a *poet*?”

”No.” He reached for her lapel. “On your credentials with the Signal Corps, which you present at the box office.”

She grabbed his collar in return. “Were you this stunningly confident with the farmer's daughter?”

The paint on the Palace Uptown was still fresh, but the theater itself looked as if it had been on the street for fifty years. Anne and Vachel stood a long time at the entrance, admiring the cathedral-like archway, stained glass, fluted columns and statues of knights and ladies. The sound of a pipe organ would not have been out of place.

Anne walked slowly around the ticket booth, tucked back from the sidewalk. It was absolutely spacious compared to most she had seen. As she noticed the girl selling tickets, their guide, with the precision of a cadet, stepped forward to introduce himself. He checked her credentials: *Anne Blackstone, Signal Corps, United States Army.*

His name, of all things, was Arthur. He was tall, had spotless white gloves and faced her in that military way which acknowledged the presence of another without making direct eye contact. It came as no surprise that his official position was head usher.

Arthur led them into the palatial lobby. A girl stood by the door, at attention, a cape of gold brocade draped over her shoulder. Hanging lanterns, like individual chandeliers, ignited sunbursts of gold leaf that smothered the high arched ceiling and massive crossbeams. At the back of the lobby was a glass case filled with ice.

“What is that for?” she asked.

"We offer fruit cup and shrimp cocktail, Ma'am.”

"Nothing like bread and cheese?” asked Vachel. “Coca-Cola? A chocolate bar?"

"No, Sir. We are not a confectionary."

As she stepped on the Persian carpet, with its ornate designs, Ann recalled the nutshells and human spit coating the floor of the St. Louis nickelodeon she once toured with Henry.

Arthur led them down a line of velvet ropes to the actual theater entrance. Inside, a great dome towered above the seats, with small pinpricks that Anne realized must be stars in a painted night sky. Rows of plush red seats cascaded toward the velvet curtain and the orchestra pit like a gentle waterfall.

"Behind the curtain,” said Arthur, “is a Wurlitzer organ. For premieres and special occasions we have a seventy-five piece orchestra. Some of our players are veterans of the symphony."

"And their pay?" Anne asked. "Is it on a par with what they were getting as professional musicians?”

"Ma'am, the musicians are employed more consistently than during the symphony season. The working conditions are equal to that of the symphony hall, and the acoustics are said to be even better."

"I didn't ask you about prestige, I asked you about their pay."

"I'm not at liberty to disclose salaries, Ma'am."

He began walking down the center aisle, a slight flick of his arm was a gentle summons for them to follow. Vachel caught up with him. “Tell me, Arthur... how does one get to be an usher in this theater?”

"Sir, an usher must be between the ages of seventeen and twenty-one, in college, or a college graduate. Our best are fresh from military academy. At least five feet seven inches tall, weighing between 125 and 145 pounds, Caucasian."

Anne stopped. "All Caucasian?"

"No, Ma'am. Messenger boys are colored, slight in build, not over five feet four inches. In other words, not as tall as an usher."

Anne said nothing, but continued to walk down the aisle.

"It's the image that the owners wish to project, Ma'am."

"Is that the only reason for the specific size?"

"No, Ma'am. In this way, a uniform can be given to another employee when one is no longer employed here."

"I appreciate your honesty," she said.

"I'm instructed to answer you in complete truthfulness, Ma'am."

"Yes, but must you always address me as *Ma'am*?"

The aisle ended at the polished railing just above the orchestra pit. Here they stopped.

"It's part of my job, Ma'am, when asked a question. Also if I make a request of a patron, say, to ask them to take a different seat or to lower their voice, I must always say 'thank you.'"

"What if I gave you a tip?"

"If I were caught, Ma'am, I'd be fired."

"What if I request that you no longer call me *Ma'am*? It unnerves me."

Vachel folded his arms and smiled.

"Is that request on behalf of the United States Army, Ma'am?"

"It is."

"Then with your permission, I'll only address you as 'Ma'am' when management or other employees are present."

"You have my permission."

Arthur pointed one gloved hand to the right of the stage. "Now if you will follow me, I can show you some of the amenities not regularly seen by the public."

He led them down a series of halls and through foyers. When they passed each door, he called out its identity: "Men's Smoking Room... Ladies Lounge... Business Office... Film Storage..."

"Any problems there?" asked Vachel. "Fire, I mean?"

"None that I've ever heard of, Sir. We are fully equipped to handle any emergencies that may arise."

Arthur opened a door behind which was a bright, airy room. "Here is our fully staffed childcare department." Anne could see a slide and a sandbox. Though there were no children, a uniformed nurse was putting things in order. "Childcare is particularly busy afternoons, during tea time shows."

Vachel blinked. "Tea time show?"

"After shopping." Arthur closed the door. "Especially popular with mothers, nannies and those with small children." He closed the door. "That concludes our look behind the scenes of the Palace Uptown. If you will kindly follow me I will take us back through the lobby to exit the building."

From the sidewalk, Anne looked up at the illuminated marquee. *Hearts of Flame,* a title she did not know, supported by a cartoon, a newsreel, a Harold Lloyd comedy short, and, of course, vaudeville. It occurred to Anne that it really made no difference what titles and short subjects were listed on the marquee. This was no theater, but, in truth, a palace. A respite after shopping or a hard day's work, a place to leave the children, rest one's bones in a cushioned seat and forget all cares for three hours.

Anne took a few steps until she stood directly beneath the marquee. "This was where the barker used to stand," she said.

"No more of him," said Vachel. "No more the traveling exhibitor and the tent shows with the prize fight pictures. No more of that, for all time."

And no more of that girl behind the screen, playing with wooden blocks and cow bells. Henry may have been right, damn him. They should have opened that nickelodeon in St. Louis. In the world of the automobile, the washing machine and the radio it would almost certainly have grown into a palace by this time.

"And now..." said Vachel. "What about that finale?"

Anne shook her head. "What?" It brought her back to this morning, staring at the wall. "I still say I'm finished."

He looked puzzled. "With Delia? Really?"

Her eyes took in the movie palace facade, the department store widows across the avenue, the traffic in between. “With everything. It's time to go home.”

*** *** ***

The mail boat was small, the color of bleached driftwood beneath a canvas roof. Lodged between bundles marked Decatur, Florence and Sioux City, Anne felt like a sack of mail herself, postmarked **Return to Sender, Marion, Iowa**.

There were no other passengers, and would likely be none by the time she reached Marion. Vachel had traveled with her as far as Omaha, then caught the train west, on one of his recital tours. He had not only poems to recite but books to sell, and his publishers were big on promotion. Of course he would make a detour to Marion upon his return. Of course.

A passenger boat that stopped in Marion was due in Council Bluffs, but it would not be for another two days. That meant a hotel stay, for which she had the funds; the sale of her Manhattan apartment had provided her with travel expenses and more besides. But she did not care to wait, not at all. Impulsively, she had talked herself aboard this little packet, not unlike the way she'd talked herself aboard the *River Queen*.

How badly that could have ended. One wrong word from Arthur and she and her carpetbag would have been thrown ashore at the next stop downriver.

Something about the mail boat reminded her of the barge her father had crewed on. She remembered it from an old picture, but also from a day standing at the town docks, her mother telling her to "Wave to your father, Anne... " as a little boat about this size left the dock and floated into the river's glare, dappled with a thousand reflected suns, so bright that she had to close her eyes, and the boat and the dark outline of her father were gone.

That was the last time she saw him, before the news of the explosion, and the sight of the plankboard coffin at the Meadows, the one that could not be opened because, as she suspected, every piece of her father had not been fished from the river.

But here she was, for the first time since her escape, coming home. Since Eddie had left town there was no one to fully appreciate her tale, of how she had become a scullery maid, seamstress, ticket taker, stage prompter, film exhibitor, scenarist, editor, director, au pair and wartime propagandist. And – however briefly – steamboat pilot.

She couldn't think of anyone back home to tell her tale to. In fact, she pictured trouble from the moment she climbed down the mail boat's little stepladder and onto the waterfront. Her first steps would have the feel of walking toward a firing squad.

For there, blocking the carriage lane between the landing and the Children's Home would be the Ladies Aid Society, and next to them the Sheriff.. Kidnapper, they would call her. Runaway. Stowaway. Liar.

"It's my town as much as yours!"

Had she said the words aloud? She glanced quickly on the deck behind her, then remembered it was only she and the mail boat crew, who had either not heard her or paid no heed to her ravings.

As the boat continued north, this whole stretch of the river – cottonwoods, patches of prairie, the wharves and town docks along the way – distant in memory yet also familiar, unfolded like a film projected in reverse. The river, the boat she traveled in, the willows; so little had changed since the day she left.

And though there were no signposts of "Marion, Just Ahead," she knew by small signs that they were close: a cluster of wharf pilings, boat shelters, the bank where her water birds waited for food and at the very last a shack and cooking fire at the Meadows.

From the river, it appeared that the Meadows had been drained long ago. Small trees had taken over a lot of the swamp – for the better, as some would say.

As the little boat thunked against the Marion landing she thanked the crew, tipped them as they handed over her baggage, and stepped down the ladder. No one at the landing looked up, or smiled. There was, of course, no committee of Church Ladies and no Sheriff with warrant in hand. What was once Fantine's Place had been rechristened the Marion Landing Hotel. That told her, without question, that Fantine was gone, most likely dead and gone.

Anne checked into the hotel, had a quick meal, then felt the pull, right down into her boots, to walk down the carriage road.

The broken windows of the brick edifice were large enough for a bat to fly through. Vines and ivy crept through windows, while more vines choked the high gables. It was empty, which was a mercy, to the three acres of soil on which it stood, and to the entire town. Anne did see some resemblance to the Gates of Hell.

She could not bring herself to step inside; the very floor looked sharp, broken, dangerous. She found a side yard where the children once had recess. In a corner, she found a tall, decaying box. Maybe it was the actual punishment box; she hoped it was. As she gave the box a kick the rotten wood caved in on itself.

The Meadows not been drained and razed completely, but there were fewer dwellings than she recalled. Ma's old cottage had been turned into a shed, stacked high with wood. Anne poked through the logs and kindling, looking for the glint of a bit of tarnished jewelry or a piece of glass, anything that might have belonged to Ma.

She heard a sound outside. A neighbor asked what her business was.

"I used to live around here." It sounded more like an admission of guilt than a statement of pride. Surely the neighbor knew the sort of people who used to live around here.

Anne continued along the shoreline, to a place that would not, could not have changed: the spot where she used to find the swans. She remembered the nesting couple that had leapt from the bulrushes when she and Eddie walked there after the school picnic.

The single swan she found did not behave like that; it returned Anne's gaze. Anne stepped just close enough to see the little beaded black spot inside the yellow of its eye.

On the following day Anne returned to the spot with her carpetbag. She removed Ma's pearl-handled comb, then tossed the bag into the Missouri River. She watched until it sank, turned on her heels and took the road back to town. *Her* town.

*** *** ***

DECEASED

Anne Blackstone March 15, 1882 – November 10, 1946

Anne Blackstone, a resident of the town of Marion, in Cole County, passed away in her sleep on November 10th. Known chiefly as one of the first film directors to break the sex barrier, Miss Blackstone involved herself in every aspect of film production.

Prior to the First World War Miss Blackstone was the principal director of the pioneering film studio Pantograph, one of a very few located in St. Louis, Missouri.

During the First World War she distinguished herself as a film editor with the U.S. Army Signal Corps. Her attempts to make a comeback in feature film production in the early 1920's proved unsuccessful, and she returned to Marion, where she was involved in the running of the Gem Theater, Marion's premier motion picture house, which had only recently been fitted for sound. Shortly before her death, she donated the prints of her existing films to the International Museum of Photography at the George Eastman House.

In 1938 she achieved the ambition of a lifetime to visit the European capitals London, Paris and Vienna.

In recent years Miss Blackstone had arranged for the purchase of a parcel of riverfront property for the establishment of a nesting ground and refuge for water birds. Since her passing the town has named it the Anne Blackstone Memorial Bird Sanctuary.